STOLEN FUTURES

M. DREWERY

EDITED BY NATE RAGOLIA

STOLEN FUTURES

M. DREWERY

edited by NATE RAGOLIA

SPACEBOY BOOKS

Denver, Colorado

Published in the United States by:
Spaceboy Books LLC
1627 Vine Street
Denver, CO 80206
www.readspaceboy.com

First printed March 2018

ISBN: 978-0-9997862-0-8

To Chloe

Thanks for buying Stolen Futures
Hope you enjoy the story

M. Drewry   18/5/19

For my grandparents

To my family and friends

1

GOODBYE

For the last nine months I have treated every meal I sit down to eat like it was the last I'd ever have on planet Earth. It was not that I have been obsessed with death, counting every moment as the end. That would have driven me crazy. Death was not even my concern. It was the very opposite. I was definitely going to live. But the Earth was running out of time.

Every day I would sit at the table on the military base where they kept me safe. I would watch my family eat and wonder if *this is going to be the last time we eat together*. Would it be the last time me and my brother would bicker over who had the largest portion of meat? The last time Mum would say grace? The last time my Dad would force me to eat my vegetables?

The meals hadn't been that good since we got to the base. The Destroyer was disrupting all international trade, and not much exotic food was getting through to the UK. The vegetables were bland, the meat dried and stringy. There was no gravy any more so the tastelessness of every type of English food showed through.

Tonight though, Mum was dishing up the very best we had left. It wasn't just our rations allotted to us by the government, but a full roast dinner. Somehow she must have sensed that we would never get a chance to eat this wonderful food if we waited much longer.

The vegetables steamed in their dishes, the meat leaked rich juices onto the chopping board and the potatoes continued to fry in their roasting tin.

It smelled amazing.

It was a shame that we weren't eating in our family house.

The Lake District military base wasn't as homey as, well, home. The walls were bare concrete and sparsely decorated with a few things we had grabbed from our house when we had been evacuated from London.

Once upon a time Cumbria had been a popular holiday destination for my family and me. Now it was not as beautiful as it once was. The lakes were virtually empty and their dried up beds were covered with rotting fish left high and dry with nowhere to go. The beaches were barren and looked more like deserts. Even the forests had turned brown and the trees were dead and bare.

We used to stay in plush hotels on holiday, and this cold, sterile army base was no comparison. I missed the way the Lake District used to look, all the greenery and water, now it was just like the aftermath of a terrible war. But then, I missed how the world used to look.

The last time I had seen the outside properly was several weeks ago. Everything beyond the base was declared off limits, not just because the air was becoming spare, but because it was no longer safe for me.

As one of the chosen, my safety and security was paramount, and no more risks would be taken. Others just like me were on the base too, unable to wait for the end in their home countries as some no longer existed or were in states of war. Factions everywhere vied for the pitiful resources that remained, fighting for air, water, and food, to be the ones to survive until the end. I had not talked to any of my future companions, even though I would be spending the rest of my life with them.

I could barely accept that the end was really coming. Let alone that I would be the only member of my family spared. I didn't want to connect with the other chosen. They represented the future I didn't want.

My mother served the food and grimaced every time the base rocked to the sound of explosions outside. She quickly wiped the expression from her face as she tried to keep up the façade of happiness. I loved her for that. She was trying to make my leaving as painless as possible.

Even while the base was under attack by hordes of people searching for a way off the planet, or for food, or just wanting shelter from the chaos sweeping the country, she kept up being my mum.

Once the food was served, Mum said grace. As she prayed I added my own that by some miracle the Earth would be spared.

We all said "amen," and I still held out for hope for a different ending than the one I was expecting. I knew though, deep down, that nothing had changed.

We all took up our cutlery to eat. My little brother was already munching away, scarfing down the food without closing his mouth.

"I don't want to see you chew," my mum scolded him, still adhering to old rules that no longer had any relevance.

Then the red phone on the wall rang.

I immediately thought, *What a waste*. I dropped my cutlery onto my plate and it bounced once and settled in the Yorkshire puds.

That was a selfish thought, that all this food was not going to be eaten, a stupid one too. Considering what was going to happen in a short while, not getting dinner was going to be inconsequential.

My dad answered the ringing phone, then bowed his head at the news he received. He didn't bother putting it back on the hook, he just left the phone to hang by its cord as he let it drop.

Things then happened fast. I was made to stand. Dad positioned me on my own in the middle of the room.

My brother was forced away from his plate by my mum. My dad's face had gone rigid as he fought back emotions, I could see muscles in his jaw twitching. He quickly gathered the bags I was allowed to take. My mother grabbed my little brother and held him close as if he too was about to be whisked away. My brother was too young to understand what was going on. Maybe he thought I was going on holiday.

Then mum and my brother stood with my dad a few feet away and just watched me, waiting for me to be plucked up and taken away, as they were left behind.

Tears formed in my eyes. This was it. I was finally going.

They would only give me five minutes to say goodbye.

I looked down, away from my family. I didn't want to see them crying. No way was that going to be my last memory of them. Hearing their sniffling and sobbing cut me to my very soul. I didn't want the image, too.

Five minutes.

What do you say in five minutes?

I suppose by then there wasn't much else to say. In nine months my family had become closer than any other on Earth. Lots of trips to fun places, celebrations, birthdays and one wedding, all spectacular and intense. We had talked, cried, yelled and wallowed together in such a short space of time.

Now it was time to let go.

"Mum I love you," I said to Mum, still without turning around, but projecting my voice over my shoulder.

She sniffed, a painful sound.

I couldn't help it, I looked.

Tears streamed down her cheeks and as I watched them fall I dragged the best words I could from my mind to express how much I loved her. "You're the best mum ever, you did everything right, I'm sorry for not listening to you all the time and making your life hell sometimes."

She wrapped me up in the tightest hug she had ever given me. Mothers always hug this strong, demonstrating the bond between mum and precious child, showing true love every time. I hugged back as strong as I could.

"I love you. I don't want to leave," I said and the tears that fell from my own eyes soaked the jumper she was wearing.

We may never have broken apart. Mother and son, why would they let go of each other in these desperate times? But my father wanted his turn with his son, and when he placed a hand on his wife's shoulder she sniffed and let me go.

The hug I got from my dad was not like the hug I got from my mother. It was not as tight. Instead it imparted warmth and reassurance that everything was going to be alright. It felt like it imparted pride, that my dad who I looked up to was proud of me and I was going with his blessing. It was amazing to feel such reassurance. Hugs from fathers were always rare and that's what made them special when you got one like a reward for being a good son.

Then the hug tightened. In the last moment, my dad didn't want to let go any more than my mum did.

"I love you son."

"I love you too, dad," I sniffed and wiped my eyes with my sleeve.

We didn't say anything more. Sons and fathers never had to. The respect and love was always unspoken. I regret that most of all. I took my parents for granted and looking back on all they ever did for me, made me realise that no words could ever express the thanks and love I have for them.

Then came the goodbye I was dreading the most.

My little brother, Jack.

It was the worst goodbye because I felt love, regret and shame all at the same time.

Love because he was my little brother, cute and funny and full of energy and wonder. He was amazing. When he was born, I had been old enough to appreciate him and not be jealous.

Dread came over me because I was going to escape and he wasn't. He was younger. I was older. By that reasoning alone he had to go, not me, he had to be saved not me.

It wasn't fair. I was glad to be chosen, and I didn't want to die, but Jack deserved to be chosen too. The reasonable part of my mind told me I had no choice. They chose me. Not him. And I didn't have any control over any of it.

I hugged my brother hard. I had never hugged him before, it wasn't the done thing between brothers, at least not us. He squirmed as I embraced him. He didn't understand its significance, it was the first and last hug we would share.

When I let go, he looked at me and was the picture of innocence. He was happy and content, seeing his big brother off for a holiday, not understanding the calamity about to befall him.

I stepped back and looked at my family: mum, dad, and Jack. They all smiled and waved, but the smiles were tight, holding back tears, save for Jack's.

I stared at them until the memory burnt into my brain. My five minutes were almost up.

The teleport would happen soon, stealing me away from everything I loved.

And the Earth's demise.

2

MY SALVATION

Despite being underground, a virtual window was on the wall of our family's 'room', which was actually more like a cell, and it showed me pictures of the outside world.

The sky was dark. Clouds pumped out from the Destroyer, a by-product of its engines' activities, were continuing to spread, blocking out the sun.

For the last four years those thick, dark clouds had spread from the Hawaiian Islands all across the world.

Australia had been in darkness for three full years. India for two, Africa for one. Europe, now the most densely populated continent on Earth, thanks to mass migrations, was the only place where the sun still sort of reached the ground

I was used to the clouds.

It was the rumblings that held my focus now.

Earthquakes had been spreading out from the Pacific, but I never felt them at home. Here, I felt them through the foundations of the base. Explosions from outside and vibrations through my feet sandwiched me between the effects of Earth's destruction.

They said this would happen, the TV experts. They said that as the weight of the world's water was removed the plates would shift and buckle. Now, the internal pressure of the Earth would suddenly find that the layer of crust it had been pushing against for millions of years was billions of tons lighter than usual. Also add that the Destroyer was getting heavier and heavier with all the water it sucked up. The crust of the earth is very thin in comparison to the rest of its layers, like a crumbly pie crust. The Destroyer was sitting on a fault line as well, where the crust was already cracked. It was breaking the Earth from the outside, while the internal pressure broke Earth from the inside.

I looked at the TV that was in the corner of the room by the window.

The program was the BBC news studio and it was nearly empty, the reporters had long left their desk. The cameraman had let the camera drop, showing the floor of the studio. I thought I heard a faint voice say "Goodbye," but the audio was muffled. It made sense. The end was nigh and so everyone had run home to be where they wanted to be. I was glad that they haven't behaved like a film cliché where it suddenly goes to static. Why would it? Who bothers to turn off studio equipment when the world is about to end?

I smiled at my pithy observation, then the severity of my situation washed over me anew.

The TV offers no new news, but I know what's happening. The five minute warning was going to happen when the world was ten minutes from destruction. By now the Hawaiian archipelago was destroyed and the explosion was cracking the surface of the Earth in new places.

Soon the Destroyer would take off and the compression wave from its engines would tear the planet to pieces.

The earthquakes were getting more intense. The base would topple soon.

Then the teleportation started, my salvation.

My body began to tingle.

I was told that this was the transmission procedure. Every atom of my body had to be identified.

Then spots started to dance in front of my vision and various body parts became disconnected. They were still there in a sense, but they were also somewhere else.

Now that it was happening I couldn't do it.

I couldn't go.

I gave up reason and logic and turned back to my family.

My mother cried. My father reached forward.

We were a family. We couldn't just be separated like this. Not forever.

The teleportation was still happening. Parts of me were disappearing. I could see the shock and sadness in my mum's eyes.

"I don't want to go mum," I cried.

"You have to," she managed to stammer back.

"Mummy, what's happening?" my brother asked in a muffled voice.

I reached out, trying to wrap my arms around all three of them. Maybe if my hands met they would be taken with me.

The tips of my fingers were centimetres away from each other. I could feel it. *Just stretch a bit more.*

Then the dancing spots filled my vision completely.

"No, no, no," I yelled. But my voice was already teleported elsewhere.

My fingertips met.

My family was gone.

More correctly, I was gone.

I gasped and stared down at my empty hands

My eyes filled with tears. I couldn't see exactly where I was, but I knew I was no longer on the army base. The air tasted different and there was a low level droning noise all around me. No more explosions or earthquakes. Just a cavernous drone. I could see through wet eyes that I was now in a much larger space.

I heard the shuffling of feet and others crying around me. I wiped my eyes on my sleeve and then saw exactly where I was.

I was on the Ark.

I had seen it before, on the tour that had been provided during our mission briefing. Then it was a virtual tour, not a real one. The Ark had already been placed in orbit by the time I was chosen

Filling the Ark around me were hundreds of other children.

Some were in the same state of shock as I was. Others were staring into space.

Then there was a collective gasp and outbursts of crying from some of my companions.

It could only be a reaction to one thing.

I turned to face the Ark's window: a giant panoramic glass shield protecting us from the cold vacuum of space.

Through it, I saw the planet Earth in its last moment of life.

3

THE ONLY ONE WATCHING

I joined the other children at the window.

A meter-high railing ran parallel to the glass for us to lean on. I grasped the rail to watch the end.

I had never seen the Earth from this vantage point before, and now could finally see just how bad things had become and how dead my world now looked.

I had seen broadcasts from around the world over the years of the chaos and fighting, which had ruined cities and the most impressive monuments on Earth.

Never though had I seen it like this. The food riots, nuclear strikes and small proxy wars were nothing compared to what my eyes now beheld.

One half of the planet was barren, a dark brown wasteland as if the deserts had multiplied and swallowed up half the Earth. The northern hemisphere was slightly blue and green in patches, but covered in dark clouds.

One whole continental plate in Africa had risen above the ones around it and was outlined bright red by the lava squeezing through the cracks. It looked like a giant version of one of those mountains in South America, from the classic film, *Up.* A section of land had risen upwards, a million square kilometre pillar of rock.

The planet had even changed shape, like a malformed, shrinking balloon.

It was a nightmare. This orb had been humanity's home for so long, and we had believed it would stand for an eternity, a bastion of safety in a harsh universe.

Now it was a dying husk.

Worst of all my family was down there, completely unable to escape.

We were right above the Indian continent. Vicious cracks were appearing on the Earth's surface. They were red, magma was rising to the surface. Down the line of children I saw one boy turn away. He had dark skin and curly hair. He must be the chosen Indian child. I didn't blame him for not looking.

I wanted to turn away, but I couldn't. I felt I owed it to those below to witness their ending.

I felt like *Superman*, or more accurately *Superman's* father, *Jor-el*. It was like watching Krypton explode. My world was crumbling beneath me.

The Ark slowly moved away from the planet, getting clear of the disaster. Earth was getting smaller by the second.

Then the Destroyer came into view.

A stupid name in my opinion, a news corporation's attempt to be dramatic. I didn't like it because it was cheesy, I hated the name because it was so finite, so hopeless. 'The Destroyer.' This thing that had invaded our planet was going to win. It was a destroyer, unable to be stopped. I wondered why the human race tried to survive after giving it that name. Must be human nature.

The Destroyer was massive, and had pierced the Earth like the tip of a spear. The point of the vessel was embedded in the middle of the Pacific Ocean where Hawaii used to be.

The part of the vessel that wasn't inside the Earth reached beyond the upper atmospheric layers. When it first landed numerous satellites that were in low orbit had smashed into it, including the International Space Station.

Snaking out from the vessel were pipes. They spread out into the atmosphere and the oceans.

They were like veins siphoning off the only two resources that matter on a habited planet, water and air.

The Earth was almost empty of both.

From where we were I saw the vessel disconnect itself from the network of pipes it had laid, like the old space rockets breaking free of the towers that held them up before they travelled to the moon. Even from thousands of miles away I saw the explosions that occurred when the Destroyer broke away.

This was it.

I knew what was going to happen next.

The monster ship began to glow as it charged an engine near its tip.

The pulse from the engine would allow the massive ship to leave the Earth's gravity.

The pulse was an intense burst of energy. On the news, I had seen a nuclear explosion on Earth before, and it was nothing compared to the flash that came from the Destroyer's engines. It was so bright that I had to raise a hand to block out the intense light, which faded as quickly as it had shone.

I saw The Destroyer leave our world and head off into space.

The pulse's shockwave, which we felt even in space, rippled through the Ark and everyone fell to the floor.

I grasped the rail and I alone stayed upright.

I was the only one to see the Earth blow up.

The pulse hit the core of the planet and through the cracks in the crust the same bright light shone outwards. For a moment my ugly, wreaked home-world glowed from within. Its last moment of beauty.

Then the Earth shattered.

The plates that made up the crust were thrown away and the glowing molten mantle of the planet was exposed.

The Ark sped away from the explosion and avoided the massive chunks of our former home that threatened to crush us.

The moon took multiple direct impacts and broke apart.

Only the iron core of the Earth remained where my homeworld had once been, a dull, dead stone floating in space.

Our home was gone.

My mum, my dad... Jack.

And I saw it all go.

Me. Callum Tasker.

SYSTEM ONLINE

CHECKING PHASE ONE PARAMETERS

1. TELEPORT SUCCESSFUL

2. OXYGEN PUMPS ONLINE

3. LIGHTING ONLINE

4. HEATING ONLINE

SOLAR SYSTEM SCAN REPORT

1. DESTROYER PROCEEDING OUT OF THE SYSTEM

2. ARK COURSE SET, TRAJECTORY IS CLEAR

3. DEBRIS FIELD CLEARED.

PHASE TWO IN EFFECT

ACTIVATING DR. GHOST FILE 1 - INTRODUCTION

THE THIEF COMES CRASHING DOWN

SEVEN YEARS AGO

On the day the Ark landed I was 8 years old.

Back then I had very little concerns in life, the world was still a normal place, with its daily routine of school work, holidays, government, sport, free time and eating/drinking. I wish I could say that I was clued in to what was going on in the world, however I confess to not having a clue about the daily issues. In hindsight, I needn't have wasted my time reading newspapers or watching the news anyway. All those problems the world had are over now. Global warming gone, terrorism gone, these things are irrelevant in my current predicament.

I remember the day very clearly however. Well who wouldn't? My dad told me that when he was very young, about my age, he watched a terrorist attack involving planes and remembered everything about that day. And so it was with me when aliens made contact with the human race for the first time.

It was not the kind of contact we were expecting.

Long before the Ark landed it was spotted by NASA and the European Space Agency. The TV reported the discovery as the passing of a very large asteroid near to Earth, which was true, the giant vessel was covered in rock and ice as it approached our homeworld over the course of two months.

Documentaries were hastily put together on the appearance of such a large lump of rock.

Tabloid newspapers put out headlines like NEAR EARTH COLLISION POSSIBLE, END OF THE WORLD? And so forth, just to drum up public panic and interest in the story.

No one was frightened though, every scientist worth their PHD said it was going to pass by us harmlessly.

I heard about it of course, but it was hardly worth my time, I had computer games to complete. The thing only appeared in the skies for eight days when it was close enough to the planet. When I first saw it in the sky it was a boring sight, just another light at night and during the day it looked like a plane that wouldn't move in the sky.

However it was kind of a new friend, I would look up and feel comforted that it was there, like we had somehow obtained a new moon.

On its final day in our skies a special late night show was on, as the asteroid was going to pass behind a full moon and the possibility of it hitting our natural satellite was still feasible.

I was ignoring the spectacle. I was only eight years old and space was not a particularly interesting place for me. Humanity at the time was not seriously considering space travel, the Mars landings had not been followed up due to cost and lack of real results, plus as I'm sure you know, space is vast. What's the point if you couldn't cross it fast enough?

My mum did however come into my room and practically drag me downstairs to watch, and managed to entice me when she said the moon might blow up under impact.

And so I watched the show and waited patiently for the asteroid to first disappear behind our natural satellite and then to reappear a few seconds later, which it did.

My parents were excited and a little relieved, no one lived on that moon so what did it matter if it was hit.

I was the only one in our house to notice something off about the asteroid.

It was no longer streaking across the heavens, instead it looked like it had stopped completely on the far left hand side of the moon.

I may have been wrong, but it looked like it was getting bigger as well.

The presenters on the show hadn't noticed, and they instead talked about how it was a rare astrological feature not seen in a generation.

It was then one of them put their finger to their ear to receive a message from the production crew, then panic and fear started to spread.

"Oh, no. Should that be happening?" the presenter said, to a scientist who had joined him in the studio.

Those were the kind of words you shouldn't say live on air.

The scientist looked behind him at the big screen showing a telescopic close-up of the asteroid.

The asteroid was getting larger and it was shedding ice and rock, that was falling into the gravity well of the moon. The close up showed impacts on its surface.

"No, it should continue on, following this path," the scientist said and traced the predicted path of the asteroid with his finger.

By now I was picking up on the fear my parents were feeling. Mum tapping at the chair's arm. Dad peering into the television.

"It seems as though the asteroid has changed course," the astronomer said in surprise. "That's not possible, how can it do that?" he added.

Then the program stopped. The screen flashed. The words "breaking news" appeared. This was news.

"This is an emergency broadcast, asteroid M5437 has changed course and is now heading directly for planet Earth. We advise everyone to seek shelter immediately, "This is an emergency broadcast...."

As the news broadcaster repeated his message, my father plucked me from the sofa, and rushed me, mum and Jack into our basement.

"What's going on? I said.

My father didn't respond. My dad went back upstairs and returned carrying bottles of water and crisps.

We sat down in the basement, I could hear screaming outside in the street.

My dad took out his mobile phone and brought up the news channel.

"Greg don't," my mum had scolded him.

"We have to know what's going on," he protested.

The same news channel we had been watching appeared on the mobile phone screen, and we gathered round.

New images were displayed showing the asteroid heading for Earth. The reporters were trying to say something constructive on the situation, but how do you report on a disaster of that magnitude.

The asteroid entered the atmosphere and huge amounts of fire obscured it from view. Rock and vaporised water left a thicker trail of debris in its wake.

"If you live in the northern hemisphere find shelter immediately," the news broadcaster said.

The images turned to another satellite in orbit tracking the asteroid.

The shots were above the Atlantic and zoomed in on the falling rock.

It was heading for Iceland.

Horrified gasps and statements came from the presenters. As cameras in orbit followed the asteroid as it moved closer to Iceland we could see ships leaving the island. The wake of the various ships gave the island the appearance of a jellyfish.

Then came the impact.

The phone vibrated in my father's hand as the thunderclap of the asteroid's impact on our atmosphere was piped through the news cameras to us.

Then the whole house vibrated as the rumble reached us in real time.

I screamed. Mother held me and Jack tight.

"It's okay boys. It's okay," I remember her saying softly.

We all saw the asteroid strike Iceland with colossal force and the impact created a flash of light that momentarily obscured the camera's view.

The images then changed to a much closer view of the island. These appeared to be taken from a plane flying off the coast.

It was a wide angle shot showing a shower of water and rock falling into the Atlantic.

A tidal wave was issuing forth from the island, the water pushed forwards by the creation of a crater caused by the asteroid impact.

The debris began to clear and I expected to see a massive hole in the ground.

"This isn't right," the scientific advisor on the news program said. "An impact of that size would have affected us by now. Where's the explosion? The debris field would not clear so quickly."

There was no hole in the ground.

What I saw instead, and what the whole world saw, had pierced the crust of the Earth, not smashed into it. It now sat in the very centre of Iceland like a newly formed mountain.

It was not an asteroid any more, it was a ship.

4

THE GHOST

The Ark sped beyond the shockwaves and rubble of the Earth's death throes and stabilised. My knuckles were white and my arms a little sore from holding so tight to the rail during the explosion.

I didn't look away from the window, but out of the corner of my eye I could sense everyone else getting to their feet and shambling forward to see the remains of our homeworld. It felt strange to think of it that way. It implied we had other worlds and that Earth needed to be identified as special. But there was nothing special about it anymore.

Everything we had known from our fifteen years of life was gone. Our nations, civilisations, people, government, society, friends, family, houses... All gone.

The Earth was now just a field of debris radiating out from the iron core of the planet that had survived the destruction.

There was crying all around - no one available to comfort another.

Why would they, anyway? We were all strangers here.

We hadn't even met during the orientation week. We met the mission specialists individually, in our home countries.

We stood there in silence, some of us walked away from the window, some sat down.

I suppose from a bunch of fifteen year olds you would expect a much more emotional or dramatic reaction. All our parents were gone. Our brothers and sisters and friends, all gone too. We were alone on an alien ship and everything that we could count on to keep us safe had been destroyed.

We should all be hysterical, maybe even frightened of each other. I should have been throwing up or crying or running around like mad. But, it wasn't like that.

We had all been prepared.

We all had the memories to guide us, implanted in us for this day. Those memories were now activating, as part of the mission, to smooth the transition to our new lives.

The day we stopped being average teenagers and became the remnants of the human race.

"Children," a voice suddenly said. These were the first words spoken by anyone since we arrived on the Ark.

Everyone except me looked up at the ceiling in response, the usual human reaction, seeking the source of a disembodied voice.

I didn't look up because I knew there was no point. The person who was speaking wasn't hanging from the ceiling. He was very much dead.

It was a voice we all knew.

It had belonged to a man named Dr. Richard Ghost, the one who had chosen us all to be here, the one who made this entire project viable, the one who had prepared us all.

"Please assemble in the theatre for your mission briefing and leadership introduction. Follow the guide strips to find the correct location on the Ark," Dr. Ghost said.

It was then that I followed the gaze of every other child and stared up at the ceiling. A thick red line of light appeared above us, don't ask me how it was projected in thin air, but there it was. As it flickered into view it was accompanied by a buzzing sound, just like some fluorescent lights make when they are activated.

I didn't immediately follow the red line.. For one thing, I was still trying to get it straight in my head that I just lost my parents, brother and home all because by some fluke I was the right kid. I was born at the right time, with the right DNA to get a place on the Ark. I had no choice in the matter. No one did. And despite being surrounded by more than two hundred other chosen children I felt all alone.

Normally I would have just collapsed onto the floor and started balling my eyes out.

But that was when I had a mum to comfort me. Now, I had responsibilities. There were things that I had to do. I needed to keep going, if not for myself, then for everyone we left behind.

I shook off my concerns and started to follow the red line, and the doctor's orders. At the time it didn't click with me that I was the first to do so, but none of the others had moved.

I hadn't even noticed that half of the others had been staring at me ever since the doctor's announcement.

Two hundred plus pairs of footsteps followed me, and the red line, deeper into the Ark, our home for the next three years.

Maybe forever.

No one spoke on the way to the theatre.

We still didn't know each other's names.

I started to wonder and silently dread the possibility of there being some kind of ice breaker session, where we'd all have to circulate around the room and learn three things about one another. The thought made me sick. I don't know why, but I guess it would just be kind of insulting for us, the last representatives of mankind, to do. This wasn't the first day of fourth grade, after all.

The corridors inside the Ark felt endless. The orientation week I had been on included a tour around a mock set up of the vessel, not the real thing. And that model was much smaller. The architecture inside the Ark was strange, and felt slightly Victorian, with unnecessary decoration and adornments on the pillars, just like the old train stations in London. It was a space ship for heaven's sake. Where was the functionality? Where were the rugged, exposed metal panels that I'd seen in space travel movies?

I was not entirely happy with the name either, *The Ark*. No doubt it was someone's hope that giving the ship a religiously important designation bestowed it with gravitas and deeper meaning. I thought it was just a lack of imagination.

I was surprised we weren't called the Genesis Crew of something obvious like that. I don't why people borrowed from the Bible in that way. As if the importance of the Bible was in the words it used instead of the meaning it imparted.

It isn't important now, though. Whomever named the Ark was gone with the rest of Earth.

The red line led us to a room with a tiered seating arrangement facing a large-format theatre screen.

Immediately this place felt familiar.

But that was to be expected.

The room was not part of the original ship, human hands had built this and designed it like any other theatre. I wouldn't call it that though. There was a stage and screen, however it was more like a cinema. Built for us, for education and entertainment during our long journey, to make us comfortable in uncomfortable times.

It was already lit up and there were three tiers of seats, which were further divided into two blocks. Subconsciously, due to my new set of implanted memories, I counted the chairs, assessing my surroundings.

There were 260 seats divided into two big blocks and ten rows of thirteen chairs each. I knew that was too many for those present, which I thought was strange. *Were more people joining us? No, that was ridiculous.* Maybe there were supposed to be more of us, but they had been rejected?

I ignored these thoughts and tried to suppress the implanted memories that had activated them.

My head clear, I decided on where to sit.

I was first into the room and I decided on a seat that adhered to the cinema seat picking policy I had used on Earth.

I chose a row halfway down, so the screen was right in front of me without me having to raise or lower my head. I also wanted to sit next to the isle because I didn't want to have to embarrass myself or annoy anyone by asked them to move aside so I can get out.

As I sat down, the rest of the crowd filled the cinema.

No one sat next to me. They left a ring of seats around me, as if I were the Sun and they the other planets. Some people would have to sit next to each other eventually. It was inevitable. But no one wanted to be the first to break another's personal space.

Some of children who spoke the same language had found each other, and were staying together. Others who probably had the benefit of geography and history found each other, too.

There were odd smiles and nods, and for the first time some normal sounding conversation, like "Anyone sitting there?" or "Excuse me" or "Hey, I want that seat!"

Once we were all seated, the lights dimmed, and the talking children fell silent.

In curiosity, I checked my watch and realised that it had been exactly fifteen minutes since the announcement. The ship was on a timer.

Then the screen lit up.

There were no logos or advertisements, this wasn't a summer blockbuster, just a white screen and fading into view was Dr. Ghost, himself.

The man looked like a thinned down version of Santa Claus.

He had lots of white hair and a short, thick beard. I wondered when he had recorded this. A week ago? Maybe more? The dwindling food supply, over the past months had ruined most people's health.

"Children," his voice boomed. "Welcome on board the Ark."

He winced for a second when he said the ship's name. It wasn't his choice for a name either.

"What we prepared for has happened. The Earth is no more. It is time for you to consider the future now, and how you will live aboard this alien space ship."

5

OUR MISSION

"First, let me outline the mission once again for you," Dr. Ghost said.

I rolled my eyes, I had heard this all before back on Earth, and I doubted anything had changed. I slumped back in my chair

The doctor's face retreated into an inset box at the top left hand corner of the screen, and a map of the solar system filled the rest. Each planet's orbital paths were traced across an inky blackness, only half the planets were on the screen.

"As you know the Destroyer was an automated space ship that arrived in our solar system and was projected to leave via this course," the doctor said.

The map focused on planet Earth, whole and healthy, and showed a blue triangle leaving the planet and heading outward to the edge of the Solar System.

"We believe it is taking the resources it stole from our world back to wherever it came from," The doctor said. "Because of this, your course will send the Ark in the opposite direction, out of the system toward a wormhole that has been orbiting our sun for millennia."

I had heard of the wormhole at orientation. It was discovered using the advanced technologies harvested from the Ark. No one has ever been through the wormhole before. I suddenly wasn't sure if I wanted to traverse a gigantic space phenomenon that no one has ever experienced.

"The wormhole has been studied by long range probes and we have determined that on the other side there is a planet similar to Earth.

We believe this is the best shot the human race has of settling a new home, one the Destroyer won't be able to reach."

That was good news. I had wondered if it was worth saving us if the Destroyer was able to find us again somewhere down the line.

"Because of limited resources due to the Destroyer's harvesting, the water and oxygen that is onboard the Ark will last four years. We've calculated that your journey to the wormhole will take a year, your journey through it a single day, and your trip to the nearest habitable planet on the other side another year and a half. You will have a year and half's back up supply with you on your journey. This has been calculated for the exact number of passengers you have, no more no less."

Where would new passengers come from anyway? I didn't think we were allowed to pick up hitchhikers.

"Over the course of the next two plus years, you must tend to the vessel and prepare yourselves to begin a colony on your new homeworld," the doctor said. "Now then, the time has come for you to learn each other's names. For security, we never allowed you to socialise on Earth, however you are now crewmates and when you reach the planet on the other side of the wormhole, hopefully you will be the beginnings of a new human race."

I knew it, I knew it, a flipping ice breaker session, I thought.

I shrank further down in my seat.

"This presentation will now cycle through all your names and photographs. Use the memory techniques implanted by Howard Carver to commit each of them to memory."

I sat up straight, this was better. Howard Carver was the fourth memory implant we were given. He had been a celebrated Memory Man able to commit vast stores of information to near perfect memory. All of us had his various techniques and ways of thinking in our minds. In fact, our brains had even been partially reorganized in order to replicate his unique mind.

We learned all of Carver's techniques through a variety of injections administered over the course of the last nine months. However it wasn't chemicals or medicines that changed all our minds it was something far more invasive.

Millions of nanites, small robots the size of germs that are able to work on a cellular level to alter our bodies were in each injection. They literally tore apart the tiniest pieces of our bodies and rebuilt them to accommodate the new techniques and memories. Some also latched onto my flesh and physically expanded my brain.

In my head right now small robots that look like insects are crawling all over my brain. Have you ever sat around a camp fire and swapped horror stories? Well I have, and the most frequently repeated was about earwigs, and how they crawl into your ear, and lay their eggs inside.

Well, that's how I feel everyday. That feeling of something crawling around inside your head is like nothing else.

In total we had 17 memory implants in our minds.

The process of programming them was very complex. The batch of nanites would first be injected into another human, one whose mind you wished to replicate. For example, Howard Carver was injected and the nanites were programed to seek his brain and copy the parts needed to transfer his ability to memorise facts, into another brain. I guess we could have been taught his methods, but it was too dangerous to risk one of us forgetting.

Once the nanites copied his mind they were extracted and reinjected into each of us.

Carter had to do this almost 260 times, for 260 injections.

I can't imagine what it was like for him and the 16 others who donated their talents to us all.

Receiving these new skills had been the most difficult and interesting part of the whole orientation process, however their full potential wasn't activated until now. Dr. Ghost didn't want our personalities to shift too dramatically while on Earth. Maybe for security, or maybe just so our families didn't see us change.

The first memory implant was the reason I was no longer capable of crying or getting angry. Even before it was fully activated it had given my mind enormous discipline I shouldn't have at the age of 15.

Implant Number One had belonged to a Captain Amis, a Royal Marine who had served across the globe, and even entered the Destroyer on a mission to destroy it from within. It was a failed mission, but the Captain made it out alive.

His memory implant imparted his sense of duty and confidence in a war zone, his courage in the face of perhaps the most terrifying place for a human visit. This was a man who kept fighting even when his fellow soldiers died around him in a frenzy of bullets.

Amis's unflappability was keeping me from having a break down right now.

As the doctor said, the screen showed the names and faces of my fellow crewmates, in alphabetical order, sorted by country of origin.

The first picture was of a boy, his name was Dehqan and he was from Afghanistan. The picture was like a passport photo. The boy wore the most neutral expression I had ever seen on a human being, and it was then that I realised mine would bare the same one too. We probably all had the same photographer at some point telling us how to hold ourselves and where to look and not to say cheese.

As I focused on the name and details about Dehgan I saw people who were probably seated next to him, turning their heads to check him out in the flesh to confirm it was him.

The next picture was a girl, the one after that a boy and I wondered if that was deliberate. No doubt there needed to be an equal boy to girl ratio. I also thought that whoever had selected us was lazy, as he had simply gone boy, girl, boy, girl, boy, girl according to country. If my luck had been different, if I had been a girl, maybe I wouldn't have been chosen? Maybe I would have been left behind? The thought made me uncomfortable.

The sequence of names and faces continued.

My name and my face finally appeared and I read the details.

Callum Tasker born in England.

I was happy with the photo. It showed me at the age of thirteen with longer hair than I had now. The army base barber was no kind of stylist, and it's not like soldiers could request the latest hairstyle. I also had more weight to my face then, not the ration-made bony features I had now. I admired my hair, it was black and curly and framed my face. And the scar wasn't there. Not yet passing vertically across my left eye from my forehead to just above my mouth. I hated that scar, another wound brought about by my selection.

Everyone in the cinema turned to me when my picture came up.

Many looked at me, then the picture, then me again. The absence of a scar obviously confused them. I knew I was going to get a lot of questions about that later.

When the next picture came up, attention returned to the screen once more.

I watched 258 faces appear and disappear, and I had them all committed to memory by the time the last face disappeared. Knowing all their names and faces didn't prompt me to go and talk to any of them, though.

The last face faded from view and fading into his dominating position in the centre of the screen was Dr. Ghost.

"Now then children, I think it is time for you to rest and relax for the next twelve hours. No doubt your day has been exceptionally trying and emotional. The whole Ark is open to you except the cargo bays, which you will gain access to in a couple of days. If you want to sleep you can find your designated apartments using the computer terminals around the ship. Service robots are already performing maintenance duties so do not be alarmed if you meet them. Dinner will be served at 8:00pm in the cafeteria. Just follow the illuminated line when it's time. Tomorrow you will meet your mission leader who will command of the Ark. Rest well."

The doctor's face was lost to blackness as the screen powered down and the cinema became quiet.

Mission Leader? I didn't know there was going to be one. I guess the governments couldn't really trust two hundred plus children to manage themselves.

In some ways I'm glad that an adult was going to take charge tomorrow. I've always been the type to step up and lead in school, on sports teams, but I hate being one of these people. I hate the responsibility and the conflict when someone else decides they would have done it better.

Faces turned toward me from all around the cinema. I sensed that they were already looking to me, probably because I was the first to follow the red line, but no one was getting out of their seat or talking.

After seeing those names and faces, our names and faces, knowing that we were all that was left of Earth. That Jack, and mum, and dad weren't on that screen... I just wanted to be alone. I got up and ascended the stairs to the exit keeping my eyes fixed on the steps, and not once looking up into the eyes that followed me.

I knew the Ark was huge and there was plenty to explore, and there was plenty on my mind that I still wanted to forget.

Without thinking, I turned left when I exited and started walking.

I stared to run when I heard footfalls following me.

I just wanted to be alone.

6

HUMANITY'S SECOND ARK

I managed to escape my fellow crew members, and began walking the halls as randomly as I could. Every time I reached a fork in the road, so to speak, I would just go with my gut instinct and go left, right or whatever. I was not looking for anything. I just wanted to find a quiet place.

It should have been easy to find a quiet place to sit down and avoid people, but no matter how long I walked nowhere seemed far enough away from everyone else, or quiet enough, so I walked on.

Sometimes at school during break times I used to the do the same thing. I would just walk away from the crowds and sit alone with my thoughts. It was impossible though. Even when I just sat down behind the hut at the farthest reach of the school grounds, someone would walk by the same place.

As I walked the corridors of the Ark, I found empty rooms, but I knew that someone would find me. The Ark is massive. Still, I couldn't trust any place to be a place of solitude.

As I wandered, sometimes turning around and going back where I had already been when I heard voices, I pondered the ship; my new home.

The Ark was city sized, not as big as the Destroyer even though they have the same basic design.

Seven years ago when the Ark pierced the atmosphere of our world to steal our water and air, it touched down over Iceland and almost completely obliterated the island. The tsunami caused by the landing crater changed the face of the northern hemisphere forever.

Humanity managed to stop the Ark from stealing our resources. The battle was fierce, and only three days long. At least from what I remember. I was a kid then.

Then the Destroyer arrived three years later and began siphoning off Earth's resources again, at a much faster rate than the Ark ever did. We never determined what alien race had created it, but it was clear that they wanted what our planet had.

Pundits on television wondered if they just wanted to replenish their own world. Maybe they were like us, poisoning their own air and water as their population grew? Maybe they sought out our resources, rather than fixing the damage they had done to their home planet?

We tried to fight the Destroyer, but they had learned from the battle against the Ark, and the new ship was too powerful.

The Ark is about one tenth the size of the Destroyer, and couldn't possibly hold all the Earth's water and air, so our scientists theorised that it was designed to strip smaller worlds, and must have been wrongly programmed to attack Earth.

The capture of the Ark was a momentous day for humanity. We gained a host of various technologies, as well as a giant intergalactic space ship.

For a while the most powerful nations debated which nation should hold rights to the ship. The United Nations spent months arguing the issue. Eventually though, international co-operation won over, and it was decided that the ship would be used solely for scientific research.

The Ark Program was born, and it began as a space exploration project. We intended to send it out into space to explore our solar system, and beyond, in far greater detail than ever possible before. By testing the alien technology on the Ark, humanity became aware that aliens existed, and that they weren't too friendly. Militaries around the world began preparing for a possible second attack.

Then the second attack happened. The Destroyer came and the Ark Program changed. No longer focused on exploration, it would work to preserve the human race so it could continue beyond Earth.

I was twelve years old when the Destroyer landed and I remember the news broadcasts of the first, second and third attacks on it. The threat it posed was better understood by that time, but every assault against it failed.

So, the governments of the world lied to the people, and told them the Ark would be dropped on the Destroyer to obliterate it. The truth was the Ark was going to be used to save a portion of the human race. World leaders assured the people that the Ark Program had a different goal, the exploration was cancelled, and instead the Ark would be a weapon. As the Destroyer stole from us, so did the Ark, taking air and water for the humans who would fly to safety away from Earth.

At orientation, Dr. Ghost explained, coldly and logically, that the planet was doomed anyway, which is why the Ark had to take even more resources.

I've spent most of the last nine months, since I knew I would be saved, thinking about his logic. It's like those situations in films where the hero has to make the hard choice, to destroy in order to protect, to weigh life for life.

A part of me cried, *Save them!*

But Dr. Ghost presented the facts. The Earth was already dead, and everyone on earth was doomed. It was the future of humanity, or its fated present, and seeking the future was the logical choice.

Logic however was cold and unfeeling.

And it didn't make me feel better, even if I wanted it to.

Despite the secrecy of the Ark Program plan, some people found out.

The rich and powerful thought they could buy their way to salvation. More than a few oligarchs, corporate CEOs, and royal families were neutralised when they tried to influence the program at the highest level.

Dr. Ghost told us that some wealthy people tried to blackmail the governments to letting them on board the Ark. And they threatened to reveal the plan to the general public.

At orientation, they explained how we were chosen. Only so much air, water and food could be stored on the Ark and that dictated how many people could go.

Dr. Ghost had insisted children be the crew of the Ark. Young enough to survive the journey, and each using less resources than a full grown adult.

Dr. Ghost also selected children across the globe based on who had the best DNA for a successful gene pool. It was important that humanity continued with the best possible chance of survival, he had reasoned. Dr. Ghost decided that one child from every nation on Earth would go so that all of humanity was represented.

I am lucky to be here. But when I think of the millions who never had a chance to be here, I feel sad, and almost ashamed.

On launch day, once Dr. Ghost and his teams had unlocked most of the alien technology on board, the whole world watched the Ark lift off into high orbit.

Only a mere hour after it was set in orbit did the questions and arguing spread around the planet. Billions of people were expecting the Ark to smash the Destroyer, as they had been told, but that didn't happen.

That was when the chaos started. Governments around the world disintegrated as people rebelled, demanding a spot on the Ark when they realised the truth.

For our protection, the chosen had to wait till the last minute to board the Ark, using the ship's teleportation system.

And now I was there.

Wandering around, just taking my new reality in.

I can't imagine how the alien builders of the Ark decided that they would just strip other planets of life. I wondered if they cared that they had destroyed a whole civilisation. I wondered why the ships were sent without any crew. I wondered if the aliens saw humans as nothing more than rodents.

I continued down the ship's various corridors pondering all we had won and lost... and what my future held.

As I turned a corner, the alien architecture of the ship changed into something that was very familiar to me.

BATTLE AGAINST THE THIEF

Three days after the giant alien ship had landed, military forces from several nations in and around the Atlantic approached Iceland. Even China sent a huge fleet.

They were followed by news helicopters and planes from around the world.

The Ark's landing had caused a tidal wave. Northern Ireland, Scotland and parts of Canada had suffered flooding on their coastal areas. The way the ship pierced the Earth's surface limited the damage, but the appearance of such a gigantic vessel was causing alarm and panic across the globe.

No one could understand why it had appeared as an asteroid when scientists started tracking it. Talking heads suggested that if it had been travelling for many years in space, it might have accumulated such debris. Others who wanted to give the fear knife an extra twist suggested that it was camouflage, so that when it approached a world little attention would be paid to it.

Either way it didn't matter now, the ship was here. Its intentions had to be determined.

Refugees fled what remained of Iceland

The Ark did nothing for three days. It just sat there, towering over the island it had ruined. It was on the fourth day after its arrival that it finally did something.

I watched it all from the comfort of my own home. We stayed in the basement for a day, then came out when the all clear was sounded. We had Scottish relatives, evacuated, now staying with us. My cousins all shared my room. It was like a giant sleep over.

The living room filled with the whole family when the actual battle started.

At the edges of the Ark, doors opened and snaking out from them came tubes that slithered over the land like writhing worms.

These tubes crawled across the island then down into the sea.

Each one was massive enough for a train to pass through, and some were larger.

Helicopters hovering nearby tracked the pipes moving underwater, seeking the deepest parts of the Atlantic Ocean.

From the top of the Ark, towers grew into the atmosphere, extending telescopically. Some stopped a mile or two above the ship, while others climbed higher still, passing beyond the airplanes observing the scene.

The battle started when one of the pipes in the sea stopped underneath a battleship.

The water above the pipe, and around the battleship, started to sink. Foam and spray kicked up as water disappeared into the pipe, eventually forming a giant whirlpool. The battleship spun around at the whirlpool's edge until finally its bow went under the water, and down towards the pipe's mouth.

At my age at the time I had no concept of the lives of on the ship, or the brave sailors who went down with it. To me it was all like a film. When my mum started to cry, I knew that something was really wrong.

When the battleship hit the end of the pipe it exploded.

The explosion was massive, a combination of all the fuel and weapons on the ship. The pipe was damaged in the blast.

The sea erupted in fire and a spray of water.

Then the Ark sent another pipe and it continued to suck up water from exactly the same spot, pulling in some of the wreckage of the destroyed ship.

The news broadcaster reported that more water was being sucked into other pipes all around the northern hemisphere. The Weather man reported the barometric pressure changes as the towers above the Ark started sucking up the Earth's air.

The battleships began firing on the Ark. Airplanes took off from the aircraft carriers to deliver their payloads upon the hull of the alien ship.

Missiles streaked towards the Ark, and it was rocked by multiple impacts that scarred its hull. Many pipes and towers damaged. The ship responded by sending out more pipes and towers. It never seemed to target the attacking ships, instead replacing its own damaged parts.

The attacks against the Ark's surface were mostly ineffective. The hull was too strong, and the replacement pipes too numerous to stop.

The navy changed its tactics.

Depth charges, mines and torpedoes were dumped around all of the pipe entrances, some of which had already reached the equator and the North American coast.

The pipes sucked up the bombs and mines, exploding in the pipes and some inside the alien ship.

After two days of detonations the Ark sustained enough damaged that it shut down.

Fifty military ships had been destroyed, not to mention thousands of other commercial vessels, and Iceland was no longer habitable.

But we had won, the alien ship had been defeated.

It was a shame that our victory was so short lived.

7

MY HOME FAR AWAY FROM HOME

By accident, I stumbled upon our rooms.

The corridor that housed them stretched on for what seemed like kilometres and every ten metres there was a door on each side.

I could tell that these had been added to the Ark by human hands. They looked nothing like the original alien design.

Since the Ark had been an automated mining and storage ship for oxygen and water, having small crew quarters was unnecessary. Additionally, each door was different like the doors you might have found on Earth's suburban housing developments. They were a mix of different colours and decorations, and some had numbers still painted only, if faintly. It was only when I noticed Icelandic writing on one of them I finally understood. These doors had been harvested from Icelandic homes. The ones destroyed and abandoned when the Ark arrived.

That gave me chills.

But we had more of Earth with us than I originally thought, too.

The transition between the alien built corridors to the human modified ones was abrupt. The alien corridors, smooth and uniform in some extraterrestrial metal ended at a crude weld and the human architecture took over. I wondered what was originally in the space they had modified, and what might have been done with all the removed alien material.

I didn't trust the human-added corridor, either. I knew little about welding, but I could tell that the materials were different, and that might mean this new part of the ship was not supported properly. I was having visions of the whole thing tumbling around inside the ship with us in it, just like a clothes dryer.

My curiosity was greater than my fear, so I stepped forward, carefully watching out for any loose plates of metal in the night, or the cracking welds.

As I strolled past the doors I saw that each one was marked in black ink with a country name. I started to think that if this was the *Enterprise* from those old *Star Trek* shows a bronze plaque would have been fixed to each door with our names engraved on them. But here, they would have seemed out of place. The Ark construction project shouldn't waste time and limited resources on personalised name plates for the doors. Some of the signs even had little smiley faces dotting the "I"s. One had a crude landscape illustration on it, as if the builder who had installed it had gotten bored with just writing names and decided to add a little flair.

The builders had signed their names on some of them, scrawled and illegible, leaving a scant record of their contributions.

There was one door that stood out most. The name of the country had been written neatly and clearly, but just underneath an insult— Murderous Pigs!—was scrawled. The writing was jagged and rough, as if the writer was shaking angrily when they had wrote it. I wondered why it was there. Had the worker realised what the Ark was really for and snapped? Leaving a last jab at the people they thought were dooming the rest of the Earth?

Otherwise, the doors were in no particular order. Not alphabetical. Not by continent or hemisphere. I guessed they had been randomised so that the representative from Zimbabwe didn't have to walk the furthest on account of her country's name.

My room was about fifty doors down.

It was painted blue, and had no lock other than the original handle installed on the door. I wondered where it had come from. Perhaps the apartment of a single guy, or a family home. The wood was dinged and knocked, telling a story that I would never know for sure. There was a scuff in the shape of a boot print near the bottom of the door. Whoever lived here had opened it once with a big kick. Maybe while carrying heavy shopping bags, or maybe it was a desperate moment, when the Ark came?. It was my door now, so I grabbed the metal handle and barged the door open with my shoulder. This was how I opened doors. Mum never liked it. She told me to be more gentle. But she was gone, and by doing it this way I was marking my territory. If only ceremonially.

What I found inside surprised me. The room was essentially a larger version of the bedroom I used to have on Earth.

The wallpaper was the same, the posters on the wall were the same, and even the cupboards, bed, and sheets appeared to have come from my old bedroom. The carpet was the same dark red colour, and as I walked across, it even had the same feel to it.

I felt a little bit of gratitude to Dr. Ghost and the team that had built the room. Everything was spot on, and for a moment, I felt like I was at home, even without any windows.

My suitcases sat at the foot of my bed.

I considered unpacking, but there was no hurry. I had over two years to do that.

I lay down on the very familiar mattress and stared at the ceiling.

Once again, I was overwhelmed with loneliness. Everyone I had known was gone and this place was the only remnant of the life I had before. That it looked just like my home was almost worse. It was fake and empty.

A headache was forming at the front of my skull. I had the same stress headaches when I was at school.

When I started secondary school, I was being bullied by a trio of boys. I think they only picked on me because I was there. Luck of the draw. It went on for months. My parents wouldn't remove me from school, no matter how much I begged, but I couldn't tell on the boy's because I wasn't a tattle tale. The headaches started then. I had to go to school, but by going to school I knew I would be bullied.

Of course the bullying stopped right after my induction into the Ark program. Captain Amis' memories made sure I was not going to be bullied again, but they weren't stopping me from feeling lonely and sad that I had survived when my family didn't.

I turned away from the ceiling and lay on my side. That's when I saw another door in the room. Finding out what was beyond it seemed like a good distraction.

It turned out to be nothing more than a simple bathroom with a shower cubicle, toilet and sink. It looked nothing like our bathroom back home. This one was basic, with just the essentials and no frills. Above the sink, a notice written in red lettering said, 'Your daily water usage is restricted to ten gallons'.

I sighed. I used to love long showers.

Even though my room was just a clone, it was pleasant surprise. I assumed we would be put up in dorms, sleeping on bunks. And I hated sharing a room.

Eager to explore more of the Ark, I left my room. In the corridor I was surprised to find the other two hundred-plus survivors of Earth.

They were searching for their rooms, with some gathering in small groups to talk.

Eerily, every conversation stopped as soon as I came near.

I didn't quite understand the effect I was having. My scar might be a point of curiosity, but there had to have been something else about me that attracted their attention.

I couldn't put off talking to them any longer, even if I still didn't want to.

"I can't believe they replicated our rooms," I said to the nearest group. I pointed into my room and tried to look incredulous.

"I mean how did they know it looked like that? Did they spy on us?" I asked. I wanted to get on their good sides, without saying too much about myself. Besides, the people who made our rooms were dead now, and I could talk about them however I wanted without causing them trouble.

The group nearest to me was made up of five children. I remembered who they all were from the introduction video. Ogwambi was to my left. He was from Uganda, tall and lithe with a shaved head. Just behind him was Ernesta, from Italy. Her wide eyes beamed from behind her straight brown hair. She was wearing a flower-pattern dress and makeup. I wondered what she had been doing when she had been picked up to be dressed so nicely. Koyla from Australia was directly opposite me. I knew what he had been doing when he was teleported aboard. He was dressed in pyjamas. He had long dirty blond hair and looked very tired. He yawned as I swept my gaze over the group. To my right were Bae and Koamalu from South Korea and Hawaii, respectively. Koamalu was dressed in mismatched clothes but that was understandable, Hawaiians were essentially a refugee race after the Destroyer landed on the archipelago. Bae was wearing jeans and a t-shirt with a manga character on the front. The character was smiling and wearing a straw hat, I didn't recognise him.

After my initial conversation starter they all just stared at me.

Then suddenly they advanced on me.

SYSTEM ONLINE

PHASE TWO COMPLETE

ALL PHASE TWO INFORMATION BRIEFINGS DELIVERED TO CREW

PHASE 3 NOW IN EFFECT

ACTIVATING DR. GHOST FILE 2 – SIMULATION

8

THE GUILTY

As they advanced on me I stepped back into my room out of instinct. The memories from Captain Amis must have made me a little jumpy. I stopped myself—mid-motion—from slamming the door in their faces.

They were asking questions. That was all. Getting closer to me to talk. Maybe the Ark makes us all a little tense.

"What happened when the Destroyer left?" Bae asked in Spanish.

"Did you see it?" Ernesta asked in Mandarin.

"Any chance of survivors?" Koamalu asked in English.

I understood each of their words perfectly. In our training, they implanted language memories for Spanish, Mandarin and English in every one of us who would be on the Ark. Some of us had other linguistic specialties, but with the memories, Dr. Ghost ensured we all stood on a common ground when it came to communication.

Apparently the English language memories are from George VII. Now that I think about it, I feel a little proud that the entire human race speaks the King's English.

"What are you talking about?" I replied.

"The end of the Earth, what did you see?" Kolya asked.

"You were the only one of us to witness it," Ogwambi said.

I snorted in contempt. The planet was gone. They may not have seen it explode, but they definitely saw the aftermath. What more could I add?

"Why do you want to know?" I replied. "It blew up. It's gone."

Their faces dropped and they turned away from me.

I sighed, feeling a little guilty for being so cold. Koamalu's question was the real reason each of them were asking. They still all hoped that whomever they had left behind was somehow alive. Maybe they thought I had seen something they had not, something that gave cause for hope.

Survivors guilt. I think that's what they call it.

Dr. Ghost wasn't a medical doctor. He was—above all his other fields of study—a psychologist. He invented the memory transference technology. The same tech that gave me the ability to speak different languages, and have Captain Amis' life in my head.

Dr. Ghost was the one who interviewed us when our genetics flagged us as potential candidates. The doctor wanted to understand our mental states, and teach us what we should expect once on the Ark.

Survivors guilt was a topic that we talked about a lot. Even with our memory implants, there was a cost to being one of the only two hundred survivors of Earth.

Dr. Ghost had told us we were heroes. He told us that we were the saviours of the human race. At the time, I saw through it, and felt like it was all a play for the more sensitive kids.

Only one thing he said really stayed with me. It was a crumb of comfort. Dr. Ghost told me that we had a responsibility to survive even if we didn't feel we deserved it. This was bigger than us, or our families and friends. The human race was in our hands, all our history, our shared suffering and potential, our dreams, and even our faults and failures. "Live to save humanity," he had said. That was what we had to do, ready or not.

And I had to do it too, which meant being kind and compassionate to my fellow survivors.

"I'm sorry," I said.

They turned back to face me.

"I did see it," I said. "The end of the Earth."

"What happened?" Bae said.

I saw hope in her eyes. It didn't make telling her the truth any easier. Nothing I was about to say was going to give them any joy, but maybe it would give them closure.

"The Destroyer left the planet just like Dr. Ghost predicted," I said. "As it lifted off of Earth, the surface dented in and then exploded outwards. The planet burst at the seams, and then the magma, bright red, swallowed everything in fire. And that was it. You all saw the aftermath."

I turned away from them. I didn't want to see. Behind me, I heard crying from some and silence from others.

The end of the Earth flashed before my eyes again, I had dug up the memory and now it wasn't ready to go away. I held back my own tears.

My fellow survivors were crying harder.

This was not going to be an easy trip, I thought.

Then the alarm sounded.

9

THE LEAK

The alarm was so high pitched and loud that it hurt. I stuck my fingers in my ears to protect them, but it barely helped.

We all looked around frantically for the cause of the alarm.

Then a red line appeared above us, like the one that led us to the theatre. Its fingers reached into everyone's rooms, including mine, and bundled together in the corridor.

We all looked at each other. Children whose rooms were further away came running to join the much larger group near me.

"What do we do?" I asked. "I don't remember being trained to recognise alarms during the orientation."

The only responses I got were shrugs.

I looked up at the red line again.

"I guess we need to follow that," I said.

I started down the hall, passing other children, still standing around confused. I collected everyone I could as I followed the red line. Many were happy to see someone who seemed to be in charge.

The line led us to the Ark's control centre—the bridge. The room featured a mix of alien and human technologies. They were all mashed together, with similar crudeness to our housing corridor, a ramshackle, hodgepodge of various systems and controls. The room had two entrances, and had the shape of a dome, like someone had nicked the top off St. Paul's cathedral, without the mural. The walls and ceiling were one giant view screen. Around the circumference were various consoles with chairs that didn't match one another, probably pieces taken from Iceland and elsewhere. The floor displayed a map of our position in space. It was also a giant screen.

I stared at the map, comforted by the image of my location in the universe, knowing exactly where the Ark was in space.

I looked up and saw something familiar in the dome. It was Mars.

The giant, red, ball hung in the centre of the view screen and was getting larger as the Ark headed toward it, and out of the solar system. On the other side of the screen we saw a vast debris field, the remains of planet Earth.

The room was filling up fast around me. The other two hundred people.

The red line ended in the centre of the room. Everyone was taking in the view. The sea of stars and the planets were a sight no human had seen before, not like this. For a second we forgot all about the alarm.

I looked around the room for the emergency. There was no clear indication as to what we should be doing next. I searched for Dr. Ghost's image, on some screen somewhere, explaining what the problem was, but there was nothing.

I went to the nearest computer, a touch screen that we humans must have added to the Ark. It showed a diagram of our ship's internal plumbing, cobbled together from various places around the world and mixed with alien architecture, just like the rest of the ship.

I heard footsteps all around the room, and now everyone was following my lead, taking a position at any available computer screen. Suddenly the alarm stopped.

I whirled around. "Who did that?" I asked.

"Me?" said Darma, from Indonesia.

"Thank you," I said.

"Yeah that was annoying," Koyla added.

The boy smiled as the others gave him nods and words of thanks.

We all turned back to our screens, trying to find the issue. Then one of the other kids spoke up.

"There's a problem in the Water Pumping Station," a boy said.

We all turned toward him. It was the Russian, named Illarion. He was very tall, easy for me to spot in the crowd.

"The blockage is causing pressure to build up in the reservoir," he said. "Automatic systems are redirecting water, but if the blockage isn't cleared then the pipes are going to burst."

"We have to clear the blockage," Bae responded.

"Does anyone have any ideas?" I asked.

We were an assemblage of children, some still in pyjamas, not one of us a scientist or engineer. No one volunteered a solution.

"We need to do something soon, we have, umm, fifteen minutes according to this computer. We need this water to survive," I said.

"Who is good with computers?" the German girl called Gerlinde cried out.

Several hands went up.

At that moment, despite our sadness and situation, we were all coming back to life. This problem was taking our attention and focusing our minds.

"You computer whizzes stay here and monitor the situation. Use the loud speaker to tell us anything we need to know. The rest of us will go and try to clear the blocked pipes," I said.

"You don't need all of us, do you?" Mathieu the boy from Canada asked.

"The pumping situation looks huge," Illarion replied, looking at his screen. "So, yes. We might need everyone." He tapped at the screen and a new line appeared on the ceiling, blue this time. "This should take you straight to the pumping station."

"Let's go people, let's go," I shouted. I rushed through the nearest doorway with several of my crewmates in tow.

***

When we reached the pumping station the complexity of its systems was immediately baffling.

The station was a nest of pipes snaking their way across a curving wall two stories high. The pipes fed into the various corridors branching off the room, extending around corners and out of view. On the opposite wall were cupboards, more from Iceland and elsewhere, and hanging next to them were various tanks that looked a lot like fire extinguishers.

A thin film of water was already seeping through the floor, and at various joints and connections, the pipes sprayed water. It felt like a light rain.

"The blockage is this way," Illarion said, pointing to our right.

I turned to the nearest cupboard. So far Dr. Ghost and his team had been pretty thorough in planning this mission. Hopefully whoever had been responsible for this pumping station also planned ahead.

Inside, I found numerous foam pads. They were all bright red, and flexible. As I opened the doors to the cupboard one fell onto the floor and into the rising water. It didn't absorb any water. Instead, the water rolled off it like it might on a wetsuit.

Among the cabinets, I also found thousands of cable ties of various lengths.

A girl came up to examine the insides of the cupboard with me. I glanced at her and I shrugged.

"You think these are useful?" I said.

Her name was Sanna and she was from Saudi Arabia. She stared at the contents of the cupboard and tilted her head to the left.

"I know what these are," she said.

"What?" I asked.

"They are used to patch leaks on pipes," she replied. "My father used things like these on oil pipes."

"How do we use them?" I asked.

"I'll show you," she said and she took two cable ties and a foam pad from the cupboard.

"Gerlinde, Illarion, take a group to find the blockage," I said. "Everyone else is going to watch Sanna fix this pipe, so we can stop all these leaks."

Gerlinde and Illarion smiled and nodded. They called out a group of children and followed Illarion toward the source of the blockage.

The rest of us watched Sanna demonstrate how to fix the leaks.

She didn't flinch under the sprays of water, even though she must have been cold and uncomfortable. I admired her. She placed a foam pad over one of the leaking pipes.

"Hold this right here," she said to me.

I came forward and placed my hand on the pad.

With delicate and nimble fingers, Sanna wrapped one cable tie around the pipe and pad, linked its tail into the lock and then pulled it tight. Then she repeated the process with a second tie.

She stepped back and inspected her work.

The leak had stopped.

"These will only work on the length of pipes, we need something else on the joints," she explained.

"Get into pairs, grab ties and pads and start fixing these leaks," I ordered. "We'll find something else to tackle the leaky intersections."

Everyone looked at the pipes above us. Some were very high up.

No one moved.

"If you don't want to die of thirst, get a move on," Sanna called out.

I grabbed some pads and ties and started to climb up the pipes to the leaks that were highest up.

Sanna followed.

I reached the highest leak I could and waited for her to catch up.

I saw everyone swarm out for the various trouble spots. Braver pairs were climbing the pipes like me and Sanna.

"I've got some *Haribo* in my suitcases," I shouted to everyone. "If you want it then fix more leaks than I can."

The motivation worked. Their paces quickened.

"Come on Sanna," I urged. "Give me the first pad, I want that *Haribo*."

"Share it with me and I'll make sure we aren't beaten," she offered.

I nodded and she handed me a pad. I slapped it in place and held it still.

She vaulted one of her legs over the pipe to sit astride it while she worked with both hands. I wondered if she had taken gymnastics. She slapped cable ties around the pad, and just like that, the leak stopped.

"Any ideas on what we do about the leaks coming from joints?" I asked.

"We might just have to use more pads," she said. "But they won't work for long."

"Hey guys look at this," called a boy beneath us, standing next to a fire extinguisher. "We can use these!"

"We want less water not more," I shouted down, which got a laugh from some of them.

"It's not water," he said. Then he took one from the wall, pulled a pin from it and used a handle on top to fire foam at the nearest wall. The foam immediately expanded like an inflating balloon.

The boy then reached out and touched the foam. I expected his hand to disappear into it, but instead I saw that it was solid.

This black-haired boy, Myles, was from Ireland. He looked up at me and smiled.

"It's some kind of epoxy or something," he said.

"Start spraying," I said. "But only on the difficult joints. We might need this stuff later."

A few children actually pushed others aside to have a chance at using the foam canisters. Our desperate task now had a fun component. They immediately started sealing the joints and cracked fittings. The rain storm we walked into in this room was turning into a drizzle.

Sanna and I climbed back down to fix a lower leak. Then the whole pipe system started vibrating and rumbling. It was not a good kind of rumble.

Gerlinde came running.

"Callum, we have a problem."

"What kind of problem?" I called back.

"Just come here," she pleaded.

"Find another helper," I said to Sanna

"Don't worry I can do this on my own," she said.

I slid down the pipe network and rushed after Gerlinde. She was already heading back to the blockage.

***

When I caught up with Gerlinde, I saw the problem immediately.

The ship's pump was a giant rotating water wheel inside a clear glass cylinder. I could see that water came from the left hand side and the wheel would push it around, then it would exit on the right hand side. But something was keeping the wheel from turning, and pressure was building up in the pipes on the left hand side, where my fellow crew mates were currently fixing leaks.

"We found multiple blockages and cleared them, but this one is worse than the others," Gerlinde said.

Illarion pointed left and right. "We have to get this wheel moving again," he reported.

"Why is it jammed?" I asked.

Gerlinde pointed up at where the wheel pushed water out on the right. There was a metal fragment lodged there.

"One of the fins of the wheel has broken off and jammed it. It can't rotate," Gerlinde explained.

"How do we clear it from the wheel?"

"I don't know," Gerlinde shot back.

"Guys! Hey," someone's voice boomed out throughout the ship.

The disembodied voice was Bae's.

"Look, I think we got the intercom system working and if you can hear me you've got two minutes left before the pressure causes catastrophic damage to the pipe network," she said.

"What do we do?" Gerlinde and Illarion said together.

I stared up at the pipes and the water wheel. Both were inaccessible, but further down the pipe on the right hand side was what looked like an access hatch.

"You think I can fit through there?" I said, realising a second later that I had just volunteered myself.

Illarion stared at the hatch, "Yes. It looks like you could enter the pipe and crawl back to the wheel to dislodge the metal fragment."

"Open the hatch," I ordered, wanting to take action before I lost my nerve.

Illarion grabbed three others and muscled the hatch open.

I got into position. Illarion and his helpers released the hatch and it fell open like the loft door of a house.

I clamoured into the access opening.

"One minute until catastrophic failure," Bae's voice said, with rather more urgency.

I army crawled down the tube as fast as I could.

The fragment of metal was lodged between the pipe and one of the wheel fins. The wheel strained against the metal.

I reached out with my hands and grasped the broken fin and started pulling. The wheel would shift back and forth as its motor strained to turn it, the metal fragment became loose only for a brief moment, and that's when I pulled at it. Inch by inch it came free.

When it was almost loose, I turned over onto my back and got ready to make the final pull. I knew what was going to happen when I dislodged it, and I wanted to be ready.

I took a deep breath and held it. Then I pulled at the metal fin. It broke free, the wheel inside the pump started to rotate.

Water came rushing down the tube, shooting me out of there like a water slide.

I crossed my arms and hoped I wouldn't shoot past the open hatch. If I did, I'd probably drown inside the plumbing, destined to be another blockage.

When I dropped out of the open hatch, I took a much needed breath. My heart raced.

I tried to yell at Illarion to close the hatch, but the words were drowned out by the sounds of rushing water.

Illarion was ready though, and he slapped the hatch closed, helped by two others to hold back the weight of the water inside.

The pump was running now, like a jet engine. We had done it.

The others gathered around me.

"Good job, everybody," I said, coughing up some water.

A cheer came over the intercom.

"Blockage cleared!"

Sanna pushed through circle of people around me.

"Well? You promised us some Haribo," she said.

SYSTEM ONLINE

PHASE 3 COMPLETED

PUMP SHUTDOWN ABORTED – LEAKS AND BLOCKAGE

RESULTS OF SIMULATION:

1. COOPERATION INITIATED

2. RESPONSE TIME SLOW

3. CREW FAILED TO UTILISE TAUGHT SKILLS EFFICIENTLY

CONCLUSION:

PROJECT ONE ACTIVATED TO PROTECT THE CREW

PHASE 4 NOW IN EFFECT

ONE MUST REVEAL HIMSELF

10

ONE

I did something I've never done before after we cleared the pump blockage and patched all the leaks: I shared my sweets.

My mother had packed plenty of the candies that she knew I liked, but could never get again once I boarded the Ark.

Now that I think about it she must have ferreted these packets of sweets away long before we had to move to the safety of the army base in the Lake District.

I'd never felt so fond of some sweets before. They never meant this much. My mum had accepted my future, and she planned ahead. That's a mother's love.

As I held my entire supply in my hands, displayed for the crowd of tired teenagers, I felt a crushing sadness. I missed my mum, dad and little brother. They had only been dead about three hours. And here we were, celebrating.

Anxious faces eyeing the sweets filled my vision. Despite my sadness, I was enjoying the camaraderie on the Ark. Everyone in front of me had banded together and worked hard to solve a problem that threatened our lives. These candies were their reward, and there was more than enough to go around. Mum and Dad would be proud of me for sharing, too.

I stood on one of the tables in the cafeteria, a sturdy bolted down table with plastic fold-out seats surrounding it.

"To the smart kids in the control centre," I yelled, and threw eight sweet packets to Bae.

She caught them, and distributed them to the kids who had helped her access the systems, and make sense of it all.

There was a cheer from that part of the crowd.

"To the kids who fixed the leaks," I added, throwing more packets to Sanna, who gave them away joyfully.

"To the kids who found and fixed the blockages," I said as a finale, showering everyone around me with sweets.

Then something I didn't expect happened. Illarion raised his hand in the crowd.

"To the one who took a swim," Illarion said. He threw a jelly fried egg up to me. I caught it, and popped it into my open mouth. Everyone applauded.

I raised my arms into the air, victoriously, and then choked briefly on the sweet. I coughed.

Everyone laughed.

That they admired me and thanked me made me feel very lucky. Maybe we were becoming like a family.

"To the crew of the Ark," Koyla cried.

Everyone cheered at that, and raised their plastic cups of water into the air. They clinked together with a dull tap. A lot of liquid was spilled as those cups struck one another.

"Another leak," shouted Pilar from Chile.

There was more laughter.

We were all smiling, chatting about our victory.

Then the purple lines that led us to the theatre before reappeared in the air above us. Dr. Ghost's voice then echoed over the ship's intercom.

"Children, it is time for dinner. Please make your way to the cafeteria to receive your evening meal," the voice said.

The recording must not know that we're already there. A Scottish boy called Carlton called out to the ship, correcting its error. Many of the kids laughed.

All around the outer walls of the cafeteria, the food dispensers activated. Each was basically a portal in the wall with a small dumb waiter that would lower a plate of steaming food down on trays. Each tray was separated into different compartments for different foodstuffs.

The cafeteria was a warm and brightly coloured room, it looked like the food court in a shopping mall. The seats and tables were smooth plastic, easy to clean, I suppose. It was nice enough to be a place I wouldn't mind eating in for two years.

No one needed prompting to start feasting. We were all starving, growing kids, so we all lined up with our trays, got our food and found our seats.

For the first time, we all started to socialise properly. We sat at tables, swapping anecdotes about what we'd just accomplished, among other things. It was nice to feel, and look, normal for a few moments.

I took my seat at a table with Gerlinde, Illarion, Koyla, Bae, Sanna, Ogwambi and Koamalu.

"Where did you learn about all that plumbing stuff?" I asked Sanna.

"My father worked on an oil pumping station on the Red Sea. My family lived on the site so he could monitor it all day. The owner of the pumping station wasn't generous with funds for repairs, so my father had to make do with things at hand. He made a patch like the ones we used with a polystyrene box that was washed ashore once," she replied. "Helping him, I picked up a few things."

"And you, Illarion?" I asked the Russian boy.

"Same kind of thing, actually," he said. "I worked as an apprentice at an oil refinery."

"An apprentice at fifteen?" I asked.

"Best to start early at the job you will be doing for the rest of your life... That's what my dad said. And when we needed every ounce of oil to keep us warm after the Destroyer arrived, they started taking on thirteen year olds. School took a back seat to survival," he said.

"I never went to school," Koyla said, somewhat bashfully.

"Luckily you never needed to, especially now that we have these memories," Ogwambi said, tapping his head.

"Without Captain Amis I wouldn't have been brave enough to climb into that pipe," I said.

"And without Mr. Gates' memories I might never have figured out those computers," Gerlinde added.

We sat in silence for a moment as we thought about those memories rattling around in our heads, and what they had just done for us.

"It's hard to believe isn't it. We carry the memories of people who are all gone now, but who still get to help us with their experiences," Gerlinde said, picking at some food with her fork as she spoke.

"We're very fortunate," Illarion said. "Not just for the skills they gave us, either. Before the memories, I had never been more than ten miles from my home. These implants opened my mind to the rest of the planet, and to their lives. Each injection was like a spectacular adventure."

"Where did you receive yours?" I asked, curious of the logistics of it all.

"When I was selected, taken from my home by government officials and brought to Moscow where Dr. Ghost was waiting for me. Afterward, my government kept me and my family in the capital. I received injections from Russian doctors in the Kremlin until the teleport," Illarion said. "The whole time there Moscovites were rebelling against the government for failing them. Every soldier and civilian in the building fought, all to protect me. When the teleport finally happened, the protestors were storming the building. A few more moments and I might not have survived to see the world end."

"Wow," I said. "We're glad you're here."

Illarion smiled and nodded.

"I was in the same base as you, Callum," Koyla chimed in.

"They must have kept us separated," I said. "For security."

Koyla agreed.

"I was in the Saudi desert," Sanna said.

"The desert? That's a weird place to stay" Bae said.

"I didn't have a choice," Sanna explained. "After I was chosen, my government took me to the home of one of the wealthiest Princes. His home in the desert was built over a spring. I lived like a princess until the teleport. All the protests happened near government buildings in the city, so they left us alone. I was probably in the safest place possible."

"I was kept along with the Japanese representative," Bae said. "We were on an aircraft carrier in the South China Sea."

"You were on the ocean?" I asked. "That must have been dangerous with the Destroyer out there sucking up all the water?"

"Not really," Bae said. "We floated around for a while, and eventually the water level dropped around us. We were isolated in a small lake of water, separated from the rest of the ocean, so the Destroyer couldn't even find us. There were a few other ships trapped with us, so the adults linked them together to form a small city. I spent the time before the teleport with the Chinese and Vietnamese representatives."

As I digested this story, I realized that my experience, spending my last days in relative comfort, surrounded by my family, was pretty easy. I tried to imagine being trapped on a ship, or sitting in a desert palace. Their stories didn't sound like real life, but like TV shows.

I scanned the table, looking for anyone else who wanted to offer a story, but Koyla broke the silence.

"I still don't understand why they had to inject the memories," he said. "Couldn't they have done it in a less painful way?"

He lifted his sleeve and checked the crook of his right arm. There in the soft, springy part of his arm was a raised scar at the site of the multiple injections we had received.

We all followed Koyla's example and showed off our scars. The one thing, other than surviving, that we all had in common.

I felt my scar. It was a memory of its own.

"How else would they have done it?" I asked.

"They should have put it in candy," Sanna said, as she swallowed her last piece of *Haribo*.

"Yeah. They could have put it in this food," Bae said, as she took a bite.

"Who's making our food here anyway?" Gerlinde asked.

I looked over my shoulder at the dispensers, which had all shut down now that we were fed.

"Robots, I guess," I said.

Illarion scoffed. "Robots? What do they know about cooking?"

"All they need to know is how to measure ingredients, chop, grate and heat them properly," Koyla said. "I think a robot could do that."

"At least this is food we recognise," I said. "Although, I wouldn't have minded the dehydrated food that astronauts eat."

"We're are all astronauts now," Bae said.

"But I always wanted to be a fireman," Koyla said.

"I dreamt of being a nurse," Gerlinde said.

"You might still get to be a nurse, too," I said.

"Well, I want to be rich," said Illarion.

We all laughed.

"The question is: What are we going to do on this ship?" Ogwambi asked. "Are we engineers, doctors, decorators? What is the daily routine around here? There must be one."

"I'm sure Dr. Ghost will tell us," I said.

"I'm not sure I want to spend two years listening to a computer," Illarion said.

"Yeah," I said. "I didn't think we'd be in here alone, you know. Some kind adult supervision would almost be nice."

As we finished our meals, the purple lines above us disappeared and were replaced by green ones. Each started at every table and pointed toward one of the entrances.

"Are we supposed to follow that?" one boy called from another table.

"I don't know," I said, standing from my seat.

We all stared at the doorway, now lit fully green. The cafeteria became eerily quiet.

Then we heard the footsteps.

They said a lot about whatever was approaching the door. Each step was purposeful and equally spaced. Plus, they were loud footfalls, but not quite stomps. The green light dimmed as the door opened.

That's when I saw the weirdest person I had ever seen.

11

QUESTIONS AND ANSWERS

We all stared at the newcomer in the cafeteria doorway. I was wondering where he had come from. He most certainly was not in the observation room when we teleported onto the Ark. Nor was he listed among us when the theatre did roll call. Plus, he was conspicuous.

He was very tall, taller than Illarion by a few inches, making him almost a foot taller than me. His clothing was very simple, just a sort of dark grey jumpsuit. It looked a little like the pre-flight suits I had seen astronauts wear. There was a long zipper going up from the waist and ending at a high collar that covered his neck.

The sleeves were rolled up to his elbows, exposing his arms, and he stood with them crossed before him, like a drill sergeant might.

His limbs were lean and muscular at the same time, bulging under his clothing, but not looking ready to burst. An electricity seemed to pulse through them, just beneath the surface of his skin,

He stood before us, all straight lines and angles, looking both sturdy and flexible at once.

His hair was brown and swept back. His eyes were narrow and his irises were as dark as his pupils. His chin was strong and his ears pointed, hugging the sides of his head.

He wasn't ugly, just alien, as unsettling to look at as he was a curiosity.

He smiled softly, not at all ill at ease at the stares he received from us.

Finally, one of the other kids asked the question we all had on our minds.

"Who are you?" Juliana asked. She was the girl from Brazil.

The newcomer turned to her swiftly, the motion as alien as his appearance.

"My name is One. I am responsible for your protection and leading you to our new home," he said in a deep, precise voice.

"Isn't 'One' an unimaginative name?" Gerlinde prodded.

One then smiled wide at her, as if he found the comment amusing.

One seemed safe enough. I figured if it meant us any harm it would have attacked by now, so I stood up.

"Where have you come from, One?" I asked. "Dr. Ghost never said anything about you."

One nodded slowly, sympathising with my lack of knowledge.

"I have been here since the Ark was first launched back into space. I was stored in a Cryo-Chamber until you were teleported aboard."

Stored, I thought, what an odd choice of word.

"There's a Cryo-Chamber?" Koyla asked urgently.

"Yes."

"If there was one Cryo-Chamber on board, why couldn't you fill the Ark with them. You could have saved thousands of people: our parents, brothers and sisters..." Koyla yelled, standing up.

The other kids had similar questions, and they bombarded One with thousands at once.

I had wondered before, if our oxygen and water were so limited, then why weren't we in placed in Cryo-Chambers. That way we'd keep our reserves intact until we got to our destination. And maybe more people could have joined us on board. Right now everyone else was having the same thought, and One was taking the brunt of our confusion.

"Follow me to the theatre," One said, walking out of the cafeteria. "There I will answer your questions."

Koyla ran after One, and we all got up to follow. One moved fast, despite not looking like it. He was already fifty metres ahead of us when we entered the corridor.

We tried to keep up, but when we reached the theatre he was already standing on the small stage under the screen waiting for us to take our seats.

I sat next to Koyla, who looked angry and impatient. He sat on the edge of his seat, watching One. Once we were all seated One started to speak.

"Well, what about these Cryo-Chambers?" Koyla interrupted.

The screen came on, and an image of the Ark appeared.

It was a 3D image looking at the ship at an angle, with the top half closer to camera.

"How old do you think the Ark is?" One asked, ignoring Koyla.

No one answered.

"It is three hundred years old," One answered.

Some of the kids expressed surprise, oohing and ahhing.

"Yes, quite old," One stated. "When it attacked the Earth, the Ark was essentially on its last legs, which was why it was so easy to defeat when compared to the Destroyer."

What One said made sense. The Destroyer had gleamed when it arrived on our planet. The Ark definitely showed its age.

"The Ark's power core is reaching entropy," One continued. "It will only last another ten years, based on the limited parameters of your present mission. To answer your previous question: if we had loaded this ship with thousands of Cryo-Chambers the power required would have drained the Ark completely in two years, stranding the inhabitants in deep space."

We all absorbed this information. Koyla pursed his lips to speak, but didn't say anything, as if any questions he still had disappeared.

"Rebuilding the Ark for this journey required difficult decisions," One said. "Thousands of scenarios were tested for feasibility. Every possibility was considered."

One turned toward the screen, and the image focused the pyramid section atop the Ark.

"When we first gained control of the Ark, the plan was to use the ship to explore our solar system," One said. A thin line appeared onscreen at the very top of the Ark. "This small section, which we now occupy, was constructed by human engineers. Back then, it was intended as a simple control centre and living quarter for the astronauts who would pilot the vessel away from Earth. Once we realized the Ark would have a different purpose, the cargo bays, your living spaces, and other necessities were also added."

The image on screen zoomed in further and One continued.

"Beneath the cargo bay is the ship's original power plant. The lower half of the vessel is filled with water and oxygen that the Ark took from the Earth on its arrival on the planet."

As One explained, it became clearer to me that this ship was not even a very good lifeboat for us.

"When the Destroyer came we had only three years to prepare everything you would need to start a colony and survive," One said. "This ship is very large, but we lacked the time to modify it to accommodate thousands of humans. We focused on making it habitable for you, and now its entire function is optimized to keep you alive for long enough to find a new home planet."

"Aren't we recycling some water and oxygen?" Gerlinde asked. "Surely if we do that it will last longer."

"Yes," One answered. "We are recycling the air and water, however, recycling resources also drains power, a resource we can only use once. I assure you that we have done the best we could, all to ensure that you children can keep the legacy of Earth alive."

We all took this in. If any of us had any more questions, we didn't speak up.

"Now, it is time for you to sleep," One said. "Tomorrow we must begin work."

Everyone squirmed in response.

"Work?" I said.

"Did you think you were just passengers on the Ark?" One said. "No. You are all going to help me maintain this ship. In thirty minutes, the Ark will power down the lights and heat, save for the living quarters you all saw earlier. Be in your rooms by then, or you will blindly wander the night away in the cold."

I looked around the room. I wasn't alone in my surprise. I wasn't expecting a holiday while on this ship, but I thought clearing the pump blockage earlier would be a rarity, rather than a daily occurrence.

"This meeting is adjourned," One said. "Tomorrow if you have more questions I will answer them. For now get some rest. In the morning we will inspect the cargo bays."

DEBATE AT THE UN

Our attacks had disabled the Ark. It had stopped sucking in our air and water, and had completely shut down. We let it sit there dormant for a whole week before any further action was discussed by what remained of our militaries.

The world had watched the battle with panic, alarm and trepidation, and now that the action had sort of paused, the world started considering the longterm impact of this ship's landing.

My dad, who was a fan of classic sci-fi films like Independence Day and Contact once said that the arrival of an alien ship, that proved to be our enemy, would either be the best or worst thing that ever happened to humanity.

The best because we finally had a reason to unite as a race against a common foe. And the worst because the alien technology and knowledge could divide us even more, if we fought over who would control it.

A year after the Ark's arrival the second, worse, scenario seemed to be the more likely outcome.

During those twelve months the British, Russian, American and Chinese navies had quarantined the site, and sent in joint recovery teams to assess the vessel. The best and brightest scientists joined the military presence and gradually new technologies were uncovered. And a new understanding of the universe.

We learned that the Ark was a long-range storage ship for the water and air it had attempted to take from us. It became apparent it had travelled not from a local star system but thousands of light years away.

That was the only information shared widely. Everything else discovered was kept secret among the big four nations.

No other countries benefitted from the discoveries, which started to change the world very quickly. New metals and alloys were created, new circuits and processors, and we even discovered the teleportation technology used to bring us aboard the Ark.

Despite a vote on the floor of the UN to force the major powers to reveal these technologies, or at least allow other nations to send in their own exploration teams, the four powers continued to deny access.

It wasn't long before the countries that had been locked out started undermining Britain, the United States, Russia, and China. Products from the big four countries ceased to be traded almost overnight. An oil embargo from the Middle East was threatened.

Britain, itself being pushed out by the other three, sided with the European nations, and shared the technologies, while demanding more access from the three nations still closely controlling the vessel.

Sadly, it looked like my Dad was right. The Ark was proving to be the worst thing ever to happen to humanity.

China, the United States, and Russia began talking about using military force against the other nations to regain control of the Ark and its resources.

In response, the UN organised a conference to bring the arguments to a head, and settle the matter before any conflict could arise. India and Pakistan, remarkably, joined together to threaten a nuclear bombardment of Iceland. They hoped to force a quorum of nations, threatening to destroy what remained of the Ark, if any nation did not attend. The threat was ultimately meaningless.

I remember hearing the varied opinions pundits and politicians were spreading around. At the time I was only ten years old and computer games were still catching my attention more than international politics.

We were required to watch the UN debates at school, though. I remember sitting on a soft play floor of our sport's hall at school, seeing it all on a big screen.

My school's population had grown since the Ark's landing. We had Icelandic refugees in every grade.

I had made friends with one boy, and he talked only of home. He hoped that the UN would allow the Icelandic people to return. I understood his homesickness, even though I didn't think there was much left to return home to.

The debate turned out to be very interesting to watch, especially when the various officials slung insults at each other.

In the end, it was the American Vice President who proposed a solution that suited everyone. I didn't realise it at the time but this was the first time I saw Dr. Ghost, he was a member of the VP's UN delegation.

The Vice President, a man named Cross, didn't look like a potential president in the wings. He was tall, gangly and had thinning black hair, not exactly the face of America.

However, he spoke precisely and with authority, more so than America's current president who was an ex-film star.

His proposal, I thought, was generally acceptable.

The Vice President proposed that America would pay billions of dollars to Britain, Russia, and China for exclusive access and control of the site. Then each nation of the world would be allowed to send delegates to Iceland to join together in what they called the Ark Project. The United States said they had a plan for how to launch the Ark into orbit, and the Vice President suggested that an international effort would be most successful.

He promised that all countries would benefit equally from the technologies discovered. To prove it, the Vice President unveiled several advanced technologies, and their schematics, for the assembled representatives at the UN.

Once the Ark had left Earth's atmosphere, the United States would fully fund rebuilding efforts in Iceland and see to the re-settlement of the country's remaining people.

Many nations appreciated this offer. Russia and Britain were eager to pay back the money they had spent on studying the Ark.

China, however, was suspicious of America's motives. The Chinese Foreign minister was extremely hostile, and on behalf of his nation declared that

China would not let the Ark come under the control of the USA. But he seemed like a non-entity to the rest of the Chinese politicians, their president boldly rejected his firm stance.

Their ambassador however sought out a few more concessions from the United States, and surprisingly, the United States gave into every one of them.

It seemed that the world's nations had come to an agreement.

Of course, there was more debate. It seemed like everyone was talking about the Ark Project and what it would mean for the future. Adults, including my parents, were always going on about it. It was the top story on the news every hour. And we even talked about it in school, our teachers eager to discuss it as a historical moment.

Another United Nations meeting was scheduled to vote on the proposal.

The United States gave over fifty billion dollars to China, Russia, and Britain. The remaining nations gained access to the technology the United States had harvested from the Ark.

The United States Vice President's offer gave the U.S. exclusive access to the Ark, and the Ark Project.

Then the Ark Project became the most important topic of the day, it was like the space race for the 21st century. It even eclipsed the Mars landings a decade before.

We watched as a crew was selected to train for the mission. My school learnt all about the reconstruction of the Ark. There was a distinct spirit of cooperation across the globe.

Every nation was part of the project, and the USA accepted all offered help.

The incredible collaboration was sadly short-lived. When the Destroyer arrived, the original Ark Project was abandoned. The partner nations scrambled to get the Ark ready for a much more desperate mission.

SYSTEM ONLINE

PHASE 4 INTRODUCTION COMPLETE

CONTINUE INDUCTION TO SHIP'S SYSTEMS

....

....

....

OXYGEN AND WATER CONSUMPTION EXCEEDING PREDICTED LEVELS

DISCOVER SOURCE OF OVER CONSUMPTION

12

BEDTIME

I used to go to church on Earth, and as inviting as the people there were, after the evening service they would start turning out lights to encourage people to leave.

I mention this because I suspected that One was doing the same thing.

We didn't know enough about One. He had just appeared and taken control of our lives. I needed to know what he was about.

"So what now, it's bedtime?" Koyla said, responding to One's order that we go to our quarters..

I looked at my watch. "It is ten o'clock Earth tim..." I began but trailed off.

"We've had a busy day," Sanna said.

We all shuffled out in groups and headed for our rooms.

When I got back to my room, and after I had said goodnight to some of the others, I dove for my suitcases.

I changed into some dry, warm clothes—jeans and jumper—and then started looking for a torch. After a few minutes of frantic searching, I realised that I must have forgotten to pack it.

Then I remembered that I had my phone. It was useless now for communicating, with all the cell towers and stations gone with the Earth, but it did have a lamp.

It still had a little power. I also had my charger, but there were no power sockets in my room.

I fiddled with the phone for a moment, checking the brightness.

The glow from the screen was strong, but it wasn't a directed beam. I tried to use the torch feature, but it no longer worked. The dim light from the screen was all I had.

It would have to do, I thought to myself.

Then I saw a notice on my phone's screen.

It was a text message.

The sender was my mum. However the message was a joint text between her, my dad, and my brother Jack.

I stared at the phone, frozen and sad. This was the last message I would ever see from them.

It felt like opening the message would mean they were definitely gone. I was overwhelmed with loneliness. My hands shook. Finally I opened the message.

The first bubble read:

Never forget that we love you. We are so proud of you and we know that you will do incredible things on your mission, Callum. Love, Mum

The second bubble read:

Son, you are a strong young man ready for the journey ahead of you. Don't doubt yourself. Live your life. Don't waste it. Love, Dad.

And a third bubble:

Hi Callum. Jack

I read the words over and over and they cut to my heart.

My mind kept telling me to delete it, to let go of them, but I couldn't. Instead, I typed a response to their text.

Hi Mum, Hi Dad, Hi Jack. I Love you. Sorry I couldn't take you with me. I will live my life and never forget you. I'm so lonely though, and all I think about is how you're no longer here. I think I'll feel alone forever. Love, Callum xxxx :)

I pressed send.

I watched the status bar move from left to right as it processed the message.

My eyes wandered to the signal strength symbol.

It was empty.

I looked back at the processing message.

Then the notification appeared:

Message not sent.

I collapsed onto the carpet. They were gone. I was alone. I didn't want to move. I didn't want anything now. Tears ran down my cheeks. All I could do was cry.

***

I woke up on the floor about an hour later.

My phone was still in my hand, on standby. I closed the text message app. I didn't want to see those words again.

I wiped my face and sniffed.

I decided to take my mind off my sadness by leaving my room. Maybe snooping for information on One would distract me.

The corridors of the ship were quiet and pitch black, just like One said. It was cold, like the middle of an autumn night.

I switched on the phone to dimly light my way.

There was no light at either end of the corridor. One was right. The whole ship was completely dark. I wouldn't admit it to anyone else, but the total darkness freaked me out.

"You had the same idea?" someone said, behind me.

I yelped and spun on the spot. I raised the phone and lit up Gerlinde's face.

"Thanks for almost giving me a heart attack," I said.

"I suppose I shouldn't have scared you like that," she replied as she fought off a smile.

"What are you doing out here?" I asked.

"The same as you probably," Gerlinde answered.

"I'm going to the bridge to check the computer for any record of One," I said.

"Oh, then we didn't have the same idea," she said.

"What was yours?" I asked.

"I'll show you."

Gerlinde took out a torch and shone it down the corridor. I put my phone away. It was useless now.

She led me to the giant room that we had all teleported into.

We stood at the panoramic window. It was the same window through which I saw the Earth end. The stars were the brightest they had ever been, and there were more in this field of vision than I had ever seen from Earth. Without any light pollution they shone brightly in the darkness of space.

Gerlinde pressed her face against the window.

"The wormhole we're heading for is on the very edge of the solar system," she said. "Most of our journey will be through empty space. A view this spectacular must be soaked up." As she looked around, her forehead squeaked against the glass.

"I think we'll see lots of stars on the journey," I replied.

"No, not the stars, Callum. Look what's coming up," she said.

I stepped closer to the window. When I stood next to her, I saw what she meant.

Mars.

I remembered that I had seen it on a display on the control centre. Now we had nearly reached it.

I stared at the Red Planet in awe. I was suddenly thankful that Gerlinde had surprised me, and led me here. This was the most amazing thing I had ever seen in my life. I was staring at a 'famous' world; a world that Mankind had dreamed about for years. A world of wonder, and made-up tales of little green men. I thought of the probes and the Mars Landings in the 2020's. I felt almost near enough to touch their remains.

"Did you ever think that you would see something like that?" Gerlinde asked, smiling wide.

"No," I replied. "And it's a shame no one else is going to see this."

"You know, despite everything that happened today, this view dulls the pain a little," Gerlinde said.

I could have stared at the view forever.

"It does help," I replied. "If only a little."

"A little will do," Gerlinde agreed.

We both stepped back from the window. For a moment I thought we might hug, but then we went back to looking at Mars.

"Do you think that they put this window here so we would have a view?" Gerlinde asked.

I shrugged. "I don't know. I'm glad they did though," I said. "Hey, how did you know that we were about to pass Mars, anyway?"

"I worked it out from the video Dr. Ghost showed us," she said.

"And you didn't tell anyone else?"

Gerlinde looked a little guilty.

"I thought about it," she said. "But there was no one I really wanted to share this with."

Though I could have been offended, I knew exactly what she meant. I was going to dig up information on One, and I didn't tell anybody else either. I felt alone, and for some reason, I wanted to be alone, too.

"I left my mum and sisters behind," Gerlinde suddenly blurted out.

I didn't know what to say in response. I experienced roughly the same thing, but I couldn't even comfort myself, so I wasn't going to try to do the same to her. Still, talking might help.

"Parents and a brother for me," I said.

We were still staring at Mars.

"I keep thinking of how they must have died," she said. "Wondering if it was painful, or if they just suddenly stopped being alive. They must have been so scared."

I knew where she was going with this, and I didn't want to think about it myself.

I turned to face her.

"Don't think like that," I said.

A single tear ran down Gerlinde's cheek.

"We were chosen to be here, and we can't change that," I added.

She cried some more. Then I started to cry too. I couldn't stop.

I took out my phone, and showed her the last messages from my parents and Jack.

She read the words.

And I said something I didn't really mean. "I can't do anything about what I lost, and dwelling on it only makes me depressed and empty. It's up to you what you do next, me I'm moving on."

I smiled at Gerlinde, willing her to take comfort in what I had just said.

She didn't say anything. She just cried. It took every bit of strength I had not to cry with her. I couldn't do this. Not now. Not again.

"Let me know if we pass by other planets. I'll want to see them too," I said to change the subject.

"I will," she said, sniffling. "Maybe we could tell the others."

"Yeah. But Mars is just ours," I said.

I took one last look at the planet. Mars was shrinking now, as we moved past it. Soon it would be nothing but a speck, almost erased from our view.

I hoped that the pain I felt would do the same.

THE GREATER THIEF

Like the Ark, The Destroyer appeared as a comet in the sky. We spotted it much sooner than we did the Ark, because of its size.

But, we mistook it for an asteroid.

It was almost the size of Great Britain. A collision with the Earth would be catastrophic, several hundred fold worse than when the Ark arrived and nearly destroyed all of Iceland.

Hawaii, the predicted impact point, was evacuated, and so were the coastlines of all the countries in the Pacific, anticipating a powerful tsunami.

Doomsayers were everywhere. After the Ark, you could hardly blame anyone for assuming the world was about to end. And besides, they turned out to be right.

A military strike was planned to destroy the asteroid. It would be televised live worldwide. We were all excited to see it happen.

My family watched it happen in town. A screen and projector had been set up outside the council offices. They had even planned celebrations for after the asteroid was destroyed.

I was eleven, then, and the prospect of a massive natural disaster really held my interest.

The attack on the asteroid was supposed to take two stages. Stage one was a missile attack designed to push the asteroid off course. China, the United States, and Russia all fired dozens of long- range missiles.

The explosions filled the sky for a day and a night and I watched them through binoculars and on television.

The news broadcasts all focused their cameras on the asteroid during the final set of explosions, each obscuring the target for a few seconds. They filled the airtime by showing us a 3D representation of the asteroid being pushed onto its new trajectory, away from the Earth.

After each missile hit the target, the trajectory line moved a bit, until finally, late at night, it was clear that we had succeeded.

The asteroid was now going to miss the Earth. The problem was solved.

People cheered all over the world in a celebration like New Years. The world was saved, we thought.

That elation only lasted five minutes.

As the newscasters traded joyful anecdotes, the 3D trajectory tracker showed something none of us were prepared for. The asteroid's course bent, almost wilfully, back to its original path.

Someone in the park next to my family yelled. "That's impossible."

Then we saw something we'd never forget. A layer of stone and ice broke off from the asteroid, and a shiny, metallic core was revealed.

We recognized the shape right away, and we were terrified by its immensity.

People all around us screamed.

I was afraid, too.

Our governments responded quickly. They shot nuclear missiles at the former asteroid. Each time a warhead hit the ship, the sky lit up with the intensity of the sun, but the Destroyer took no damage, aside from scorch marks. Ironically, the pattern of the scorches vaguely resembled a skull.

Death.

The ship pierced our atmosphere with a powerful pop that resonated around the world. The shockwaves rattled skyscrapers and tossed satellites off their orbits. Then the Destroyer stabbed the planet like a knife, its blade driven into the Hawaii archipelago.

The cut was so clean that there was no flash of light like the Ark's landing. The crust of the planet split cleanly, and magma oozed up around the edges of the Destroyer. Stream surrounded it, the ocean boiling, and obscured our view. Several tectonic plates slipped all around the planet, a terrible chain reaction, and earthquakes rippled everywhere.

On the opposite side to the planet, volcanoes erupted suddenly. Even the Ark, still embedded in Iceland, bobbed from the surge of pressure throughout the Earth's crust.

Then a tidal wave rolled out from the ship, sweeping across the Pacific, and crashing upon the shores of Japan, Australia, New Zealand Alaska, North and South America. Millions were hurt and killed.

Two days later the ship began leeching our natural resources.

The Destroyer would never stop. It would take everything from our world.

13

THE MIDNIGHT DISCOVERY

I reached the Control Centre after some back tracking, and I admit, tripping over myself in the dark. My phone screen didn't provide much light, but luckily, someone was inside the Control Centre, so I followed the glow inside the room. I pocketed my phone so whomever was in there wouldn't see me coming.

Was One still awake too? I wondered. Maybe One didn't sleep.

I didn't feel like being too stealthy. My breath was condensing in the ship's cold air. My fingers were going numb, too. I hoped the heat was on inside.

I edged close to the door and peered through its small window. It was One. He was standing with his back to the door, tapping at the controls on some screen.

I have revealed myself," I overheard One say aloud.

On the screen a familiar face, Dr. Ghost, nodded.

"How did the crew respond?" Dr. Ghost asked.

For a moment, I wondered if Dr. Ghost were alive somewhere, but then the image twitched and paused, just as it had when we watched the orientation video. Somehow the doctor had infused an artificial intelligence of himself into the Ark.

"They were naturally surprised by my appearance," One replied. "And they asked a lot of questions."

Dr Ghost's image remained frozen for a moment, and then spoke again.

"Did they accept your authority?" Dr. Ghost asked.

"I do not think so. Though, for the time being they seem content to follow my instructions. They are scared and looking for guidance in an unfamiliar world, but soon they will start to question my leadership," One said.

I ducked below the window, not wanting to be seen. I was actively questioning One's leadership, after all.

I heard Dr. Ghost sigh. "You cannot force them to follow you," he said. "I doubt they will get lazy or complacent to their situation, and the memories we gave them will prevent such behaviors. When they realise what work they have before them, they will want a leader, and you are perfectly suited to that task."

"What if they choose one of their own as leader?" One asked.

"That may happen," Dr. Ghost replied. You can't force them to accept their leadership. Just protect them until they reach their new home. I have no doubts that they will see you as invaluable in due time."

One nodded.

"You have taught me how the human race often divides itself, by race or views or geographies. How can I hope to keep these children from repeating the same mistakes of the past. Might they ultimately destroy themselves?"

"One of the biggest mistakes humanity ever made was assuming they had all the answers," Dr. Ghost replied. "But that flaw of ego is also what makes us fundamentally human. They will resist you. That is their nature. In return, you can show them why you are their best chance at survival."

"And if they would rather destroy themselves?" One asked.

"It would mean the end of humanity, forever. It is unlikely, but if that is their destiny, you would not be able to overpower them all if you wanted, son," Dr Ghost answered.

What did he mean when he called One his son?

"Very well, Father, I will proceed as you suggest," One said.

Dr. Ghost, in the machine, nodded.

"Tomorrow you must inspect the cargo bays and insure that supplies are stored properly," he said. "The computers contain additional memory implants should the children need continuing education."

"Understood," One said.

"I know you will make me proud, One," Dr. Ghost said. "I hope that this program can help. I am sorry that I am not there to see you save the human race."

I had heard enough, and fearing getting caught, I returned to my bedroom. I lay on my bed, staring at the ceiling, replaying what I had just heard between One and Dr. Ghost. I had a new respect, and trust, for One. At least for now.

"Hello Callum of England," One suddenly said, standing in my doorway.

I sat up with a start, confused as to how he arrived so silently, and quickly.

"He-hello One?" I said.

"You have questions regarding the conversation you overheard," One said.

I wasn't about to try lying to him now. Besides, he was being direct with me.

"I do," I said. "Who are you, exactly?"

"I am Dr Ghost's son. He placed me on board to protect you and the other children until you arrive at your new home."

"Why did you get to survive, when so many others didn't?" I asked.

"My father chose me to become the leader of this mission. I had little choice in the matter."

If One was lying, I couldn't tell.

"How can we be sure that you won't harm us?" I asked. The question had been on my mind since One first appeared, and though I believed what I just saw in the Control Centre, I couldn't pass up the chance to test this strange man.

"You can't," One replied without hesitation. "But as you overheard, I will have to work hard to prove it."

I shuffled to my feet,

"Now, may I ask you a question?" One asked.

"Go on," I said, figuring I owed him that much.

"Would you be able to accept my leadership?" he asked.

I looked into One's dark expressionless eyes. They weren't soulless and frightening, they were almost toy-like.

"I could," I said, not wanting to lead myself. "But like Dr. Ghost said you will have to prove yourself to everyone else."

One nodded.

I climbed onto my bed. One stood still in the doorway.

"I'm going to go to bed now," I said.

"Please do," One said. "You need your sleep."

"How did you see me outside the Control Centre?" I asked.

"I didn't see you," One said. "I heard your heart beat."

14

BREAKFAST AND BAYS

I woke up the next day aching and tired. Then I snoozed for half an hour, which is, in my opinion, better than sleep itself because you get to be awake just long enough to enjoy it.

I woke with a start when I remembered that breakfast was served at a specific time. I didn't want to miss it.

I rolled off my bed and onto my suitcases. Still full of clothes, they cushioned my fall.

I just lay there with my face buried in my jumpers, using one hand to grab the clothes I would wear. Bleary eyed I managed to dress and make it to my door. I didn't bother with shoes. It's not as if the ship was dirty anyway.

Outside in the corridor I met a few other kids who were also struggling to wake themselves.

"Morning, Callum," Ogwambi said. His door was opposite mine.

I yawned in his face, which of course caused him to yawn.

"Morning, Ogwambi," I said, stretching. "Sleep well?"

"Not bad," Ogwambi replied. "I've never slept somewhere that has a constant rumbling noise though. It's nothing like traffic or city noise."

"I didn't notice anything," I replied.

"Heavy sleeper?" he asked.

"I guess so," I said, wiping my eyes, "Shall we get breakfast?"

"Good idea! What do you think we'll be eating?" Ogwambi asked, as we walked toward the cafeteria.

"I don't know, probably cereal or something dehydrated, since those will last for ages," I suggested.

"Milk?" he inquired.

"Probably that dry stuff that just needs water," I suggested.

"I hate that stuff," Ogwambi said. "In Uganda real milk is—*was* a luxury. I only ever managed to have it a few times a year."

"I haven't had milk since the rationings began," I said.

The Destroyer had made raising crops and animals very difficult in the last months of the Earth's life. Parliament took control of all livestock and crops to ensure proper food was provided for the British people. Given the resource costs, milk was especially rare.

"I thought you Brits needed milk for your tea," Ogwambi said, smiling.

"I never developed a taste for it," I said, smiling back. "I did love chocolate cake though."

Then I realized that I was probably never going to taste chocolate cake, with whipped cream and sprinkles again. At least not for a few years, if we could make it on our new planet, and grow what I needed to make one.

"What do you think this inspection of the cargo bays is all about?" Ogwambi said, changing the subject.

"I don't know," I said. "Maybe it's just to make sure everything we need is on board?"

"What? We don't have everything?" Ogwambi said. "It's not like we're going back to Earth to reload."

"Good point," I said. "It's probably all there."

We entered the cafeteria and found it mostly empty. The food dispensers offered us cereal and surprisingly, some fruit, along with a glass of apple juice. I had never felt so excited for something so relatively plain.

I waited for Ogwambi to collect his tray from the dispenser. Other kids had started to funnel into the cafeteria.

We took our seats at the same table we had sat at last night. Koyla and Illarion had just sat down as well. We were forming a bit of a clique.

"Guys," I said, greeting them.

"Mates," Koyla said.

"Dah," Illarion replied in his native Russian. Then he scooped a spoonful of cereal into his mouth.

Drifting into the hall came more and more kids.

"I'm surprised to see everyone coming in at the same time," I said, "I didn't hear an alarm. Did you?"

"Nope," Ogwambi said, prodding at the fruit on his tray. "It's probably the memories we have floating around in our minds. Seems like they could make us punctual, as well as smarter." He took a bite of his food, chewed, and then spit it out on the tray.

"Not a fan of mango?" I asked.

"No," he replied. "Tastes soapy to me."

"You should have said, I don't want my apple," Koyla said.

"Why did you eat it if it tastes like soap?" I asked.

"My mind is telling me I like them," Ogwambi said. "I keep thinking it looks good, and then my tongue says otherwise."

"It's those memories again!" Illarion said. "Captain Yuri likes oranges but I know that I hated them." He took the orange from his tray and tossed it onto the floor. Then, almost immediately, Illarion stood up, gathered the orange, and put it back on his tray.

"Captain Yuri?" I asked.

"He was the military mind I got to help me adapt to my role as Russian representative," Illarion said.

"Oh, I got a Captain Amis," I said.

"We probably all got a mix that would help us work together," Ogwambi said.

"Did you get any of their military training?" Koyla asked. "Special ops? Guns and war? Anything cool?"

The three of us shook our heads. Captain Amis gave me many things, but nothing like that.

"Me neither," Koyla replied sullenly.

Then, a boy named Kaam, from Bangladesh entered the room. I remembered him from yesterday when we were fixing leaky pipes. He had jumped and climbed with the agility of an Olympian to reach pipes really high up.

Once he had his food he asked to join us and we all gestured to an empty seat.

"Thank you," he said. Then Kaam sat and ate in silence waiting for us to either resume our conversation or talk to him.

A thought hit me. We weren't children or really teenagers any more. There were no adults, save for One, if One was an adult. There weren't younger kids anymore either. It didn't seem right referring to everyone as 'kids' anymore.

I tapped my spoon against my cereal bowl to command attention.

"We need a proper name for what we are," I said.

"What do you mean?" Illarion asked.

"We need a title for who we are now. Now that Earth is gone. What should we call ourselves?" I said.

"We're astronauts aren't we?" Koyla said, "We're on a spaceship travelling through space."

"Yeah, but we pretty much live here now. Space isn't somewhere we're exploring. We kind of live in it," Illarion said.

"We're survivors," Ogwambi said. "Or the last humans," he said seriously.

"Arkonauts," Kaam suddenly said.

"Arkonauts," I repeated testing the new word.

"It's good," Koyla said. "I like it."

"From now on, we are Arkonauts," Ogwambi said.

We raised our cups of juice and clinked glasses to cement our new name.

"Comrades," Illarion then said, in a hushed whisper. "It's here."

He nodded back toward the door. One had just entered the cafeteria for his breakfast. One was the last to arrive and sat down alone.

"At least we know he's human," Koyla said. "He eats actual food."

"I don't think we know that for sure," I said. "But I wouldn't speak badly of One, just to be safe."

"Why?" Ogwambi said.

"He hears everything," I replied.

We all turned to him to see if Koyla's earlier comment led One to look in our direction, but his focus remained on the food dispenser.

"How old do you think he is?" Ogwambi whispered. "He looks like a kid and an adult."

"He must be a few years older than us at least," Kaam said. "He's so tall."

One suddenly set down his spoon and raised his hands into the air, clearly signalling to us. One held all ten fingers up to signify ten, then closed his hands once to signify another ten, then held up another five.

"Twenty-five?" I guessed.

One nodded his head, and then went back to eating.

"See," I whispered to the others at the table. "One hears everything."

***

For an hour the cafeteria was a buzz with conversation. All the Arkonauts discussed their rooms and how they slept. Some shared their sadness at leaving Earth. The mourning would take some time.

Eventually, the last few stragglers sat with One at the last empty table. One tried to talk to the other Arkonauts, but they were clearly guarded and cold, talking amongst themselves.

After an hour, One stood up and surveyed the room.

"Crew of the Ark," he said loudly.

A few conversations became quieter, but for the most part everyone ignored him. One tried again, slightly louder, and saw the same result. The others were too absorbed in their food and each other to pay him any attention.

Then Koyla stood up on the table and shouted. "Arkonauts!"

That quieted the room, as everyone looked at Koyla.

One stared at Koyla, clearly taken aback.

"We're Arkonauts," Koyla said. "That's what we're calling ourselves now. You know, like astronauts, but on the Ark."

Some of the others cheered as Koyla said it. One just watched, scanning the room, observing.

Then One stepped up onto the table where he was seated and in a boom voice said, "Arkonauts!"

We all listened to him now.

"We must all inspect the cargo bays today," One said. "It is time to assess our supplies, and recover equipment essential for our daily survival. Most of the equipment and material stored on the Ark is for our eventual arrival at a new planet, therefore it will be left in the bay. The service robots will be the only ones to utilise the bays after today. You will randomly be assigned into teams and given areas of the bay to record and inventory. Please assemble in the observation room in thirty minutes. The cargo bays are refrigerated areas, for good reason, so dress warmly. Gloves and scarves may be necessary."

"What if we don't have gloves and scarves?" a girl called out.

"Why don't you have them?" One asked.

"I come from Mexico." It was Gloria, I remember her from the orientation video. "We don't really do winter."

"I've brought extra," Illarion said.

"Me too," said Eirikur the Icelander.

"Looks like some sharing will solve your conundrum, Gloria," One said. "See you in the cargo bay in half an hour." One stepped down from the table, turned, and walked out of the room.

"Where do you think he sleeps?" Ogwambi asked.

"Maybe he doesn't," Koyla suggested.

"You're making One sound almost superhuman," Kaam said.

I remembered his speed and stealth, and hearing my heart beat. I couldn't discount the possibility.

We all went back to our rooms to change. I used the time to shower and forgot about the water limit. I used up my daily supply with soap still in my hair. Life on the Ark would take some getting used to.

I dressed in jeans, a jumper, and grabbed gloves and a scarf.

I met up with Koyla, Bae, Gerlinde and Illarion, and we walked together to the observation room. We chatted about what we imagined was in the cargo bay, and what we hoped we would find.

The common theme was chocolate. Chocolate in some form or another would be the greatest treasure. None of us had enjoyed a decent chocolate bar for some time.

We gathered with the rest of the Arkonauts in the observation deck. Outside the window a comet passed by.

Everyone herded to the window to watch it fly, it's burning tail painting the blackness of space.

I stood next to Gerlinde. We shared a subtle smile, as we had experienced Mars together the other night. We watched the comet as it burned. It was no Mars, but it was still impressive.

As the object left our view, One spoke up.

"Arkonauts," he called out.

We all turned dutifully to face him, but stayed at the window.

"I will call names separating you into groups of six," One said. "Each group will receive a tablet with maps of the cargo bay and your assignments. Please pay careful attention, especially if you're checking the food supply areas.

"Do not worry," One continued. "I will be observing each group and offering assistance with assignments as necessary. At the entrance to the cargo bay you will notice a single isolated stack of crates. You will have thirty minutes to inspect their contents."

"What's inside them?" Gloria asked.

"That is the purpose of inspecting them," One replied.

One called out names in quick lists of six. When the team gathered before him, One handed out a tablet.

One repeated the process until we were split into about forty groups, each assigned a tablet.

"Now, follow me," One said, striding out of the observation room.

My group put me with five other Arkonauts I had not yet met. We were the closest behind One, trying to keep pace.

For the first time since arriving on board we encountered a staircase. It was built into a steep downward sloping tunnel, much like one of the old underground stations in London.

The stairs led a few levels down to a gigantic cogwheel door that had been rolled into position on giant teeth, like a vault.

"Welcome to the cargo bay," One said. "When I open it there will be a rush of air as the vacuum that was put in place to help maintain the food supply displaces. Please brace yourselves."

One went up to a control panel next to the door and activated the locking mechanism.

A small cog near the base of the door started to turn, activating another mechanism, and the huge door started to roll open.

As it broke free of the door frame, breaking the seal, there was no sound. I felt no rush of air.

I looked at One. He was frowning.

"Shouldn't there have been an air rush?" I asked.

One didn't answer, still staring at the door.

"One?" I said.

"The seal has already been broken," One answered. "There is a leak in the bay somewhere or—"

"Or?" I asked.

"Never mind," One said. "I misspoke. Proceed with your instructions."

One then sprinted into the bay ahead of us. He was like a blur disappearing through the widening gap in the door.

I turned back to my group, and then toward everyone else.

We all seemed to share the same concern, but no one said anything aloud.

I followed One into the bay, with the others close behind. This was not going to be an easy task after all.

15

ANCIENT HISTORY

The bay was as three kilometres in diameter. It was a sight to see, surprising until I remembered that the Ark once landed on Iceland and took out half the island nation. Much of the Ark's internal space was for the storage of water and air, and the bay we were in was part of the ship originally dedicated to that purpose.

Human engineers and technicians had converted it into a vast storage space, two stories high, and criss-crossed with the kind of pillars and supports that you would find at Waterloo station in London.

Stacked to the ceiling were crates like you would see in any warehouse.

It was an unfathomable amount of supplies. I knew it was meant to last us until we reach another planet, but it didn't seem possible that we'd ever go through it all. I wondered if the space could have been used for something else, or someone, but the thought passed quickly.

Just as One had said, there was an isolated stack of crates in the front. Each one had stamps on the sides, featuring the names of our former home countries.

We looked at each other in anticipation. It was clear that there was a crate in the stack for each one of us. The question was what was inside.

Koyla was the first to have a look, bounding toward the stack and grabbing his crate. He put his hands on the handle to open it, and the Koyla stopped.

He looked up and stared at all of us. The rest of the Arkonauts stared back, hanging on the moment.

"Wait," Koyla said. "I don't want to do this alone."

"Go on," Sanna coaxed. "Don't be scared."

Koyla frowned, turned his head, covering his face with his free arm, and then opened his crate.

The package clicked open. After a moment, satisfied that it was safe, Koyla opened his eyes and looked inside.

"Wow," he uttered.

He reached in and pulled out some Australian Aboriginal Artwork. He held it up for all of us to see.

"This was in the National Museum," he said.

Intrigued, I looked for my own crate, and I wasn't alone. The other Arkonauts dug through the pile, grabbing their carton and slipping aside to open them.

When I opened mine, the first thing that caught my eye were the jewels, embedded in a crown and sceptre.

They were the crown jewels. The artefacts cherished by British royalty for centuries. Underneath the jewels there was a sword, some paintings, a faded tapestry, a document called Carta in a glass frame, and numerous other old things. My crate was a treasure chest of English history.

I looked around at the others opening their crates.

They displayed various artworks, documents, weapons and old knick-knacks from their crates. Each one held objects of historical significance, some of the most valuable and rare things from Earth.

Sanna pulled out a black stone and held it up, reverently. Ernesta held up the Mona Lisa, and Koamalu was inspecting a piece of black volcanic rock with a tag attached to it. I could barely make out the writing, but it read: Naha Stone.

I dug further into my crate and saw a similar piece of rough rock that was also labelled. It read: Stonehenge.

In my hands I held ancient history.

I don't know how to describe the sense of wonder I felt.

I set down my piece of Stonehenge and took up the crown jewels, placing the crown on my head and holding the sceptre aloft. I put on a posh accent and said, "Bow peasants!"

Illarion immediately scoffed. "No! You bow," he said. Atop his head was a bigger crown than mine.

"What is that?" I asked, pointing.

"The Romanov crown jewels," Illarion said proudly.

Then we heard another scoff.

Oda, from Japan, stood tall and said, "Technically, my country has the oldest monarchy on Earth, so both of you should bow to me."

Illarion and I were about to say something snarky, but Oda was holding a sword. That shut us up.

"Plus, the *Kusanagi-no-Tsurugi,* or Sword of the Gathering Clouds of Heaven, insists," he added.

I turned by to my crate and drew up the sword I had been given.

"Ah ha," I declared.

"Ah ho," Illiarion said, too, holding his own sword.

Oda, Illiarion and I stood in a circle, pointing our sword at each other in a bizarre standoff, grinning.

The other Arkonauts, all around us, showed off their own ancient weapons.

We were all smiling. We were having fun, genuinely, for the first time since we came onboard.

"Have you forgotten my country's weapon of choice?" Maiara, the United States representative asked, brandishing an old Smith and Wesson.

I dropped my sword as a goof. "I surrender," I said.

The other Arkonauts did the same. Maiara laughed and mimicked blowing smoke off the end of the gun's barrel.

"U. S. A.!" she chanted, laughing.

She put the revolver away, and then retrieved an old bow.

"This bow belonged to Geronimo," Maiara said. "I've got two, so the rest of you are outgunned."

We all laughed at that, and put our weapons away in our crates.

"I guess history is ours now," said Abubakar, the Egyptian representative. His voice was muffled by the mask of Tutankhamun he wore.

Ernesta sighed. "It's just a shame that the rest couldn't be saved," she mused.

"The pyramids are gone, the Sphinx too," Abubakar said. "All that history, all that work, and these crates are all we have left."

I started to think about every statue, building and artwork that burned with the Earth. We had admired those things for generations, preserving them, and now they were all gone.

I took the crown off my head and carefully placed it back in my crate. Then I closed and locked the lid.

Abubakar's comment had sent a wave of reflection throughout the room. All the Arkonauts were carefully storing their nation's historical artifacts back in their crates. The fun part was over.

We set all the boxes into their places in the original stack, and then took up our tablets to get on with our work.

My group consisted of Alba from Spain, Mathieu from Canada, Moana from New Zealand, Saibou from Niger, and Ivaylo from Bulgaria.

According to our tablet, our designated inspection area was in the right, back corner of the bay, furthest from the entrance. The walk there would take about forty-five minutes. Plus, we couldn't go straight there. An array of crates and pillars divided the bay into blocks, kind of like a city. We would have to go in straight lines, turning and cutting our way through the many aisles until we'd snaked to our area.

We opted for the least number of turns, walking down one aisle to the back wall and then taking a right to go toward our destination. The bay was big enough that we could have gotten lost, and none of us wanted that.

During our walk, we got to know each other. I remembered what I had overheard One and Dr. Ghost discussing, about us breaking into factions if we didn't have a true leader. I didn't want that to happen, and the best solution for me was to connect with every other Arkonaut, as best as I could.

If we all became friends, then we'd all stick together. At least that was my theory. Plus, if I set an example of being open to everyone, maybe the other Arkonauts would do the same.

I suspect that One thought of this, and had put us in groups so we would be sure to meet new Arkonauts. One had very carefully watched us as we joined our inspection groups after breakfast. He was definitely trying to control our behaviours, if for good reasons.

Plus, it was working. We had only been on the ship for one day and no one seemed to have formed a clique or tried to exclude anyone else.

Besides, I never travelled much, and the other Arkonauts were a window to countries I had never known.

Saibou, for example, was an orphan who had lived on the streets of Niger's capital city, Niamey. Saibou was glad that Dr. Ghost had chosen him because it was an escape from a difficult life; the kind of life I couldn't imagine.

I was more fortunate in my life, with my family and home, than I ever realized.

Alba was from Barcelona. A tall dark haired girl who like to talk about Catalonian independence, she was also overjoyed that Spanish was one of the languages chosen for the Arkonauts.

Her love of the Spanish language prompted debate with Mathieu from Canada, who was the same height as me with blond hair and glasses.

"Just because Spanish was spoken by lots of people," Mathieu said. "Doesn't mean we should forget French. French was spoken all over the world, too, you know."

Alba wasn't persuaded, but I agreed that I would try to learn French once we found our new planet, if Mathieu would teach me.

Ivaylo liked asking questions.

She was a short girl, and she would ask just about anything whenever there was a lull in the conversation.

During one lull she asked, "Where do you suppose our poop goes? Does it stay in the Ark, or do they shoot it out into space?"

During another she asked, "If we run out of food, do you suppose we'll have to eat each other?"

She followed that with, "What's your favourite kind of soil? Mine is loam."

Ivaylo kept things interesting.

Moana and I spoke the most. She came from New Zealand, a place I always wanted to visit. I had seen its rolling, green landscapes in films, but I never got the chance to see it myself.

She told us about how the tsunami, that the Destroyer created when it landed, wrecked New Zealand

"The only positive was that lots of water got trapped inland during the flood," she said. "We could boil it and drink it that way. It gave people a sense of hope. Not that it mattered."

I didn't share memories of home with them. I couldn't. Thinking of Mum and Dad and Jack still made me choke up. Instead, I made up a story about my favourite fish and chips restaurant, and how sad I was when they couldn't bring in fish for us to eat.

My new friends were kind, and they said nice things to me.

Our conversation stopped when we reached our corner of the cargo bay.

"Where do we start?" I asked.

Mathieu looked at the tablet.

"The boxes in this sector are supposed to contain seeds and farming equipment," he said.

"Seeds?" Moana asked.

"Probably for when we arrive at new Earth," Saibou said.

"New Earth?" I said. "Is that what we're calling it?"

"We need to call it something," he said.

I didn't have any better names, so I shrugged my shoulders.

"What do we do with these seeds?" I asked.

"According to One's instructions we have to check the container labels for the listed seed combinations," Mathieu said.

"Where do we start?" Alba asked.

Mathieu turned the tablet around for us all to see. It showed an overhead view of our sector.

"It's the size of a football pitch," Alba exclaimed.

"I propose that we split up and leap frog one another," Mathieu said. "If we spiral inwards, three of us can check the crates on one side and the rest check the inside crates. At every junction I can call out what you need to check, I'm sure you'll hear me."

I looked at the tower of crates. Each stack had a ladder next to it formed out of the pillars holding the ceiling up.

"Do we have to check every crate in every stack?" I asked.

"Yep," Mathieu said.

"This is going to take ages," Saibou said.

"I'll take the inner track," I volunteered, having realised that the inner track will have less to look at. Moana and Ivaylo came with me. The other three took to the outside set of crates.

So we marched around, methodically checking that each box contained what the label said they should. We found a few that were mislabelled. Each time we had Mathieu record the error on our tablet.

I did most of the climbing, checking the crates at the top of the stacks. I didn't mind because each time I went up, I got a really impressive view of the rest of the cargo bay. The other Arkonauts were buzzing about among the aisles and stacks like a hive of bees.

But on one climb I noticed something strange.

There was an open crate, and we were the ones who were supposed to check it.

I climbed back down and pointed out the open crate to Moana and Ivaylo.

When we got to the crate we saw that someone, or something, had jimmied it open. The lock was smashed and the farming tools inside had spilled out across the floor.

"It's completely smashed," Ivaylo said.

"Who could have done this?" Moana asked.

"I don't know," I said. "We should find One."

The other two nodded.

"We should tell Mathieu and the others first," Moana said. "Then we can go and find One."

"It's going to take ages to find him in this cavern," Ivaylo commented.

"There must be a communication system somewhere," I said. "Maybe on the tablet. Let's go."

We searched the center of our area, where the others should have been. Alba and Saibou were nowhere to be seen.

Mathieu was there, alone, slumped on the floor with a red puddle oozing from his head.

WORLD WAR III

Like the Ark, the much larger Destroyer extended towers into the sky and pipes into the sea, some reaching as far from Hawaii as the Atlantic.

Militaries from around the world engaged the Destroyer immediately. Airplanes started bombing, but the battleships had to sail from the Atlantic and Indian Ocean, after the tsunami destroyed most Pacific fleets.

Unlike the Ark, the Destroyer had its own defences and actively fought back. It used the pipes draining our oceans to smash and obliterate approaching warships. Its towers would fire blasts of air and water at our airplanes, tossing them into the ocean or snapping off their wings like insects. Nothing we tried seemed to work. The Destroyer even knocked down our missiles, blasting them off course with air or snuffing their engines with shots of water.

Despite all our efforts, the Destroyer remained undamaged.

The alien ship even warded off the bombs we tried sending up its water-leeching pipes. The Destroyer seemed to sense the bombs, and just sent them shooting back into the ocean.

Whoever the aliens were, they had learned something from our battle with the Ark.

We were terrified.

With few options left, we deployed ground forces to attack the Destroyer. Marines from every nation attacked the Destroyer, hoping to infiltrate its inner workings.

In response, the Destroyer filled its interior with water. Thousands of soldiers drowned.

Our final option was the one we dreaded the most, nuclear strikes.

We fired every nuclear missile and bomb from every remaining arsenal on Earth. We destroyed every last speck of life in the centre of the Pacific, but the Destroyer was undamaged.

The combined might of our world's militaries was powerless against the alien ship.

The Destroyer had won.

And it was stealing our water and air every second.

What remained of the world's nations needed a new plan.

16

THE FIRST ARKONAUTS

I couldn't move.

I was too shocked by what I saw.

Ivaylo was the first to rush to Mathieu's side to see what had happened.

It was only when Moana brushed by me that I snapped out of my shocked trance.

Mathieu wasn't moving. There was blood coming from a wound near his temple. The puddle was still small, though, so I figured he hadn't lost too much blood. Then I realised that we didn't have a doctor on board. I didn't know how we were going to treat him. Maybe One knew first aid?

Ivaylo knelt beside Mathieu and touched the side of his neck.

"He's dead," Ivaylo said.

"What?" I asked, hoping I misheard.

"He is dead," Ivaylo repeated, choking on his words.

Moana just stared at Mathieu's body and bawled.

I couldn't believe it, so I reached for Mathieu's wrist and felt for a pulse. There was none.

I placed my hand over his mouth, but there was no breath. It didn't make sense.

"Does anyone know CPR?" I pleaded.

"He has been dead for five minutes," a voice I had not heard before said. It wasn't an Arkonaut's voice. It was deeper, the voice of an adult.

From behind a stack of crates appeared a man. He was seven feet tall and heavily muscular. His head was shaven, patchy and imprecise, as if done with a butter knife and without a mirror. The man wore tattered workman's overalls. And he stank of body odour, enough that we could smell it strongly from five metres away.

He held Alba in one massive hand, dangling as a cat might a mouse. In his other hand was a pair of bloody garden sheers.

Four other men, shorter than the first, emerged behind the giant. They wore similarly torn workman's overalls. One of them held Saibou in an arm lock. The others held garden tools in their hands like weapons.

"More children," one of the other men said.

"Grab them," the giant commanded.

Moana, Ivaylo and I didn't run. We should have, but we were too scared and too shocked at Mathieu's death. One of the men grabbed me by the arm and dragged me to my feet. This man, even smellier than the giant, pulled me up to his face, appraising me with beady eyes.

"Why are there children on this ship?" he asked his companions.

"Why don't we ask them?" the giant said softly. Then he turned to me, and asked, "What are you doing here?"

"Why don't you tell us what you're doing here first?" I said.

The man holding me shook me like a rag doll. I thought my shoulder might dislocate. "Answer him," he said.

"We're Arkonauts," I said. And I immediately regretted sharing our name with them.

"Arko-whats?" the giant asked.

"We're the crew of this ship," I said. "We were teleported on board when the Earth was destroyed."

I looked at Mathieu's body. He was supposed to be a survivor and now he was as dead as everyone we left behind.

"You killed him," I said.

The giant nodded.

"He caught us scavenging," the giant said.

"He was just a boy," I yelled. "He couldn't have hurt you."

The giant didn't respond.

"What are you doing here?" I yelled.

Again the giant didn't respond.

Instead he asked his own question: "How many of you are on the ship?"

"Two hundred and fifty," I said.

"Two hundred and fifty children?" the man holding me asked.

"We can take two hundred and fifty children," said the man who held Saibou.

"I just hope there are many more girls," said the greasy man, holding Moana. He stroked her hair.

Moana recoiled in disgust.

Her captor eyed her lecherously. "Get used to it girl," he said.

"Take them back to camp. We can interrogate them more there," the giant said.

The other men nodded. They dragged us across the cargo bay to another section. All I could do was hope that one of the Arkonauts or One would see us, or find Mathieu's body, or the blood, and come to rescue us. I wanted One to appear most of all. He must have heard with his super-hearing, and surely he could save us with his super-speed and strength.

The men had made their camp inside a group of crates from which they'd fashioned three walls. They had used canvas material, for our shelters when we landed on our new planet, to make beds and smaller rooms. There were packs of food everywhere, some empty, some still sealed. There were buckets filled with water, though I didn't know where they would have found it. I thought it was all rationed.

In the centre of the living space, a naked flame danced atop a gas cylinder. It gave off enough heat to survive the cold nights on the Ark. It was clear that these men had been here for a while.

Saibou, Ivaylo, Alba and I were dropped on the floor, but the man holding Moana clutched her tighter.

The giant took his place on the biggest of the beds. The other men took their own places, making a circle.

The giant set down his garden sheers and picked up a shotgun. He cocked the gun, and the *crack - crack* noise it made drove a chill down my spine.

He didn't aim it at us, but we got the message.

"Are there any adults on this ship?" the giant asked.

I shook my head, and tried to look as afraid as possible. He had to know that I was prepared to tell him everything. What they didn't know is that Captain Amis's memories were advising me.

"Keep him talking. He will give away information," the soldier said inside my head. "You don't know anything valuable. Stay alive until help arrives. And remember, a shotgun will do lots of damage up close but it is useless at long range. When you can, run, and use the crates for cover."

I kept an eye on the giant, knowing that he was the leader. He wasn't going to talk, though. He proved as much earlier. But, my beady eyed captor seemed to be the chatty type.

I turned to him and asked, "How did you get aboard?"

Beady Eyes laughed. "Get aboard? We've been here since we started to work on this ship. Longer than you, boy."

"So you stowed away?" I prodded.

"We made this ship run again," he snarled. "We knew what was going to happen to us if we stayed on Earth. No way were we going to be left to die when we did all the work."

This revelation coaxed words from the giant.

"We saw these crates being loaded on board. They were making a lifeboat, not a research ship or a weapon to drop on the Destroyer. We deserved to survive."

Behind me, Moana whimpered.

I turned around to see her struggling against the man who held her.

"Now that the cargo bay is open, we have access to the entire ship," the giant said.

Captain Amis's advice rang through my mind.

"No, it's not," I lied. "We were all teleported into the bay with instructions to check the cargo until the bay door was opened from the outside."

I hoped my lie would keep our captors in their makeshift base, and maybe that One would find us.

The giant raised the shotgun and pressed the barrel against my forehead.

I started to shake, and I worried I might pee myself.

"Keep calm," Captain Amis said at the back of my mind.

"Why would you be sent into a sealed cargo bay?" the giant asked.

"I'm only fifteen," I said, shrugging. "I don't know what's going on."

"Just waiting for instructions, right?" the giant asked.

"That's right," I said.

He reached into a pocket on his overalls and brought out the tablet Mathieu held.

"I think you've already had them," he replied. "And I think you came from outside the cargo bay."

"I can't wait," the greasy haired man holding Moana said. "I'm having some fun now."

He dragged Moana away.

She screamed.

Ivaylo reached out for Moana, trying to grab her leg. Another of the men kicked her in the stomach.

Ivaylo winced and doubled over, the breath knocked out him. He fell to the floor and held his side in pain.

I turned to the giant, hoping that there was some moral compass inside him that would stop his fellow stowaway.

Moana screamed again.

I prayed that someone heard her.

The greasy haired man covered her mouth, and dragged her away.

When they disappeared behind the wall of crates, the beady eyed one holding me chuckled.

"You can't let him—" I said.

"Where are the adults?" the giant interrupted.

I couldn't speak. Even Captain Amis wasn't getting through to me. I was afraid for Moana, Ivaylo, Saibou and Alba, fearful of what these awful men were going to do to us, and to the others if they found them.

Suddenly there was a loud snap, and I could hear Moana scream again. There were fast footfalls echoing through the air, someone was running away.

This distracted the other men. They stopped looking at me, or the others in their tents, and went toward the section of crates where the greasy one had taken Moana.

The giant dropped his guard and peered out of the tent, too.

From around the wall of crates, the greasy one stepped forward in short, clumsy steps. Something was weird. He looked more like a marionette than a person.

Then he tumbled forward, collapsing, face first, in a pile on the floor. His neck bent at an angle it shouldn't have.

That's when I realised what that snap was.

And that's when One stepped into view.

17

THE PROTECTOR

It took a moment for our captors to register what had happened.

The giant finally raised the shotgun, the barrel pointed at One's face, and growled.

One didn't flinch, his jaw clenched.

"There is no ammunition in that gun," One said cooly.

The giant sneered.

"Care to test that," he said to One.

"I don't have to," One said. "All of the weapons and ammunition were stored separately. And none of the ammunition crates have been opened."

The giant drew a pistol from a holster on his ankle.

"This one is loaded," he said. "I brought it myself, just in case."

One remained cool and calm.

"Callum, Saibou, Ivaylo, Alba, please stand and step toward me," One said.

We watched the giant. He couldn't hit all of us with his gun. And One seemed to know what he was doing. We stood and moved toward One as we were told.

The giant watched us with eyes like a hungry cat.

His companions did nothing. They were still fixated on the greasy one's lifeless body.

We had only made a couple of steps before the giant aimed his pistol at us.

"Stop right there," he said.

We stopped. He aimed the gun at Saibou, who was standing next to One.

"I guess you're the one in charge," the giant said to One. "I assume you've seen what we're capable of."

"I did see. You murdered a defenceless boy," One said. "His name was Mathieu."

"I don't care about his name," the giant spat. "I just want to be sure you know what I'm going to do you. And the rest of them."

"You will not harm my crew ever again," One said.

"You're going to stop me?" the giant said.

Then the giant fired his gun.

One dove into the bullet's path. The projectile struck him in the chest.

One fell to the floor.

He was dead for sure.

We were stunned. One had saved Saibou, but now we had no great protector between us, the giant, and his men.

The giant smiled, stood, and walked over to One, holding the pistol loosely at his side. He leaned forward over One's body, smiled again, and then glared at us.

"Too easy," he said. "This one was almost interesting."

One suddenly sprang up from the floor, landing a powerful uppercut to the giant's chin. With his free hand, One grabbed the gun, the giant's hand slack from the punch, and tossed it away into the darkness beyond the lamp light.

One whirled around and landed another punch to the side of the giant's head, throwing the man into a nearby crate. The giant collapsed to the floor, dazed.

One, without a breath, turned to face the other men.

"You have killed a child, and attempted assault on others in my crew," One said. "You will now experience the consequences of those actions."

The men looked at the giant, breathing but unconscious, and then lunged for their improvised weapons, grabbing a shovel, a garden fork, and a pickaxe. The men fanned out to surround One.

One casually stepped forward into the middle of the triangle they had formed.

Captain Amis began analysing the situation. My brain flooded with observation and calculation.

"One will die," Captain Amis said to me. "This is a no-win scenario. He is outnumbered."

"He survived a gunshot to the chest," I thought to the captain. "Maybe he can survive this."

One didn't wait for the men to strike first. He attacked the man nearest to him.

The man swung his shovel around like a medieval polearm, but it didn't matter.

One was too fast. One's palm struck him square on the nose, the blow ignited an explosion of blood.

One moved like a snake, one minute standing straight, the next sliding across the room and striking.

The man, his face shattered by the blow, fell to the floor, dead.

Captain Amis whispered, "Maybe I was wrong."

The other two men had not moved, still soaking up their friend's demise.

The moment of grief was brief, as the man with the fork took a mighty swing at One.

One ducked under the swing.

His assailant, off balance, tried to correct his mistake with a back-handed swing.

One caught the shaft of the fork, pulled the man toward him, and hooked his fingers under the man's jaw. With a brutal spin, One snapped the man's neck, nearly taking off his head.

Now, the man with beady eyes, who had captured me, was the only one left. He stared in shock, seething with anger. The man swung his pickaxe at One's head.

One, still holding the fork, swung it upwards, deflecting the pickaxe. The man with beady eyes corrected his swing, aiming for One's side.

Before the swing could come close to landing, One slipped around the man and staked three prongs of the garden tool into the man's back.

It was like One had planted a flag as he drove the man's body into the floor.

Captain Amis whispered, "Impressive." And then withdrew into my mind.

We Arkonaut members released a deep sigh, and took in the carnage.

It was wrong of me to feel joy that One had taken out those men, but that's exactly what I felt. Their deaths felt right. They had killed Mathieu.

I was also lost in awe of what One could do.

Then the giant got back up.

One watched him rise, and even waited for the giant to gather himself.

"Surrender now and you will be allowed to live," One said. "You will be placed in a cell, but you will remain alive."

The giant roared, mad, veins pulsing in his head and neck.

The giant, a full head or two taller than One, surged toward our protector, throwing his massive fist at One's head.

One raised a hand and caught the punch.

I'd never seen anything like that in real life.

When the giant's fist hit One's palm there was a crack like a lightning strike.

But, One didn't give any ground.

"I will kill you," the man grunted, throwing punch after punch.

One deflected them all, and then retaliated with a strike of his own, direct to the giant's neck.

"Surrender now," One said.

The giant growled again, and then jumped toward Saibou.

One gripped the giant's left wrist, twisted the man's arm, and then threw a knee toward the giant's elbow.

The giant's arm broke instantly. The man shrieked and looked at his now useless limb in shock.

Without a beat, One kicked at the man's knees, and he collapsed to the floor, clenching his jaw in pain.

One grabbed the giant by the back of the neck, and dragged him over to the buckets of water they had inside their makeshift tent. Then One forced the giant's head into the bucket, holding his head under the water.

The giant kicked and writhed, but it was useless. One just held his head down, harder, keeping the giant from stealing a breath.

One drowned the man with little emotion on his face. There were no action movie quips.

Only when the giant stopped struggling, when he was clearly dead, did I realise that none of us tried to stop One.

We let it happen.

And I didn't know if that bothered me or not.

Finally, One checked the giant's pulse. Certain he was dead, One stood up, surveyed his work, and then looked at the four of us.

Ivaylo uttered something in Bulgarian. It was probably a swear.

"I am sorry you all had to see that," One said to us. "Your survival is paramount, and these men were a direct threat to you. I did what was necessary."

None of us said anything.

All I could do was stare and wonder who One really was.

18

MOURNING

The other Arkonauts came rushing to us, drawn by the gunshots.

One wiped the blood from his hands on the giant's shirt, and stood up.

Our crewmates gasped. There was a wave of chatter through the crowd. Even after years of war on Earth, most of us hadn't seen such carnage up close.

Sanna hugged Moana as she cried, still shaking from the attack.

One moved through the men's makeshift camp, shutting down their fire, collecting their weapons and unused supplies. He was still protecting us, perhaps now from the reminders of what we had just seen.

"What happened?" Illarion asked. "Who are these men?"

"They are former workmen on the Ark Project," One said. "They stowed away on board, hoping to escape the Earth's destruction. They valued their lives above all of yours, so they had to be neutralized."

I looked at Moana. She had managed to compose herself, though her eyes were still red with tears. She looked at the greasy man. There was rage in her eyes.

"Are you alright?" I asked her.

After a pause, she nodded. Then she nodded again, as if trying to convince herself that she was okay.

"He didn't... Did he?" I asked.

She shook her head. "One stopped him," she said.

"Did One kill these men?" Gerlinde asked.

Saibou chimed in. "He took them down in seconds." Then he mimed some martial arts moves, throwing punches and kicks in the air.

One didn't speak. He was still absorbed with disassembling the men's camp.

"He even took a bullet for me," Saibou boasted.

There was a bloodstain on One's jumpsuit, in the middle of chest, but it was strangely small. One reached for the wound, slipping his nimble fingers inside, and after a moment, plucking the bullet as simply as picking up a marble.

The bullet was flattened into a mushroom. One dropped it to the cargo bay floor.

"How is that possible?" Koyla asked.

"What are you, One?" I asked.

One looked at us. There was softness in his eyes.

"I will answer your questions later," he said. "This inspection is cancelled. Everyone return to the residential area while I clear the area. We will hold a service for Mathieu later."

"Mathieu's dead?" someone asked.

"Yes," Alba said solemnly. "The man stabbed him with shee—"

Alba couldn't finish. Everyone became silent.

"Return to the residential area now," One commanded.

We knew he was serious, and all of us backed away, eventually turning toward the cargo bay's exit.

As we walked to the cafeteria, the other Arkonauts bombarded Saibou, Ivaylo, Alba and me with questions.

I would have thought that experiencing something like this, a scene from an action movie, would have left me more excited, but I struggled to answer their questions. We all did.

The others were especially kind to Moana, though, offering concern and comforting words.

"He killed them?" they asked.

"He moved how fast?" they asked.

"He was *that* strong?" they asked.

"How did he survive getting shot?" they asked.

"What is One?" someone asked.

I had never felt so strange. I was as curious about One's powers as everyone else, but it didn't seem right to talk about it.

"Everyone," I yelled. "Please. Mathieu died today. Let's take a moment to remember him. He deserves that much."

The other Arkonauts fell silent.

We walked into the cafeteria, our eyes on the floor, the only sounds coming from the kids who cried, knowing that Mathieu was gone.

"Poor Mathieu. He was the last Canadian," Saibou said finally.

That hit us all hard. He was the last Canadian. An entire nation of people was now completely gone. All we had left were the contents of his crate.

My thoughts drifted to myself. I felt embarrassed of that, but I couldn't help it. I was the last Englishman, and I carried the weight of thousands of years of history, of pride and accomplishments on my shoulders. I was the last ambassador for all of that. Forever. When I died, England would die with me.

The other Arkonauts must have felt similarly. We were all gazing into the middle distance, lost in thought and in mourning.

Then, a voice broke the silence.

"Can we trust One?"

Some of us began to chatter, debating the question.

"Listen," I said. "One almost died to protect us. He did exactly what he said he would. I see no reason not to trust him. And, honestly, when those men had us, the only thing I could think was that I wanted One there to save us."

"I thought that too," Saibou said.

"Same here," Ivaylo added.

Alba nodded.

The room went silent once again.

One entered the cafeteria, carrying Mathieu's body, wrapped in a sheet, in his arms.

We all stared.

One laid the body on a table, and stepped back.

Without a word, we all gathered around.

"I'm sorry I let you down," One said. "I was supposed to protect you all."

"But, you saved me," Moana said.

One nodded, but he didn't look away from the body.

"Mathieu's body will be stored in the cargo bay," One said. "He deserves to be buried in the soil of our new home once we reach it. Before I seal the body away, we will hold a funeral. Though I am not certain how."

No one spoke. We were all fifteen years old. We didn't know much about funerals, either.

"We could say a few words about him," Gerlinde said finally. "That's what we did when my grandfather died."

The Arkonauts seemed to agree.

"We shouldn't do it here," I said. "We need a more appropriate place than a cafeteria."

The others nodded in agreement.

"I know a place," Gerlinde said.

***

Gerlinde was right. The observation deck was perfect.

Outside the window a tapestry of stars served as backdrop, a mural of the infinite; the heavens themselves.

Mathieu's body was in the centre of the room.

We gathered in a circle, two rows deep.

One stood inside the circle, pacing around the body, as if marching to a bugle call on Armistice Day.

We all had our heads bowed. We were all silent.

"Who would like to say something?" One asked.

No one came forward. We had only known Mathieu for a day, and not all of us had even spoken with him.

Sanna was the first to step forward.

"I – I didn't know Mathieu, not really," she said. "But I would like to pray for him and for us."

One nodded.

Sanna bowed her head. She prayed in Arabic, words flowing from her lips in a wonderful, musical way.

When she was finished, many of the Arkonauts whispered interjections. I heard "amens" and "namastes" among others.

Gerlinde then raised a hand to speak.

One nodded to yield the floor.

"I spoke to Mathieu quite a bit yesterday," Gerlinde said. "He was the one who first noticed the blockage in the pumping station. He came from a large family, and he was sad that he had left them behind. But he was also strong. He did his part when we needed him. I think we would have been great friends... if... if..."

She trailed off and started to cry. She backed into the circle, and was enveloped by comforting hugs and words.

I decided to speak next. I took a deep breath and raised my hand.

"I only met Mathieu when we were assigned to the same team in the cargo bay," I said. "He proved himself as a great leader and coordinator. He seemed very kind and honest."

I was surprised how choked up I felt.

Some of the other Arkonauts nodded at my words. Then there was another silence, until Alba stepped forward.

"I'm only alive because Mathieu defended me," Alba said. "That man would have stabbed me if not for him. What's worse is that we argued before he died, about Spanish being one of our spoken languages instead of French. He was a clever guy and a great Arkonaut. For him I will speak French."

Alba paused, took a deep breath, and spoke.

"Bon voyage, mon ami."

More eulogies followed. Arkonauts talked about the moments and conversations they had shared with Mathieu the previous night. Koamalu even shared that they had snuck off together during the night to search the ship. He laughed, telling us that they returned to the wrong room in the dark of night, waking up Illarion.

The Russian smiled and said, "It was the worst alarm ever."

We all laughed at that. It felt okay to laugh. It brought Mathieu back to life, if only for a moment.

There were other prayers, and we all said amen to every one.

A few kids shared bible verses.

Once we had all had a chance to speak, One spoke up again.

"I believe it would be appropriate for me to say a few words from the Canadian national anthem," One said. "Ô Canada! Terre de nos aïeux, Ton front est ceint de fleurons glorieux! Car ton bras sait porter l'épée, Il sait porter la croix! Ton histoire est une epopee Des plus brillants exploits. Translated this means O Canada! Land of our forefathers, Thy brow is wreathed with a glorious garland of flowers. As is thy arm ready to wield the sword, So also is it ready to carry the cross. Thy history is an epic of the most brilliant exploits."

Some of us cried again. A tear or two rolled down my cheek.

One then took up Mathieu's body and walked out of the room, slowly, and ceremonially. Our circle open for One to pass. It was our last moment with Mathieu, at least until we reached our new home, where we could bury him properly.

As the crowd dispersed, the others walking back to their rooms, I stared out at the vastness of space.

We were only one day into our journey, and we had already lost an Arkonaut.

I wondered how many of us would survive to see our new home.

SYSTEM ONLINE

CARGO INSPECTION POSTPONED FOUR DAYS

CANADIAN REPRESENTATIVE - DECEASED

STOWAWAYS NEUTRALISED

FULL REPORT LOGGED

PHASE 5 NOW ACTIVE

ROUTINE ASSIGNMENTS TO BE ISSUED

CREW MEMBERS TO FAMILIARISE THEMSELVES WITH THE SHIP'S SYSTEMS

"ARKONAUT" LOGGED AS OFFICIAL DESIGNATION OF THE CREW

THE COLLAPSE OF SOCIETY

The Destroyer's victory had left humanity with very few options. We could only watch as the oceans retreated from the coasts and the air grew thinner.

The alien ship absorbed the resources it wanted in bursts, sometimes taking long breaks, during which we'd hope that the Destroyer would stop, or leave. Weeks later it would start up again.

The air would grow thinner over the next couple of years, but luckily the ship wasn't taking it all. It was even returning some. Scientists theorized that the ship was stripping our atmosphere of specific gases, and venting those it didn't want back to us. It made sense. The Destroyer wasn't large enough to take all our air and water at once. It only stole what it wanted.

Beyond stealing our air and water, the Destroyer was taking our sense of security from us. We controlled nothing any longer. We were left to wait for the air and water to run out. People really started to panic.

The governments of the world only managed to maintain control by telling the biggest lie ever told to the human race.

The President of the United States appeared on television to tell the world that there was a plan. More, the plan would be a last ditch effort to defeat the Destroyer, and by proxy, return our water and air to us.

According to this plan, the Ark would be launched into orbit around the Earth. Then, instead of becoming a research and exploration vessel, the Ark would be propelled into the Destroyer as a massive missile. The impact would tear through the Destroyer, disabling it and releasing the stolen resources within.

People cheered in the street outside our house when the announcement was made. That popularity overflowed from every place on the globe.

Preparations took three and a half years, which still kept us ahead of the rate at which the Destroyer mined our air and water. Launch Day was watched by every person on the planet.

We could hear the Ark's engines all the way in England. We could even see the Ark ascend slowly into the upper atmosphere, with a tail of flame.

But the Ark never came back down. World leaders kept pushing back the attack against the Destroyer, citing winds, solar flares, and fine-tunings that the Ark required to make the impact powerful enough. The Ark sat in Earth's orbit for six months. And then I was teleported aboard.

When I walked home from school, I would sometimes see groups of people looking up into the sky, pointing at the Ark as it passed overhead. Some people even prayed to it, asking it, and whatever god they put their faith into, to come down from the sky and put a stop to the Destroyer.

That six-month period saw the human race almost destroy itself. The people demanded answers. Their governments kept pushing back time lines.

I spent those six months living in fear. I knew the truth from the moment Dr. Ghost recruited me for the program. Yet, my family and I helped maintain the lie that the Ark would save the Earth.

My parents were especially strict about me not sharing a word. They wanted to protect Jack and me. We had seen the riots on television. Mum came to me crying one night because she had a nightmare that a mob came for me, knowing I'd be saved. In her nightmare, they tore me limb from limb.

I never said a word. None of us did.

The riots eventually turned into rebellions.

Rival factions battled for food stores. The world's economies collapsed. Raiding parties pillaged farms and slaughtered livestock. The strongest, and those aligned with them, hoarded canned goods and other provisions. Even military bases were under constant attack by thieves looking for MREs.

The wealthiest classes tried to use their money and influence to hire their own factions, trading access to food, water, and shelter for private security armies. Soon, the rioters and militant groups overran their gated communities, palaces, and mansions, often backed by the remains of local police forces.

Soon, all the auspices of the old order fell. Security forces assassinated the politicians they were once hired to protect. Military servicemen and women ripped the flags from their uniforms and joined the factions of their choice.

The British Royal family fared better than most, having opened their palaces as shelters, opening access to their food, game preserves, and security.

Surviving governments withdrew to secret, well-defended locations, dedicating their remaining resources to protecting the chosen representative from their country.

What remained of human history was now focused on protecting a couple hundred fifteen year olds.

That is how my family and I ended up at the army base in the Lake District.

And we watched the world die, in relative safety.

Those were not good days.

19

FUN

Two days passed before we saw One again.

Those days were a time of healing for us all.

The first day we just stayed in our rooms and moped around.

On the second day life started getting back to normal. At least the new normal we lived in. Other Arkonauts brought out packs of cards and board games for us to play.

On the third day Ogwambi, Gerlinde, Moana and I decided to roam the residential level of the ship. We had seen the control centre, the theatre, the water pumping station, the observation room, the cafeteria and our living quarters, but that only made up about one-third of our level's deck space.

In our exploration, we found other observation rooms, closets for pipes and wires, and a couple of rooms filled with more doors from Iceland; unused when the Ark was retrofitted. The best thing we found was an antigravity room.

It was the size of a sports hall and inside, as the name suggests, gravity was non-existent.

The walls, ceiling, and floor were lined with foam.

Moana was the first to enter.

As soon as she had crossed the threshold she flew into the air. She spun in mid-air, her momentum carrying her. Moana screamed, at first in fear, but then in joyous surprise.

Ogwambi, Gerlinde, and I stood at the entrance watching her float, almost swimming in mid-air, bouncing from padded wall to padded wall. We looked at each other and nodded.

"This is going to be fun," I said, leaping into the room.

The sensation was extraordinary. My jump propelled me upwards as if I was flying or leaping like the Incredible Hulk. I had never felt so powerful and free.

I buzzed past Moana.

She was still figuring out how to go where she wanted to go, spinning, and tumbling.

Gerlinde and Ogwambi followed us, floating along too.

I soared toward the ceiling, and with no way to slow down, I ricocheted back toward the floor.

Moana hit the ceiling next, tucked into a ball, and kicked off the padded surface, heading straight at me.

As she passed by Moana grabbed my leg and spun me in mid-air.

I couldn't stop myself and I was getting dizzy, spinning like a top. All I could hear was Ogwambi and Gerlinde roaring with laughter.

"This isn't funny," I said, my last meal churning in my stomach. "When I puke you're going to regret it when you float into a cloud of sick."

They all made vomiting sounds to mock me.

Luckily, I grabbed a bit of padding on the floor to steady myself. I hovered there, waiting for the dizziness to pass.

It wasn't long before I jumped back into the fray. All four of us bobbed and soared around the room. We made up games, trying a kind of two-on-two Red Rover, and then racing each other from corner to corner. Ogwambi beat me, but not by much.

Then Gerlinde sneezed, propelling herself for a few metres. We held another race, each of us powered only by our breath. It took ages, and I nearly passed out, but I won that race.

And I ran into a control panel we hadn't noticed before. Using the touchscreen we could adjust the gravity in the room, increasing and decreasing it.

I added a little gravity, making the room closer to the surface of Earth's moon. We spent quite some time leaping about like we were in a bouncy castle.

Then I had a great idea. I ran back to my living quarters, grabbed my phone and brought it into the antigravity room. I had to get some video of us flying around. On the way back I ran into Bae and Koyla, so I led them to our discovery.

Back in the antigravity room, I filmed us doing crazy martial arts moves as if we were in a Wushu movie.

Bae and Koyla would jump at each other and one would do a pretend punch while the other did an outrageous dive.

Ogwambi and I did Jedi impressions and mock lightsaber duels as we leapt around the room.

I don't know how long we were in there, but I recorded almost an hour of video.

Exhausted, we went back to the living area to show our movies to the other Arkonauts. I passed my phone around for everyone to watch, and laugh at.

That afternoon the whole crew was queued up to use the antigravity room. Other kids were making films, and there were more competitions.

One of the Arkonauts turned up the gravity in the room and challenged the rest of us to do push ups.

Illarion was the only one who managed not just one, but two.

I barely made it a few inches off the floor.

Our fun only stopped when Koyla turned the gravity up even more. The rest of us had to slither like snakes to the doorway to reach the controls.

Then on the third day One came back, ready to reassign us to our cargo inspections.

"I have done a thorough search of the cargo bay," One told us. "There is no one else there."

Dutifully, we all went back down to the cavernous cargo bay. Saibou, Alba, Ivaylo, and I were grouped together. For good reason, Moana didn't join us. She stayed back in her quarters.

We completed our inspection as quickly as we could, and then we waited at the entrance for the other groups to finish.

When Gerlinde's team returned, she shared what they had seen in their section, the section where the men had set up their camp.

"It was completely tided up," she said. "You'd never know anyone was there. Even the blood was gone."

"One must have cleaned," I said.

"Or the service robots did," Gerlinde said.

"I still haven't seen one of these robots," I replied.

"Me neither," Ogwambi added. "I have seen strange shadows in corridors, but when I called out they didn't respond."

"As long as it's not more stowaways," I said.

As the other Arkonauts completed their inspections we all congregated at the entrance. With little else to do but wait, we discussed the crates we'd seen and their contents.

"Ours had lots of food," Koamalu said. "But some crates had been opened and emptied."

"There are tents," Illarion said. "And lots of camping equipment."

"Whoever organised this cargo bay has thought of everything." Koyla said. "There are crates in there with construction equipment."

"Looks like we're going to be doing some building when we reach New Earth," I said.

"I don't know how to do any of that kind of stuff?" Koyla said, "Do you?"

We all shook our heads.

"One will tell us what to do," Gerlinde said.

"Maybe there are new memories we can receive. Then we'll just know," I said.

"I'm not sure I want new memories," Illarion said. "It's getting hard to distance them from my own."

"It's better than going to school," I said.

"Thank goodness," Koyla said.

"Careful," Ogwambi said. "One might hear you both. And besides, school wasn't a bad thing."

As if he had heard us, One came strolling through the cargo bay carrying a sports bags in each hand.

"Place your tablets in the bags, please," One said.

We did as instructed.

"Well done, Arkonauts," One said. "Now I have a surprise. After a headcount."

One scanned the group quickly, and then nodded.

"Everyone appears to be accounted for," One said. He waved his arms to shuffle us outside, into the ship's corridor.

Then he stepped up to the control panel next to the door. One cocked his head, listening the way a dog might, and when he heard nothing, he activated the controls to shut the door.

The giant door rolled into position. One tapped again at the controls and there was a hiss as the vacuum seal pressurized.

"Access to the cargo bay is now off limits," One said. "The vacuum will prevent our food from expiring. Now it is time for some fun."

Everyone started murmuring. One and fun, while rhyming, didn't seem to go together.

One reached into the bags he had used to collect our tablets. Inside were footballs, bats, cones and balls.

"Anyone for a game of rounders?" One asked.

The observation lounge was the perfect place to play. With two tiers, some Arkonauts could play while others watched, just like at a stadium.

We spent the rest of the afternoon playing rounders, forming ad-hoc teams and rotating them so everyone got to play and watch equally.

After a few hours, we stopped to eat dinner, and worn by the work and play, we crawled into our quarters, sleepy and happy.

As I lie in bed, I felt something wonderful.

We might make it through this journey, after all.

20

MISSING HOME

We had been on the Ark for a week, and I was starting to make new friends much the same way I used to on Earth. The Ark felt like a school class. We had all been enrolled, piled into a room, and through a variety of projects and activities we were bonding.

It didn't feel like a mission to save the human race. Not really. It was starting to feel a lot like home.

And the Ark really was like home in a lot of ways. The other Arkonauts and I didn't choose to be there, but one day we just appeared, and were part of a family that we didn't pick, and didn't know. What was clear is that we were together, pure coincidence or not.

We had been through a lot together already. We shared a loss. We worked and we played. Those kinds of experiences bring people together, and it wasn't different on the Ark.

I just hoped that my closest circle of new friends and new family wasn't becoming a clique.

I always found myself eating meals with Illarion. I liked that he was quiet. He said very little, and he liked to listen to me talk. Whenever he did talk, Illarion would say brilliant things, too.

Sanna and I would always reference when we met in the pumping station. We bonded that day, both taking charge, and we both felt proud of ourselves and each other that we had stepped up.

I often sought out Koyla's company. He liked to joke and play pranks on the other Arkonauts, He always seemed to make us laugh when we needed it most. After Mathieu died, Koyla showed up at my room with two pencils in his nose. He kept yelling "Space walrus" and clapping his hands.

Gerlinde and I disagree on most things, but in a good way that's fun. It's like a game. One night we argued for an hour about which part of the observation room window was best for seeing planets. After yelling at each other for a while, we both broke down laughing.

These were the kids I spent time with. This was my new family.

Most nights we all ended up in one another's rooms chilling and playing cards and board games, wondering about what our new planet will be like, and even gossiping about the other boys and girls on the ship. We are fifteen year olds, after all. Most often, though, we talk about our present. We share one thing first and foremost, a life on the Ark, drifting through space, trying to make sense of it all.

We had one of our best discussions the night after One sealed the cargo bay doors.

We were in my room. Illarion, Sanna, and Koyla sat on my bed. Gerlinde and I sat on the floor, using some of my pillows and jumpers as cushions.

"So, this dump was your room back home?" Koyla joked.

"Yep," I replied. "And you're a guest in it."

Koyla stuck his tongue out, and then smiled. "I don't like it. Were all British kids' rooms like this?"

"Everyone had different kinds of rooms, just like anywhere else," I said. "I bet your room looked a lot like this too."

Koyla nodded. "Yeah, but I had better pennants. I don't know how you guys like soccer so much. Boring!"

Then Koyla looked around the room and saw he was outnumbered.

We all sneered at him.

He blushed and looked at the floor.

"What's really missing is a window," I said, changing the subject.

"I never thought I would miss windows as much as I do," Sanna said.

"I miss grass," Illarion added.

"Who cares about windows," Gerlinde sniped. "This room needs travel posters, and more band posters. That would make it a lot less lame."

"Hey, why don't we stop poking holes in my choice of decorations," I said.

Gerlinde shrugged.

"If you had done a better job, it never would have come up," she said.

We all laughed.

"Why don't we talk about what we don't miss from Earth? That could be fun," Sanna suggested.

"Ooh ooh," Koyla said. "I don't miss social media at all."

Gerlinde jumped up like her feet were on fire.

"What?" she said. "I'd give anything to look at Facebook or Netfly again."

"I never did any social media," Illarion said.

The rest of us stared at him.

"How is that possible?" I asked.

"I didn't have a phone or a computer," Illarion said.

"How is *that* possible?" Gerlinde gasped,

"Everyone I knew lived on the same street as me," Illarion said. "I would just walk across the street to see them, unlike you Westerners."

"Are you calling Westerners lazy?" I asked.

"I am," Illarion replied. "Of course, you all are different. I have seen you work."

"You know what I don't miss," Koyla said. "Labels."

"What do you mean?" I asked.

"Like we can be anything we want to be now," he said. "You don't have to be a Westerner. Illarion does have to be a bed wetter. Gerlinde doesn't have to be a chocolatier."

Illarion scowled at Koyla's joke.

Gerlinde made a pouty face at him.

"And you must be so happy about that because you don't want to be a big dork anymore, huh, Koyla?" Gerlinde said.

"I'll be a big dork forever," Koyla said. "I like it because we Arkonauts get to make our own ideas. We can be anything we want. We don't even have to be from where we were from."

"Excuse me, but I'm Saudi Arabian and proud of it," Sanna said.

"But you're the only one now," Koyla said. "It's not like you have to listen to anyone or team up with anyone. You can be whoever you want."

"I think you're just trying to divide us up so you can hatch some evil plan," Gerlinde said.

We all laughed at that.

I had wondered where Koyla was going with this, too.

"Nah," Koala said. "I'm just saying that none of us can stick to labels anymore, and none of us have to. It's like a real melting pot in space."

"Maybe I like being English," I said. "Just like how Sanna is proud to be Saudi."

"And that's cool," Koyla said. "But why does that matter, really?"

I tried to come up with an answer for him. but the truth was I couldn't think of one. Sure, there was a lot of history and invention and culture that my country had produced, but now it was all gone.

146

And it wasn't like I had anyone to share it with, anyway. I was the only English person on board.

I could do my best to preserve the relics in my crate in the cargo bay, but it wasn't like anyone was going to reminisce with me about watching *Mitchell & Webb* or seeing Wayne Rooney in person when I was eleven. And when we reached our new planet, it wasn't like I would plant Saint George's Cross and claim it for England.

"I don't have an answer," I said.

"Great," Koyla said. "No more ties to old conflicts or wars with the other nations on board. We're a human race now!"

"Do you suppose that's why they only selected children?" Illarion asked.

"You mean because we're not stuck in our ways?" Gerlinde asked.

Illarion nodded. "I never believed that junk about teenagers needing less resources and medical care than adults being the only reason. But if they took us because we were young, and would work together, and wouldn't care so much about our home countries, that could make sense," he said. "I like Russian history and culture, but I don't like it more than I like all of you."

"So, when we get to this new Earth, we get to start over," Koyla said. "And when we have our own kids they won't be from this country or that country. They'll just be humans."

The room went silent.

I noticed Gerlinde blush. She looked away as soon as I looked at her.

I was horrified. We were going to have to get married and have babies, with each other. I wasn't ready for that.

"When we're older, guys," Koyla said, trying to break the silence.

"I'm going to the anti-grav room," Sanna said, rolling off the bed.

"I'm hungry. I will be in the cafeteria," Illarion said. Then he left.

"Observation room," Gerlinde said tersely, standing up and zipping out my door.

"What was that about?" he asked me.

I couldn't say anything. I felt myself about to blush.

"I didn't mean that we'd all have to, you know, right now, or something," Koyla said. "I just meant that in the future, when we're grown up we'd—"

Koyla gathered himself and moved toward the door.

I just shook my head, trying not to laugh, and ushered him out into the corridor.

21

ROUTINE

In the days after the cargo bay was resealed, life on the Ark became serious. We would no longer be passengers. From then on we were crew.

One assembled us all in the theatre for an introduction to the ships systems. One projected a giant hologram of the Ark in the centre of the room.

The briefing took hours. One spared no details from stem to stern, deck-to-deck, electrical to plumbing to life support to propulsion. All the information was actually incredibly interesting. I was most intrigued by the ion-drive engines, that worked almost like oars on a boat, pushing us forward while constantly adjusting our course, in three dimensions.

The Ark is shaped like a diamond. An acute pyramid forms the ship's base serving as storage space for water and air. The top is an obtuse pyramid, and the decks within were where we lived. These decks also included the observation room, the pumping station, the cafeteria, and the room we were in now, among others.

The cargo bay lay directly beneath us.

The schematic One projected focused on the inverted pyramid that formed the ship's base.

"This region, originally designed to store the air and water stolen from Earth, remains half-full with water all taken from the Atlantic Ocean," One told us. "When the Ark Project took control of the ship, we were unable to break the system of locks protecting this area. And as the ship was still embedded in the Icelandic landscape, the water would have released underground, making opening this section a low priority.

"When Dr. Ghost realized the Ark's current purpose, we elected to keep the water, and perhaps the building blocks of life within, for use on a new Earth-like planet."

One explained that only the top half of the ship had been explored or studied in any detail.

"Dr. Ghost and his team focused on that which was above ground," One said. "The Ark's power core has about ten years of life remaining, limited to a degree by the life support system that was added to the ship prior to your arrival. That concludes the technical study of the Ark. Now we will discuss roles and responsibilities.

"Over the next two years each of you will experience each of the ship's tasks and responsibilities in a rotating fashion. This will include maintenance, systems monitoring, and roles in leadership and in support," One continued. "Once we have passed through the wormhole, with a course set for the new home planet, you will choose a permanent position on the ship for the remainder of the journey. Upon arrival on the new planet, we will work in teams to hone our survival skills, and establish food sources and shelters.

"There are five major systems on the Ark. They are as follows: Engines, water supply, air supply, control centre and recycling."

One projected a new hologram in the centre of the room, highlighting the Engines first.

The engines would require weekly maintenance because of their age, and the limits of retrofitting Earth technology with the alien technology. One zoomed in on the individual directional thrusters.

"The Ark's main launch engine will not be used," One said. "However these smaller engines are necessary to maintain our course."

Then One showed us the water and air pumping systems.

"As these systems are vital to all of your lives, you will need to take special care in proactive maintenance and speedy repairs of leaks and blockages," One said. "Many of you have already experienced the water system and pumping station, and I ask that you share your experiences with other Arkonauts to expedite their understanding."

The control centre was the next focus point. Essentially the Ark's brain, the control centre roles came down to monitoring the ship's systems for errors, keeping records of operations, and anything we see that needed to be remembered, and issuing instructions to the crew in times of need or emergency.

"Finally, the recycling system," One said, zooming in on another area of the ship. "All of the air you breathe and water you use on the Ark is filtered, purified and reused. This system will also process and reuse uneaten food and human waste."

A chorus of "eww" rose among us.

Gerlinde looked at me, her tongue out. "Are we going to eat poop someday?"

"Gross," I said. "I hope not."

"With what you English eat, I doubt it's much worse," Koyla said.

Gerlinde laughed.

Then I laughed too.

"If I may continue," One said, looking right at us.

Blushing, I nodded.

I thought I saw One smirk. Then he continued.

Everyone received their assigned tasks and stations. I would start in the water pumping station alongside 45 other Arkonauts. Waiting as One read everyone's names and their roles was tedious, but when it was finished, he brought up a new hologram, showing a room we hadn't yet visited.

"Now then it is time to learn how to do each of these tasks," One said. "Follow me to the medical bay."

The medical bay was down the corridor past the observation room and control centre. A long, rectangular room, it was filled with fifty beds. Cupboards of medical equipment lined the outer walls. A counter covered in laboratory equipment filled the back of the room. And beyond it, a door marked "surgery."

One led us inside.

"If you are wondering about the surgical robots, they are on these recharging stations, in stasis to conserve energy," One said, pointing to a group of robots standing on round metal pads.

A couple of kids said "See?" in the accusatory tones of one who has just won a bet.

"If necessary, these robots will tend to you," One explained.

"I hope they do a better job than the last ones," I muttered to myself, touching the scar across my eye.

One looked at me, nodded, and said nothing. No one else seemed to hear me.

We walked past the robots to the laboratory. One stopped behind the counter and opened a drawer. He withdrew a metal, self-sterilizing syringe and a handful of small bottles filled with shimmering liquid.

I recognised the vials instantly. They were memory nanites.

The nanites were tiny robots programmed with memories from a donor, like Captain Amis. Once injected into our blood the nanites would latch onto the memory centre in our brains, importing the new with our own, original memories. The process was easier in theory than in practice. When Captain Amis's memories joined with mine, I felt like I was going crazy. It's not fun having thoughts that aren't yours. Especially when they insist on being heard.

Another batch of nanites, my second injection, came from a Buddhist monk who had achieved deep inner peace. The monk had volunteered to have the nanites learn her methods for self-control and self-centring. After that injection, my mind calmed down. I was able to focus on my own memories and thoughts, while also hearing Captain Amis.

"Each group will receive a nanite injection corresponding to their assigned starting location," One said, filling the syringe. "You will know everything you need for success almost instantly."

One held up the syringe and squirted a tiny amount of nanite fluid from the needle's tip.

"Engine crew first," he declared.

No one volunteered to go first.

"Is there a problem?" One asked.

"Can our brains handle any more memories?" Illarion asked, sheepishly.

"Yeah," Koyla agreed. "Sometimes it feels like a punk rock show in my head."

Some of the other Arkonauts echoed their concerns.

"The average human mind can handle forty injections, before schizophrenia like symptoms or possible multiple personalities occur," One said.

"I don't feel any better," Koyla quipped.

"It is perfectly safe," One reiterated. "You do not have to fear these changes. I propose a question. Do any of you remember what it was like to be seven years old? Not specific moments or events. Do you recall what you were like when you were seven years old?"

A carousel of moments flashed before me. There were visits to the park, a night getting ice cream with Mum, a group of street musicians that my father forced me to listen to... But One was right, I couldn't remember what I was like, just what I had seen.

Judging by the Arkonauts shaking their heads, I wasn't alone.

"In the last 8 years you have all gained new memories," One said. "You have all also changed, and yet, the person that each of you were at seven is not completely gone. You have all adapted, and with these new memories you will adapt again."

Then Gerlinde stepped forward, her sleeve rolled up, and offered up her arm.

Her bravery impressed me.

One smiled and then inserted the needle into Gerlinde's arm.

She winced, but didn't make a sound.

After the injection, the needle of the syringe retracted into itself. A tone sounded, and then the needle extended again, sterilized.

After the Arkonauts assigned to the engine room received their nanites, my group, the water pumping station group queued up. Next were water pumps and I, still not keen, was the last to be injected.

I hung at the back of the pack, still not eager to receive my injection.

To his credit, One made it very quick.

Barely a moment passed before I could feel the new memories digging into my mind. I thought I understood plenty about the pumping station, after fixing leaks and removing a blockage, but now I had the complete system schematics in my mind, as well as fourteen improvised methods for repair. In a blink, I was imagining new ways to re-route the pumping system to make it more efficient.

I had a job.

22

THE FISH

Those of us assigned to the pumping station were all equal. No one was the boss. And we really liked it that way.

Every morning, the control centre sent us a schedule of tasks, which was basically a checklist. Whenever we found a problem with one of the items on the list, we fixed it.

It had been pretty boring. We didn't have any major projects like the leaks and blockages of our first day on the Ark. And we knew so much more than we did then thanks to our new memory injections. Every day ended up being like the one before. We'd choose a leader for the day, look at whatever problems we were assigned, and then solve them.

That is, until the day that I was elected to lead the group.

We came to call that day 'Nemo Day.'

On Nemo Day, my checks and evaluations took me to an isolated section of the pumping station. I was patching a minor leak on a copper water line, over a glass pipe that fed into the pump from the ship's main cistern. The hole I was patching had already been patched before, so I had to remove the old repair to ensure my fix would have a proper seal. After I removed the old patch, I welded a permanent metal one over it. After I welded the last joint I stepped back to admire my work.

Something orange, I couldn't tell what, zipped by in the glass tube. I only caught it from the corner of my eye.

I knew, for sure, that there shouldn't be anything orange in the water system, so I chased after it, to get a better look.

That's when I saw it had fins and a tail.

It was a fish; a goldfish.

I could only guess at how it got inside. Maybe when the Ark first sucked water from the Atlantic Ocean? Or maybe it was in someone's house in Iceland, caught by the extending water vacuum by pure chance. But, now it was stuck in these pumps.

I tracked the pipe, following the fish, until I reached one of many larger sections that surrounded the pump, ensuring that the water pressure wouldn't get too high.

The water pressure was not very strong in this section so the fish swam by me slowly. I pushed my face up against the tube to get a good view, and I swear the fish turned and looked right at me.

It had those big, bulbous eyes, and its dorsal fin was scarred.

After looking at me, it turned and let the current sweep it further along the pipes.

I ran after the goldfish, or at least where I thought it was going. Since all the pipes lead back to the pumping station, I could have stayed put and the fish would pass by again, but I was worried for the little guy. Who knows how long it had been inside the ship, swimming in circles?

As I chased the fish, I passed by Ogwambi.

"What are you doing?" he shouted.

"Fish," I said, pointing at the pipe.

Ogwambi peered at me, then dropped what he was doing and ran after me.

"Did you say 'fish?'" he asked.

"Yes. There's a fish in the water pipes," I replied.

I stopped at another section of glass piping, hoping to see the fish again.

Ogwambi caught up, gasping for air, and stared at me as I stared at the tube.

"There can't be a fish in the pipes, Callum," he said. "Maybe you need to take a rest?"

"Just watch," I said, pointing sat the pipe.

That's when the fish appeared in the tube.

Ogwambi's jaw dropped and he stood on his tiptoes trying to get a closer look.

This time, the fish saw me again, and it definitely tried to stay in place, fighting the current.

"I think he recognises me," I said.

The fish couldn't swim against the current for long, and floated down the pipe again.

Ogwambi and I chased it again, passing Ivaylo and Koyla on our way.

"Where are you going?" Koyla asked.

"There's a fish in the pipes," Ogwambi and I yelled.

Now Koyla and Ivaylo were chasing the fish with us.

As we traced the spaghetti-like network of tubes, we picked up ten more Arkonauts, and then twenty. Finally, all of us in the pumping station were gathered around a testing pool.

The pool was a squat cylinder with an access hatch so we could test the pH of the water, or remove any foreign objects in the system. It was about as big as a hot tub.

We Arkonauts gathered around and waited for the tiny orange creature to appear. The fish soon popped out into the pool, swimming down toward its bottom, where the current was weakest. Still, there was too much current and the fish drifted toward the pool's exit.

"We need to save it," I declared.

"How?" Ogwambi said.

"I wasn't planning on fishing," Koyla said. "I don't even have my wading boots."

"Does anyone have a baseball hat?" I asked.

Evan from Wales, part of the pumping station group, volunteered that he did. He passed the ball cap through the group to me.

"The fish is about to re-enter the pipe system," Ivaylo said.

"We need to stop the flow so I can catch it," I said.

A team of three ran to the control panel.

"Great job, guys," I said. "Now we just need something to keep it in."

"I know just the thing," Ogwambi said, running over to a bin where we had stored spare parts.

Ogwambi grabbed a small section of pipe, a metal hatch, and some repair foam. He used the foam to glue the hatch over one end of the pipe, creating a closed bottom cylinder. Ogwambi quickly tested his invention, and it held water, so he filled it and ran over to us.

Then the fish disappeared from the pool, pulled into the tube on the other side.

"Come on," I said. "We've got to reverse the flow."

I heard one of the Arkonauts at the control panel yell, "Just a minute."

I opened the lid of the pool and waited, clutching the hat by its brim.

"Got it," one of the others yelled. "Flow reversed!"

"It should be here any second," Ogwambi said.

I watched the pool for that glint of orange.

"Water Station," Moana said, through the intercom. "This is the control centre. We're hearing complaints that the water isn't running. Is there a problem?"

"Hang on Moana," I called. "We're just waiting on a new friend."

"A new friend?" she asked.

That's when the fish popped out in the pool. I carefully scooped at the fish with the ball cap. The fish was a little scared, darting out of the way. My hand was shaking. I just wanted to catch it without hurting it.

"Callum, this is One," we heard over the intercom. "What is occurring in the pumping station? Moana has reported that you have found someone there."

I didn't reply right away, focused on the fish, the hat, and my shaking hand. With one more scoop, I caught it. It flopped around inside the cap, water quickly draining through the eyelets in the fabric.

Ogwambi held his makeshift bowl before me, and I carefully dropped the fish inside.

We all watched it swim about, looking almost happy to be free from the pipes.

"One," I said, finally. "We have a new Arkonaut on board."

23

LIGHTS

We named the fish Nemo.

I had never seen so much excitement surrounding a fish. You'd have thought it was a puppy or a kitten with how the Arkonauts crowded around, vying for time beside the tiny tank.

We kept Nemo's tank in the observation lounge, right next to the window. We figured that he deserved a bigger view, since he had only seen the inside of pipes for a long time.

We even decorated the inside of Nemo's tank. We put a bowl and cup at the bottom. One even made a contribution, cleaning a beaker from the laboratory, and giving it to Nemo to use as a cave.

"We should see how he likes the anti-grav room," Koyla suggested. "Fish in space!"

"I don't think that's a good idea," Gerlinde replied.

We spent much of that first day watching Koyla to make sure he didn't take Nemo to the anti-grav room.

A few days later, I went to the observation deck to visit Nemo before breakfast. I tapped Nemo's tank and he swum over to my finger. I really believed that he liked me the most. It was nice to have a pet. Nemo was another reminder of home.

And I felt happy. Not just because of Nemo, but because we Arkonauts were turning into a family. Nemo was just a bit of icing on a cake that got sweeter every day.

One sidled up beside me at the window. I didn't see him coming. He was so quiet, so swift.

"How is Nemo?" he asked.

"He seems happy to me," I said. "Assuming fish can be happy."

"I do not know if fish can feel," One said. "But Nemo is definitely resourceful. There is no fish food on the Ark, but I did discover a clump of seaweed growing where the water store connects to the pumping system. Nemo must have nibbled on those plants to feed, eating whatever it could on each pass through the system. I have taken the liberty of cultivating a small crop of the seaweed to sustain Nemo for our journey."

"Thanks, One," I said.

I felt awkward talking to One, and I knew why. One wasn't like us. He had so easily killed the men who had stowed aboard. And even though he was warm and gentle with us, I only had to close my eyes to see the incredible power he possessed. Even if he was that way so he could protect us, I had questions.

"One, why are you so strong and fast?" I asked, almost choking on the question.

One didn't look at me, instead he stared out the observation window.

"Do you remember when you were listening in on my conversation with Dr. Ghost?" One asked.

I nodded sheepishly.

"When my father conceived of the plan to send you Arkonauts into space, he argued that each child must be fifteen years old, to ensure peak physical conditioning upon arrival on the new planet, and also to prevent infighting from occurring due to ingrained biases," One said. "I was never meant to go with you, both because I am older, and because of my condition."

"Your condition?" I asked, perplexed.

"I have a developmental condition called autism," One said. "It makes it difficult for me to comprehend the emotions and motivations of others."

I had heard of autism. It was only just beginning to be understood when the Ark arrived, and everything changed on Earth.

"My father did not intend for me to travel with you," One continued. "I was never considered fully healthy."

"Then how did you end up on the Ark?" I asked.

"After months of debate over how to protect and lead your crew, my father decided to modify my capabilities in secret," One said. "He reasoned that my condition would prevent me from becoming distracted or too emotional to complete my duties, and that by augmenting my reflexes and abilities, I could become the ultimate guardian."

"It doesn't sound like you had much of a choice," I said.

"I did not," One said. "My father knew what was best and I trusted him."

"Still, it must have been hard to be a guinea pig," I said.

"It was not always easy, no," One said. "But we must all make sacrifices for the greater good."

"Do you ever miss him?" I asked. "Dr. Ghost? Your dad?"

One looked me in the eyes.

"I do not know," One said. "There are moments when I believe that I am sad that my father is no longer with me, but they are brief, and then the memories he gave me redirect my focus on the task at hand."

"I feel sad sometimes, too," I said. "I miss my mum and dad and my brother Jack. I miss the Tube and footie matches and—"

Tears welled up in my eyes so I stopped talking.

"We were all chosen," One said. "And we must not forget those who were not."

My thoughts drifted to my cousins, my teachers, my school friends.

I looked at One. "How do you do that? How do you remember and keep from getting sad?"

"It takes practice," One said.

"Maybe you just don't feel things the same way," I said, sniffling.

"I am still human," One said emphatically.

I had not seen him respond this way before.

"Despite my condition, and my modifications, I am still human," One said. "I have my own feelings, plus the memories of forty others, informing me constantly of my tasks and skills. That is not an easy feat."

"Forty different personalities?" I gasped. "Don't they all make you crazy?"

"Sometimes it can be almost painful," One said. "But, they are a gift from my father, from the world we left behind. It is a gift for me to feel too much, when for so long I could not express my feelings."

I never imagined how much One had been through. I always assumed he was a robot or an experiment. Instead he was a boy just like me, who took on everything that his father asked of him, even when it was more than I could ever conceive.

One and I stood in silence, and stared out into the vastness of space.

Our course had the Ark just days from exiting the solar system. Right now we were traveling the great distance between Neptune and Pluto. I wasn't sure what was beyond it, other than an endless field of twinkling stars.

"Did you have another name?" I asked. "Before 'One,' I mean?"

"Before I received the designation of One, my name was Joshua."

"Can I call you Joshua?" I asked.

"It is no longer my name," One replied. "But perhaps it will be again when my duty to you all is complete."

"You take your duty very seriously." I said.

"I have no other choice," One said.

"Well, I think you deserve to relax and have some fun. I bet the rest of the Arkonauts feel the same way," I said. "And maybe if you do the others will have an easier time getting to know you, and even like you."

"Does no one like me?" One asked.

I floundered. "We all respect you, and trust you, but we don't know you. Or at least they don't. I feel like I know you better now."

"And do you like me, Callum?" One asked.

"I do," I said, smiling. And it was true.

"Then perhaps I will let the others know about me as well," One stated.

"Come to breakfast," I said. "Chatting over food is a great place to start."

One nodded.

We gazed, one last time, out the window. The stars were twinkling, almost flashing. I hadn't seen anything like that before, but I was hungry, so I stepped away from the observation window.

One didn't move. He kept staring out at the flashing stars.

"One?" I asked. "Are you coming?"

One remained transfixed on the flashing stars.

When I followed his gaze back to the stars, I understood why.

They weren't stars, and they were coming toward us, fast.

MY PLACE

A computer gave me my spot on the Ark. It had sifted through DNA samples from all over the world, choosing each of us Arkonauts by comparing Dr. Ghost's desired genetic profile against every nation's DNA database.

My name popped up because I had no hereditary diseases to pass onto any children, I was the right age and I was reasonably fit and healthy.

The government approached me with my selection in complete secrecy. After being told of my golden ticket to the stars I was allowed to return home for a time. It wasn't until things went really bad that I was pulled from class, and my family and I were carted to the military base in the Lake District where we would soon live until my departure.

I had been chosen months before my family was told. My name was filed away and as Dr. Ghost's team completed preparations on the Ark, I was watched. The secrecy and tight timeline was to avoid anyone finding out who we eventual Arkonauts were, for our safety.

The day they notified me, there was a knock on the front door. I peered out the front window and saw a plumber's van parked in front of our house. When I answered the door, there were three plumbers standing on our stoop.

"Callum Tasker?" one of them said. "May we come inside?"

I nodded. I had never been sought out by plumbers before, but I was not concerned.

They had me call my father, and then sat us both down. They showed us government IDs. My father didn't object or question their credentials.

We were herded outside, with two men flanking us and another staying back, watching the street. They led us into the back of the plumber's van. Then we drove. We didn't know where. There were no windows in the back of the van.

After a few hours, we pulled into a garage below a facility. The place was crawling with police and military. Scientists in white lab coats walked the halls and corridors.

I spent the time silent and feeling paralyzed. I worried that I was in some kind of trouble, and the many men and women in uniforms and suits didn't make me feel any better.

I could tell my dad was afraid, too, but he never said anything.

The plumbers led us from the van to a bank of elevators. We travelled down for so long I couldn't believe it was possible. We must have been deeper underground than the Tube or the Chunnel. Once the elevator opened, we were ushered down a long white hall, and at the end we entered an office with the name Dr. Ghost etched on the door.

The doctor had a tan when we met, likely from explaining the Ark Project to a foreign dignitary somewhere warmer than England.

He greeted us with a smile.

"I'm happy to see you both," he said. "I trust my colleagues made your trip comfortable enough."

"Yes," my father said.

I didn't speak.

"Mr Tasker," Dr. Ghost continued. "You have been chosen to participate in the Ark Project." He said.

I looked at my dad who kept his gaze fixed on the good doctor.

"You're putting me on a ship that you're going to drop on the Destroyer?" I asked.

I looked at my dad, but he didn't seem concerned.

"The Ark Project has been modified," Dr. Ghost said. "It will not be used to crush Destroyer. Now, the Ark will be used to transport the remains of the human race to find a new homeworld."

"A new homeworld?" I asked.

My dad put his hand on my shoulder and squeezed.

I suddenly knew something was terribly wrong. "In our studies of the Ark vessel, we discovered the incredible destructive power stored in the ship's engines," Dr. Ghost said. "The Destroyer's engines are many times larger and more powerful than the Ark's, and they have already penetrated the Earth's crust. We believe that when the Destroyer takes its fill of our resources, its engines will fire, creating a shockwave that will destroy the Earth. We need to save as many people as we can from the Destroyer's inevitable destructive exit.*

"How long does the Earth have?" I asked. "We have to do something."*

My father's grip on my shoulder tightened.

"Son," he said. "It's too late for that."*

"Your father is correct," Dr. Ghost said. "There is no way to stop the Destroyer now."*

"What about the plan to drop the Ark onto the Destroyer?" I asked.*

"That is a..." and Dr Ghost paused to consider his words carefully. "A misrepresentation. The Destroyer has an engine powerful enough to destroy a planet. Dropping the Ark onto would cause a detonation easily capable of wiping out the Planet Earth anyway. No, the Ark is to be used as a lifeboat a far more efficient use of its capabilities.*

 My colleagues have already pre-empted this conversation with a phone call to your parents where everything was explained to your parents by phone, we have no choice but to pursue this alternative."

I wasn't sure how to process the information. And, really, I didn't fully process it until the day that I was teleported onto the Ark, when I saw the Earth die... when I said goodbye to them.

"For the human race to survive, a group must begin again on another world," Dr Ghost said.*

"You said there would be one traveller from each country?" my dad asked.*

"Yes," Dr Ghost responded. "Including representatives from large ethnic groups, tribes and regions, there will be two-hundred fifty odd in all."

"Two-hundred fifty?" I asked. "That's it?"

My father gripped my shoulder again.

"You'll be with all other kids your age," he said. "It'll be a lot like a summer camp, but in space."

"How can we fly a spaceship?" I asked.

"There will also be a protector on the ship," Dr. Ghost said. "Their role will be to keep you on course and safe. Not to worry, Callum."

I looked back at my dad. He was trying to keep a stern look, but I could tell he wasn't as confident as he appeared.

"Will you be able to take my younger son?" my father asked. "Jack?"

Dr. Ghost pursed his lips. "Callum's genetics are most suitable. Jack has several common, but undesirable recessive genes. There are millions of others like him."

"They told me that it was still a possibility," my dad said.

"My apologies, Mr. Tasker," Dr. Ghost said. "They should not have misrepresented our intentions. We have only selected Callum."

Dad stood up, angry, and behind us, the plumbers entered the room. They flanked my father, waiting for a command from Dr. Ghost.

"Mr. Tasker, everything has long been decided," Dr. Ghost said. "This meeting is to inform Callum of his duty. In the coming weeks, your family will move to the Lake District, for your protection, and so that Callum can attend orientations. You will tell no one outside your immediate family that your son has been chosen. We will know if you do and there will be severe consequences."

My father sat still.

Dr. Ghost then withdrew a syringe and vial of shimmering liquid from inside his desk.

"This will be your first memory injection, Callum, I'm sure you've heard of nanites and what they can do," the doctor said. "This and many like it will properly prepare you for your journey. Please roll up your sleeve and take a deep breath."

I complied.

Dr. Ghost stuck the needle in my arm and I cried.

The nanites crawled up my arm and into my brain. That was the first time Captain Amis whispered inside my head.

"What did you do to me?" I asked.

"Do not worry," Dr. Ghost replied. "It is perfectly safe. And entirely beneficial."

My father shook his head at the scene, but said nothing.

"I know that this is a lot of information to absorb in one day," Dr. Ghost said. "However, I trust that both of you, and your family members, will come to respect the gravity of your roles in the survival of the human race."

One of the plumbers stepped forward and handed my father an envelope.

"Take heart, Mr. Tasker," Dr. Ghost continued. "Your bloodline will outlive almost every other one on Earth. That's quite a legacy."

"You're not known for your bedside manner, are you?" my father quipped.

Dr. Ghost just laughed, and then turned to me.

"Callum," he said. "You will carry the future of your country. You will be the last Englishman."

24

ANOTHER REMNANT

"We must access the control centre immediately," One said.

One ran out of the observation room, so fast that I could barely keep up.

What were those lights? What did One know?

As we sprinted to the control centre, One accessed the intercom.

"Arkonauts, please report to the control centre," One's voice boomed throughout the ship. "Daily work is cancelled. You will receive new instructions."

When I reached the control centre, One had already opened a hologram projection in the middle of the room. The image focused on the part of space we just saw in the observation room.

The stars were actually space shuttles. There was a dozen of them heading directly for the Ark.

"Those are human shuttles," I said.

"Correct," One said. He tapped at the control panel, showing the shuttles' shared course on the hologram.

Arkonauts rushed into the control centre. Koyla, Koamalu and Illarion came to my side, and we all stared up at the screen.

"Shuttles?" Illarion asked.

"Yeah," I said. "Human shuttles."

"Other survivors?" Koyla said. "Man, I thought we were special. Now everyone wants to be an Arkonaut."

"This should not be possible," One said. "The Ark is faster than any Earth ship."

In the hologram, a new wave of shuttles appeared, coming up alongside the first group. I counted fifteen more ships.

"Look," I said. "There's more of them."

One tapped madly at the control panel, zooming in on the two groups, so we could see the shuttles up close.

The first group were sleek ships with huge engines. On their hulls were the red, white and blue flags of the United States of America.

The second group of ships were boxier and simpler, more closely resembling rockets. They bore the flag of the People's Republic of China.

Immediately, Maiara and Nuan, our Chinese and American representatives, shifted on their feet nervously. Our eyes fell on them, looking for answers we knew they didn't have. Though we'd have preferred either girls' answers to the one we heard next.

"They are invaders," One said.

"Invaders?" Illarion asked.

"No ship could have caught up to the Ark," One said. "These long-range ships have been retrofitted with technologies we discovered from the Ark. They must have been launched months ago. They have been waiting for us to reach the edge of the solar system."

"Maybe they just want to party?" Koyla said. "How do we get them on board?"

One stared at Koyla. "This is not the time for your unique sense of humour."

Koyla shrugged. "They're humans aren't they? Shouldn't we let them inside?"

"Those ships can carry hundreds of people," One said. "Even if they can be trusted, the Ark is not equipped to accommodate them."

"One, we can't leave them to die," I said.

A few of the other Arkonauts agreed with me, but the room erupted in arguments. Many of us feared that these people would be like the stowaways. We had already lost Mathieu. What if the people on these ships killed more of us?

"We cannot allow them aboard," One said, finally.

"Why not?" I asked.

"They are not here peacefully," One said. "These formations are military in nature. The ships are attempting to flank the Ark. This is an attack."

One of the American ships broke from its group suddenly, firing its engines and soaring toward the Chinese group. Immediately, a Chinese ship powered up to intercept. The other ships jockeyed for position, circling in an attempt to isolate us and the other ships.

Then the battle began.

Two American ships peeled off, firing rockets at the Chinese ships. Then the Chinese ships fired back.

Four of the ships exploded, one American, and three Chinese. The American ships had launched a kind of countermeasure that detonated the missiles before they hit them. Soon, more ships on both sides flew into the fray, firing more rockets.

If this were a science fiction movie, it would have been brilliant, but watching the very last remains of Earth fighting to the death over the Ark was terrifying.

"They can't get onto the Ark, can they?" I asked.

"There are docking ports on the ship," One said. "They will likely try to enter the ship through one of them."

"How are we going to defend ourselves?" Illarion asked.

"We can't fight them," Koyla said, seriously.

The space battle reached a stalemate. There were only four ships from each side left and they stopped firing on each other. Instead, they were racing toward the Ark, to be the first to enter and claim the vessel.

"Everyone follow me to the cargo bay," One said. "I will seal you all inside for your safety and deal with the threat."

Sirens blared in the control centre. Something was very wrong now.

One brought up a hologram of the Ark's exterior.

"The ships are cutting open the docking hatches," One said. "They will be able to board soon. Everyone go to the cargo bay now."

We were panicked. It was hard for all of us to exit the control centre quickly, but before long we were running down the stairs to the cargo bay.

"Wait, Arkonauts," Nuan shouted.

"What is the problem?" One asked.

"There's a group from the engineering crew checking the engines," Nuan said.

"Yes, before breakfast we're supposed to check the engines quickly. They're not here with us," Maiara added.

One quickly counted us, and then a frown set over his face.

"I'll go get them," I volunteered. "You've got to protect us, One."

One looked at me, and something close to a smile crossed his lips.

"Nuan, Maiara show me where the engine room is," I said.

The girls nodded.

"Meet everyone else at the cargo bay the moment that you have found the others," One said. "Do not attempt anything heroic."

I nodded.

"Don't worry, One."

We dashed off, the girls leading the way to the engines.

Once we were out of earshot of the other Arkonauts and, hopefully One, I placed a hand on each of the girls' shoulders to make them stop.

"Nuan, Maiara I need to ask..." I trailed off, realising that asking for their loyalty was a dumb move. And actually showed a lack of trust on my part, trust that these girls had earned simply by being a part of the crew for the last month.

"Never mind," I said blushing and moving past them. "Let's get to the engine room."

Both girls then grabbed my arms to stop me.

"I think we both know what you were going to ask," Maiara said.

"Yeah. It was obvious," Nuan added.

"Sorry," I said sheepishly.

"Don't worry, I'm an Arkonaut," Nuan declared.

"Me too," Maiara said.

I nodded. "Well I'm glad we got that straightened out."

"Next time, ask us when we aren't in a life and death situation," Nuan said sarcastically.

"Yeah," Maiara said shaking her head at him and tutting.

The girls led the way once more.

I then remembered that we were about to be in the middle of a fire fight. My heart was racing.

***

We ran so fast to the engine room that we barely touched the stairs.

The engine room was massive, the size of a city block. Rings of metal planks and access ramps encircled the giant power plant in the middle. A spider web of conduits funnelled energy from the core to the rest of the ship.

Gerlinde, Koamalu and Bae were working at the engine console.

"What are you guys doing down here?" Gerlinde asked.

"Didn't you hear One's announcement?" I asked.

"We heard something, but it was drowned out by the engines," Gerlinde said. "Why?"

I took Gerlinde's hand and tugged her toward the stairs. She slapped my hand away.

"We're being invaded," I said. "We have to get to the cargo bay."

"Invaded?" Gerlinde replied. "You have to be kidding."

"Eight ships from Earth are boarding us as we speak," Nuan said. "It is not a joke."

"One will deal with the invaders," I added. "But we need to get to safety."

"If they're humans, why aren't we letting them onboard?" Bae asked.

"There was a space battle, okay?" I said. "An American and a Chinese fleet fought each other, and the remaining ships are trying to make the Ark their final battleground."

"One doesn't think they are friendly," Maiara answered. "And based on the rockets they were firing at each other, I don't think so either."

Gerlinde nodded. She turned to Bae and Koamalu.

"I think we should go," she said.

"Right," I said. "It's like there's an echo in here."

"Don't be such a boy about it," Gerlinde chided.

I sighed. "I'm not trying to be anything, but we have to go. Are your checks complete?"

"Yes, the engines are fine," Gerlinde replied. "Sir." She hit her last word with a defiant tone.

Gerlinde smiled at me. Then she led us up to the cargo bay. Most of the Arkonauts were already inside. Illarion and Koyla were at the back of the pack, stepping through as we arrived.

"Alright, you made it," Koyla shouted. "We were worried you'd end up as Nemo food, or worse."

One stepped through the door, counted us silently and then abruptly cocked his head the way a dog might, focusing its ears.

I didn't hear anything, but One tapped at the control panel, closing the doors, and started up the stairs to the main part of the ship.

"Hey, One! Wait. We're not inside yet," I cried out. "What did you—"

The door rolled closed, sealing the other Arkonauts inside, and us outside.

One turned fast and ran towards us. He pulled Illarion and Koyla away from the door just as a blast of gunfire struck it. The shots came from the main steps.

"Go back down the stairs to the engine room," One said. "I will be right behind you."

More shots struck the cargo bay door. We all ran. Gerlinde had taken my hand this time. I didn't think she noticed that she had.

None of this made sense to me. The other ships were miles away. I didn't understand how they closed in on us so quickly.

Behind us, One had taken cover around the corner from the cargo bay. A man wearing an astronaut's flight suit came around the corner. He was holding a gun, but he didn't see One.

One moved like lightning, kicking the astronaut in the stomach. Then One spun the man around, ripping the gun from his hand, and locking his arm behind him.

I watched as One flung the man at the staircase we were on. I held out my arms, sweeping my friends up against the sidewalls of the stairwell.

The astronaut tumbled down and rolled past us, his body too limp for him to be alive.

When the body stopped rolling, I knelt beside the astronaut to investigate. There were two facts I could discern in a single look: He was facing the back of his suit, his neck broken, and he was Chinese, a red flag with gold stars on the suit's lapel.

We heard a handful of gunshots behind us. Then One came running down the stairs toward us.

"Go!" he yelled.

***

When we stopped in the engine room, One counted his gun's ammunition, then appeared to make several calculations in his head.

"We must find a safe place for you to hide," One said.

"Our assailants will be heading for the control centre to capture it. The cargo bay is sealed with a password, but once they access the control centre they will be able to crack it."

"Where do we go?" I asked.

"The residential areas will be safest for now. There are so many rooms, it will be hard for the other astronauts to search them effectively. Odds are they will ignore them completely."

We crossed the gangplanks surrounding the engine and used another stairwell on this side to get back to the residential level, listening for other gunshots. When we got back to the residence level, One cautiously peaked out, clearing the area, before waving us through.

"Stay tight against the wall," One said. "If we are attacked, take cover and retreat as soon as it is safe. I will hold off the attack."

We inched along the wall. Nuan and Koyla were holding hands now too. From the distance the sounds of an engine, and more gunfire, echoed down the corridor.

"Sounds like they are fighting each other," Illarion said.

"They are," One said. "And they are growing near."

"What about the engine noise?" Gerlinde asked.

"I cannot pinpoint it," One said, "It is motor driven and mechanical, but I do not know what it is."

One looked genuinely perplexed.

I wasn't sure how to feel about that.

"The path to the living quarters is clear," One said. "Move."

One led us to Illarion's room. It was the farthest from any other main corridors.

We piled inside. The room was dark. We didn't even bother to switch the light on. We felt safe in the darkness.

"Stay here," One said. "Do not come out until I say."

Right as the door closed behind him there was a cacophony of gunshots. We heard One slump against the door to Illarion's room.

I couldn't move. I had to know if One was okay, but I was frozen.

"Got him," someone shouted outside.

I crawled through the darkness to the door, and slid it open just a centimetre. I peeked through the crack. One was still, bleeding profusely from wounds in his chest and head. I could only barely see that he was breathing.

Gerlinde crowded behind me, wanting to look too.

I pushed her back, and thankfully, Illarion grabbed her foot to keep her from moving.

"He's hurt," she whispered.

Illarion held his finger to his lips.

We heard footsteps outside. Someone was looking at One.

As the footsteps grew louder, I shepherded us all into Illarion's bathroom.

Outside we heard a pair of men talking.

"This one's dead," said one man.

"A bit young, isn't he?" another said.

"Looks like he was trying to get into this room," said the first.

We all tensed up, waiting for them to enter.

"Well, he sure didn't make it," the other said.

"The Colonel wants all prisoners brought to him."

"This ain't a prisoner," said the other. "He's just a corpse now. Leave him."

We listened closely as the footsteps moved away from the door and grew quieter until they disappeared down the corridor.

I pushed out of the bathroom and then quietly opened Illarion's door. One was still alive, barely, and he had lost a lot of blood.

"We need to get him to the medical bay," Gerlinde said.

Illarion and I draped One's arms over our shoulders and hoisted him off the floor.

"Koyla, Maiara, take his legs," I said.

We lifted One together and started down the corridor.

One muttered quietly, and winced from pain as we lifted him.

Gerlinde picked up One's gun and aimed it down the hall.

"Let's go," she said. "I will cover us."

We made the tense trek to the medical bay, watching our backs and listening carefully. I had never heard Koyla stay so quiet for so long.

We laid One on the first bed we could.

"How do we turn the robots on?" Gerlinde asked. "They're his only chance."

One reached out and grabbed my blood-soaked shirt. He pulled me close to him, so that my ear was at his mouth.

"Fifth drawer down, mem-memo," he gurgled.

Then One's head fell back. His arms went slack, and his eyes closed. A final laboured breath rose and fell in his chest.

Then One didn't move.

We were all paralyzed.

"One?" I asked.

No response.

"Joshua," I said next.

"Josh—?" Koyla said.

"Wake up," I demanded, shaking One's shoulder. "We need you."

Gerlinde put two fingers to One's neck. Then she moved her fingers slightly and tried again. Finally, she shook her head.

"He's... gone," Gerlinde said.

Koyla yelped.

I buried my face in my hands and started to cry.

25

ONE OF US

We stood there in silence, tears in our eyes, leaderless and directionless.

"What do we do now?" Nuan asked.

"What did One say to you, Callum?" Illarion asked.

I didn't answer, my thoughts bouncing between my conversation with One, and an intense fear that the invaders would win, and not just kill all of us, but ruin the Ark's mission.

"Callum?" Illarion repeated, more urgently.

"Fifth drawer. Something about mem—" I trailed off when I realised what 'mem' and 'memo' meant. "Memory!"

I rushed to the lab at the rear of the medical bay. I opened the drawer that contained syringes, took one, and then opened the fifth drawer down.

Inside were memories all labelled for One. There was 'military training,' 'survival training,' 'combat training' and more.

"Find anything?" Illarion asked.

"It's One's memories," I said. "There's a vial for just about everything."

"Is there a vial labelled 'come back to life?'" Koyla asked.

I shook my head, and then dug through the drawer. There was nothing inside to help One. One was dead. Completely. And we were on our own.

"The memories aren't exclusive to One," Captain Amis whispered.

Suddenly, I knew what to do. I took a syringe and picked up a vial labelled 'military training.' I stuck the vial and pulled back the syringe filling it. Then I rolled up my sleeve.

"What are you doing, Callum?" Gerlinde asked. "I thought those were for One."

"We need to fight back," I said. "I'm guessing this will make me like One."

"And what if it drives you crazy?" Gerlinde asked. "What if it kills you?"

"The only alternative is to the give ourselves up," I said. "I'll take this chance."

Gerlinde nodded reluctantly.

"It might be the only way," Illarion said.

"Plus, we'll get to hang out with Super Callum," Koyla added.

"Okay," I said. "Here goes."

I held the needle close to my arm.

"We have to get control of the Ark," I said. "For One, and for ourselves."

"Do you have a plan?" Nuan said.

"Not yet," I said. "I hope these memories do that part."

"Don't move!" a voice bellowed from the doorway.

I dropped the nearly empty vial. It crashed to the floor, and shattered.

In the doorway, five soldiers had their guns aimed at us.

"Drop the weapon," one of them shouted.

Illarion dropped the gun he had been holding, and raised his hands.

I slipped the syringe in my trouser pocket and raised my hands, too.

The soldiers sneered at us.

"These are American soldiers," Captain Amis whispered in my head. "See those rank insignias?"

The soldiers carried guns and other weapons, but they also wore some kind of whirring backpacks, each pack connected with a network of straps, and each strap lined with small wheels. I waited for Captain Amis to tell me what they were, but my mind was clear.

"Just kids," the captain of the soldiers said.

"This the UN's plan?" the sergeant among them said. "Send kids into space?"

The soldiers strode toward us, never lowering their weapons.

They stopped by One's body. A soldier prodded him with the barrel of her gun. "This one's not much older," she reported. "Definitely dead."

They sauntered up to us in a line. When they stopped, the captain lowered his gun, but the others kept theirs on us.

"Who are you kids?" the captain asked. "Children of the crew?"

"We are the crew," I replied.

"You can't be," the captain growled, and then turned to the other soldiers. "You imagine, this ship manned by a bunch of eleven and twelve year olds?"

The soldiers laughed.

"We're fifteen," I said.

"Are you?" the captain said. "Well you're still not bulletproof. Let's go. You're coming with us to the command centre."

The soldier who jabbed One's body circled behind us and stuck the barrel in my back.

"Move it, smart guy," she said. "Hands on your heads now!"

They took us to the control centre. Inside five more soldiers cradled guns. In the middle of the pack, a grey-haired man stood with his back to us. He stared up at the viewscreen, currently focused on the remains of his space fleet. He wore the same backpack as his soldiers, with straps and wheels surrounding the man's joints.

He motioned at the viewscreen, the pack hummed, the wheels turned and the straps stretched and tensed.

The backpack was helping him move.

"Brave men and woman, journeying across the stars to seek safety," the grey-haired man said. "True patriots."

The man saluted the viewscreen, took a deep breath, and then craned his neck to acknowledge us.

"This is an impressive vessel. No doubt about that," he said. "Ridiculous that it was left in the care of children from lesser nations."

He then turned to look at us.

His face was scarred and weathered. He was pale, gaunt, and his eyes were wet and tired. He looked the way my great-grandfather did near the end of his life. Maybe he was sick. Based on the insignia on his uniform, he was a colonel, and the officer in charge.

He looked us all over and scowled.

"You," he barked at Nuan. "Are you Chinese?"

"No," I said before Nuan could speak. "She's French Canadian."

The man studied her. "You all look the same, anyway, don't you?" he said. "Long as you're not a Communist."

The radio on his belt beeped, so he turned away from us to answer.

"What's the situation, lieutenant?"

The radio crackled. "The enemy has secured the entrance to the cargo bay and are holding up there," the lieutenant said. "We have the stairwells locked down. They don't have anywhere to go."

"Keep them contained for now," the colonel ordered.

"Yes, sir," the radio replied. "They haven't accessed the cargo bay yet, but they were trying to communicate with someone in the bay. We believe that the remaining crew might be inside."

"Very good," the colonel said, placing the radio back on his belt.

"We need to scan the interior of this ship."

A soldier shook her head. "We are still figuring out the controls, sir."

"Double time," the colonel barked. "I want those communists tracked."

The colonel turned back to us.

"Is there an American representative on this ship?"

Maiara slowly raised her hand.

"Your fellow countrymen are in the cargo bay," I said.

The colonel looked at me and then back at Maiara.

"What were you going to say, girl?" he asked.

"Same—same as him," she said, nodding at me.

The colonel looked at Maiara. "Who do you really represent?" he growled. "You look more like an Indian to me."

"She's—" I started.

The colonel whipped around and backhanded me in the face. My ears rang.

"Stop answering for her," he whispered menacingly. He turned back to Maiara. "Now who do you represent? Really?"

She didn't reply. She just stared back at him.

"Oh, I get it," the colonel snorted. "Those bleeding heart, U.N. bureaucrats, didn't even bother to save a real American patriot."

Then he slapped Maiara.

"My father was a Texan," Maiara spat back.

She sneered at the colonel, her jaw square and proud. "Is that American enough for you?"

The colonel raised his hand again.

Maiara didn't flinch.

Wow, I thought to myself

"You're lucky to be here, girl," he said. "My country paid for this vessel, fought for it, and what did we get? A bunch of child freaks from every dark corner of the planet. Well, no more. This ship is ours now, and it will uphold real American culture."

"Sir," a soldier interrupted. "Internal cameras are now functional."

"Show me the cargo bay," the colonel ordered.

The feed showed outside the main door of the cargo bay. Thirty soldiers, all dressed in astronaut garb bearing the Chinese flag clutched their guns and looked around alertly. Leading their group was a portly man flanked by a smaller man holding a clipboard. The Chinese group also had computers and something resembling a coffin on wheels. Surprisingly, they also had motorbikes, not petrol driven ones, but electric ones, to help them traverse the long corridors of the gigantic ship more effectively.

"The Minister of Defence of the People's Republic," the colonel said. "I'm surprised the slob managed to save his own life."

"Shall we contact them via intercom, sir?" the captain asked.

"No. I prefer a more personal touch," the colonel said. "After all, we're about to give our Chinese friends the terms of their surrender."

"Sir?"

"We have two able-bodied messengers right here," the colonel said, peering at Nuan and me.

The colonel smiled.

I've never felt so scared of a smile.

26

REPUBLIC VS REPUBLIC

The colonel and two other soldiers marched us to stairs leading to the cargo bay.

"Jeeves, you take the Asian girl down to the Chinese, deliver this radio, and then come back to us," the colonel said.

"What if they don't let us come back?" I asked.

"That's not really my problem, Jeeves," he replied.

He shoved us toward the stairs.

"Why are you doing this?" Nuan asked.

"I am a survivor," the colonel said. "I've survived wars. I even survived cancer. I'm not about to stop surviving just because some paper pushers and lab geeks came up with a coward's plan."

"You're bullying kids," Nuan muttered.

"A firm hand is necessary to lead," the colonel said. "My country may have forgotten itself, but I will fight forever for the U.S.A., even against you twerps."

The colonel smiled again and then motioned to the soldiers with us. They pointed their guns at us, urging us down the steps.

"What are we going to do, Callum?" Nuan asked me as soon as we left the soldiers' earshot.

"I don't know," I said. "But we'll figure it out."

We walked slowly, trying not to make a sound. It was terrifying. The last thing we needed was another group of soldiers shooting at us.

"I don't want to see my countrymen again," Nuan said.

"Why?" I asked, surprised.

"When I was chosen, the government came for me," she said. "They demanded that I help them stow away on the Ark."

"I thought they were part of the international committee," I said.

"They threatened my family," Nuan said. "They said they would do horrible things to them unless I gave them the teleportation transmitter."

"But you didn't," I said.

Nuan shook her head. "No. I told Dr. Ghost, and he moved my family and me to a different country. Our government must have been furious."

"That was very brave," I said.

"I always wanted to be free," Nuan said. "I was an orphan, until my family adopted me. I spent ten years in a state orphanage, and then the last five in a small village where we barely had enough food to survive. The Ark meant I would make my own destiny. I would be free of the poverty and free to start again."

"We can make a better world together, Nuan," I said.

She nodded. "That is all I want. But—," she said, her tone becoming worried. "What if these people recognize me?"

"They won't," I said. "I mean, they've been in space for a while, so it's unlikely they even received a notice on you. Just follow my lead and we'll be fine."

"What's that?" Nuan said.

"Cower like a little boy," I replied.

She snorted. "Good idea. But I'll cower like a little girl."

I smiled.

When we came into view of the Chinese group we both raised our hands over our heads. It didn't matter. Twenty guns aimed right at us.

"Please, don't shoot," I said. "We're unarmed. Just kids."

"Let them come," the minister, the man in charge of this group wheezed. He was a fat man wearing a suit straining to keep him contained. His black hair was slicked back over his head. I noticed that his fellow countrymen were thin as if he had been eating all the rations on their ships, like a despot clinging to a serfdom in space.

Half of the Chinese soldiers lowered their guns, and one of them waved us forward.

The cargo bay door was still closed. Everyone inside must still be safe.

"Search them," the minister ordered.

The soldiers patted us down.

I was surprised the Americans hadn't bothered, but then the colonel dismissed us as nothing but children.

The Chinese soldiers found the radio, and the syringe.

"What's this?" the minister asked of the syringe.

"My insulin, sir," I lied.

The minister nodded, and his jowls wobbled like jelly. It was a feasible enough story.

"And this?" he asked, pointing at the radio.

"A radio," I said. "The American colonel told us to bring it to you."

"You are Callum Tasker, aren't you?" the minister said.

"How do you know who I am?"

"I know everything about this mission," he boasted. "Are the Americans here to defend you?"

"No, they invaded us, just lik—" I trailed off, hoping not to insult them.

Then the radio crackled with static.

"Minister," the colonel said. "I trust the children have delivered this to you by now."

"Yes," the minister replied. "And I offer you the terms of your surrender. This vessel now belongs to the people of China, and you are trespassing."

The colonel laughed. The static on the radio made it sound almost animal.

"You are hardly in a position to make demands," the colonel said.

The radio clicked off, and then started beeping rapidly. The tone grew louder and faster each second.

"Take cover," Captain Amis said in my mind.

Nuan was faster than me. She grabbed me and threw us both to the floor.

The tone got faster.

The minister grabbed the small man with the clipboard and used him as a human shield.

It was so loud I thought I might go deaf.

The radio exploded, flinging the soldier holding it back in a cloud a blood and shrapnel. The man holding the clipboard collapsed. So did three of the soldiers. The others were only stunned.

A body fell on top of Nuan and me.

"Are you okay?" I mouthed.

Nuan nodded.

Smoke was everywhere. Nuan and I pushed the dead soldier off of us. Everything stank of metal.

The minister and his men spun around wildly, aiming their guns for an expected attack by the Americans. The minister coughed and wiped some of his assistant off his astronaut suit. He focused on Nuan and me.

"Get them up," he ordered, drawing his pistol.

"You have betrayed your people," he said, pointing the gun at Nuan. "You have earned a traitor's death."

"Wait," I yelled. "We didn't know the radio was a bomb."

The minister just shook his head and pulled the trigger.

The shot hit Nuan in the heart.

She gasped.

"She betrayed her people long before today," the minister growled. "There is no place in the new China for those who do not serve the Party."

Nuan collapsed.

I knelt beside her.

"Nuan," I said. "You're going to be fine. Just stay with me, okay?"

I knew that what I was saying was a lie and cliché statement, but I needed her to think there was a chance and not die in terror. And I needed to believe she could survive too.

There was blood everywhere. The bullet had gone straight through her.

She coughed.

"I was proud to be an Arkonaut," she whispered.

Then her eyes closed.

I could only stare at her body. Time seemed to stop.

I bit my lower lip. My mind raced. Captain Amis was quiet, but I was not. My blood boiled.

I lunged at the minister, wanting nothing more than to tear him limb from limb.

Two soldiers grabbed me before I could land a single punch. They laughed and threw me back to the floor.

"You'll die soon enough," the minister bragged.

Then the minister walked to the base of the stairwell and cleared his throat.

"Colonel," he yelled. "You didn't kill me, and you and your American pigs will die for that mistake."

27

THE NEW SOLDIER

A Chinese soldier stood guard over me as I stared at Nuan's dead body.

They hadn't even covered her.

They just left her where she fell.

I had never been so disgusted, or so scared. They could do the same to me in an instant. I was no more a bargaining chip than Nuan was. I worried about my friends, all of them safe for now behind the cargo bay door. There were the others, upstairs with the colonel, too. How much time did they have? How far were the minister and the colonel willing to go to win?

I waited for Captain Amis, but he wouldn't speak to me. Maybe, like the adage, he had nothing nice to say so he said nothing at all.

Then I thought of One, and I remembered the syringe. The soldier who had taken it from me paced back and forth, watching over the minister. I couldn't see it in his hands.

Without drawing attention to myself, I scanned the floor around me until a glint caught my eye. The syringe was tucked next to Nuan's leg. The soldier must have dropped it during the explosion and no one noticed.

I carefully scooted forward, closer to Nuan's still face. It really looked like she could just wake up, if only this were a horrible nightmare. I leaned toward her, hoping to slip my hand along her side.

"What are you doing?" my guard yelled.

My hands quivered, my fingers nearly on the syringe.

Then the guard grabbed me by the collar, and pulled me back.

"I'm sorry, sir," I said, letting my voice shake as much as possible. "We were... I... I loved her."

"So what?" the guard said.

"Can I... can I just sit with her for a minute," I begged. "Just one more minute... to say goodbye."

A tear rolled down my cheek.

The guard looked down the line toward the minister, who was busy ordering the other soldiers around, and then turned back to me.

"Make it quick," he said.

I sniffled and nodded. "Thank you, sir," I said.

I slid back toward Nuan, grabbed the syringe, and said a prayer over her. I felt immediately horrible for using her in the moment, but I hoped that she'd think it made her a hero.

Sitting next to her, I couldn't inject myself in the arm without giving myself away, but I could inject myself in the butt.

Forcing the needle in was excruciatingly painful. I bit my lip so as not to cry out. The tears that did fall only helped my story. The guard looked at me, and for a moment, I think he felt a bit of sympathy.

Or maybe he thought I just had an itch.

Immediately, I felt the nanites crawling to my brain. There's nothing stranger than literally having something under your skin, traveling your bloodstream.

The new memories took hold quickly.

"Know your enemy," the new tactics memories told me. "The minister is a coward and a blowhard. He is more concerned with his power than his responsibility."

I watched the minister stroll around issuing orders. Like the memories said, he stayed in the centre of the groups of soldiers. And like Nuan's, he hadn't bothered to move the body of his assistant. He had no respect for anyone but himself. If only his soldiers would see that.

"You can escape," Captain Amis chimed in. "You're outgunned, but there's always a way out. Find the exit where guns can't be used"

Then the new memories whispered, "When you have many enemies, make one your ally."

I understood immediately.

"Hey, minister," I said. "Why are you defending this area, anyway?"

The minister scowled.

"Shut up, boy," he said.

"The engine room hasn't been taken yet, and it powers everything," I said. "Including the control centre where the Americans are. And the cameras watching you right now."

The minister looked up and saw the camera monitoring the corridor. He peered at his own reflection, bent and oblong.

"Where are the monitors for these cameras?" the minister asked.

"In the control centre," I said. "You'll never surprise the Americans until you shut them down."

The minister threw up his hands. "Destroy this camera! Now!"

One of his soldiers rushed forward and whacked the camera with the butt of his rifle until it shattered.

"If you want to live you will show us to the engine room," the minister said to me.

I tried to look as scared as I've ever been.

"Anything, sir," I cried. "Just don't hurt me."

The minister smiled proudly and then motioned for my guard to pick me up. The guard poke me in the back with his rifle.

"Go on," he snarled.

"It's down there," I said pointing to the stairwell at the end of the corridor.

"We're moving," the minister barked. "Trap the base of the steps leading to our Yankee friends."

Four soldiers circled the minister. The others picked up the invaders' equipment and set the trap as instructed. Then we all set off for the engine room.

Leaving Nuan, and the dead assistant, behind.

When we arrived, the breathtaking sight of the engine's glowing core distracted the soldiers.

"Where are the controls, boy?" the minister demanded.

I pointed, silently, to the control station.

"We have the Americans now," the minister boasted. "You, boy, show us how to shut this down."

My guard jabbed me with his gun's barrel again.

I stepped up to the console, but I hadn't rotated to the engine room yet. I had no idea how to do anything.

"Breathe," my new memories whispered. "You only need to create a diversion."

I scanned the control panel, I was just here. Gerlinde was checking the power conduits and exhaust vents. Where were her hands? Then I saw it, an icon of two tubes with wavy lines coming from them. It must be the vents.

I tapped the icon, and the viewscreen beside it read: Plasma ventilation not advised, life signs detected near plasma vents.

Then the screen showed me two openings on the sides of the engine core. The Chinese soldiers, still examining the core, were right in the way.

"Stop wasting time and show me how to turn off the systems," my guard said.

"First you have to vent the plasma, so it doesn't overload when you turn it off," I lied, pointing at the icon. "If you don't the core fills up like a balloon and can explode."

I stepped to my side, trying to block the viewscreen with my body.

"Fine," the guard said.

Then he tapped the vent icon again.

"Nothing happened," he said. "Don't mess with me."

"You have to hit it twice," I said.

The guard tapped the icon again.

The vents on the core opened like eyelids. Plasma erupted from them like fingers of lightning, snaking toward the metal floor. The soldiers around the core covered their eyes and dropped to the ground. Then the plasma cooled, reforming as a gas cloud.

I couldn't see a thing. I coughed and then held my breath, just trying to feel my way out of control room.

I could hear the Chinese soldiers coughing too.

Then the vents closed, on some kind of automatic timer, and the cloud began to dissipate.

As I ran for the door, I heard the minister yell.

"Kill him, you idiots!"

I could feel someone on my tail as I ran for the stairwell. It had to be my guard.

I darted through up the stairs, and heard a pair of gunshots behind me ricochet off the metal steps. Then a third shot flung sparks

"His magazine is empty," my new memories whispered. "Run."

The soldier was faster. He caught up with me halfway up the stairs, dove, and swiped my legs out from under me. As I fell he leapt at me, his hands going straight for my neck.

"He is powerful, but you are fast," the memories told me. "Split his hands."

I interlocked my hands and speared between his, as if I was doing a breaststroke. Then I pulled my arms apart in a swift motion, knocking his hands away.

"Now go for the jaw," it was Captain Amis this time.

I swung my right fist and hit the guard right where his jawbone connected to his skull. It really hurt. My knuckles felt like I had punched tarmac.

The guard reeled and reached for his jaw.

"Now uppercut," the new memories said. "Left hand."

My left fist struck the soft spot under his chin. He lurched back, stumbled on the edge of a step and fell back.

The soldier crashed to the bottom of the stairwell. I saw his shadow rise, pressing off the railing. Then he was after me again.

I gathered myself and sprinted up the stairs, but he caught up, and grabbed me by the back of the shirt.

I tried to wrestle free, but he pulled me back and clutched the back of my neck, his fingers pressing on my throat.

"You have no choice now," my new memories whispered.

Choking I reached into my pocket for the syringe.

For a moment, I hesitated.

"Now," Captain Amis whispered. "Now, or never."

I took a deep breath, spun around with all my strength, and jabbed the needle into the man's neck.

He gasped, and lunged for me, but that only dragged the needle under his skin, making a tiny wound into a gash.

Blood spurted from the guard's neck. He grabbed his neck and fell back down the steps.

He didn't get up.

I collapsed back onto the steps. I stared at the trail of blood leading down. I half hoped that I would see his shadow suddenly rise up again. I had killed him. I was no better than the colonel or the minister, was I?

"You did what had to be done," Captain Amis whispered.

"He would have killed you," the new memories added. "And then your friends, too."

I felt a little relieved. Maybe One felt like this too. But it didn't last. My stomach started to turn. I swallowed hard, trying to keep the contents of my stomach down. I picked myself up and headed for my friends.

There wasn't time to waste.

28

THE RETURN

I ran up. I didn't notice how far. My eyes filled with tears. My stomach churned. Images of the soldier's neck, the syringe, the gushes of blood.

I stumbled on a step. Sweat poured from my brow. I stopped, bent over and vomited. I could barely move my feet out of the way.

I had killed someone.

Just a few weeks ago, I was bickering with Jack over who got the last ration cookie.

Now, I was a murderer.

"You had no choice," my memories said.

I suppose it wasn't really me, but the new military tactics I had injected.

Plus, I really didn't have a choice, did I? That's how a soldier thinks. There is an enemy. They are a threat. You kill them. Or better you *neutralize the threat*. Simple. Direct. Justified.

I looked down and saw that I was still clutching the syringe, my knuckles white. I threw it at the wall and it shattered into pieces. The last few nanites inside, no more than a glistening puddle, the things that had made me a murderer, splashed on the wall and gathered together seeking the brain they were programmed to assist, until they gave up and dribbled to the floor.

I buried my face in my hands and tried to wipe my tears away.

"It wasn't your fault," I said to myself. "You had to do it."

I swallowed, and the taste of sick made me wince. I spat. The taste wouldn't leave my mouth. There was something metallic and rancid about it, a taste like death.

"You had to do it," I repeated.

I clung to those words, making them a mantra. Someday it would become truth.

"Focus," Captain Amis whispered.

"They're still out there," the new memories added.

I breathed deep. The colonel and his men would still be in the control centre, believing that they had the Chinese contained below.

I could move to the residence level, then take the stairwell leading up to the floor above that. One never had a chance to show us. The colonel would be too busy trying to find the Chinese soldiers to bother with me.

When I reached the floor above the residences, I went through the first door I saw. Inside was an army of robots. They were lined up, like terracotta warriors, across the entire open level, at least a football pitch long.

They all stood motionless, waiting for someone to activate them.

The robots came in almost every shape. There were new models, shiny and freshly painted lined up with older ones, showing their wear and tear.

What was clear was that humans had set up this room. Our technologies were cobbled together with those of the Ark. Each robot's little space was marked in duct tape, a quick job. They were never properly stencilled and painted. They were in a hurry, especially near the end.

A few of the pads were empty, their robots either elsewhere or forgotten.

Suddenly, a robot activated. It was almost humanoid. I recognised the model from my school. It was old, its white surface had yellowed. The robot stepped forward with a jerky, long stride.

"Hello," I said to it.

It ignored me and kept moving.

I didn't know what its function was. I just watched it walk to an empty square on the floor and stop.

The robot stiffened, and then the square upon which it was standing clunked and started moving downward like a lift.

The robot descended below the floor. I ran over and watched it go. Once the lift stopped, about twenty metres down, the robot stepped off the platform and the lift came back again.

Then I understood why we hadn't seen a robot yet. They moved on lifts, not through the stairs we used. They could descend, do their work, and then ascend back without ever crossing our paths.

"Use the lift and you'll surprise him," my new memories told me.

I liked the idea, but I didn't know how to navigate the passages the robots used. What good would I do if I got lost? What good was any of it if the colonel and his men killed me immediately?

"A little knowledge goes a long way," Captain Amis whispered.

He was right. There were more of One's memories in the lab. If I got to them then I might learn enough to do help the Arkonauts.

I searched the hall for a medical robot. I had no real idea what they looked like. I paced the lines of robots, looking for any indication. Then I remembered the robots on the military base in the Lake District. They had lots of arms, and were always clean. They always looked brand new. I ran up and down the ranks of metal automatons, and then I spotted them: a large group, all clean and shiny and new, with lots of arms covered in various medical tools. Each one had a control panel and small screen on its front that currently read: Please enter procedure.

I found an empty lift square, but I had to get the robot working.

The robots had no switches. I tapped at the screen, but it didn't respond.

I pushed it toward the lift, hoping that it might start up if it was in motion, but nothing happened.

I went back to the screen and tapped at it furiously. Nothing changed. It just offered the same message: Please enter procedure.

It needed a reason to wake up. I felt stupid at how obvious it was.

"Robot," I said. "Perform brain surgery."

It was the first thing that popped into my head.

The robot came to life.

"Perform brain surgery," it repeated. "Provide bed number."

"Bed... uh... fifteen," I said.

The robot straightened and moved onto the lift. After a beat, the lift clanked and began to lower.

I jumped on, holding tight onto the robot, as we both descended on the lift into the medical bay.

When we stopped the robot moved over to Bed 15, and began performing brain surgery on the air above the empty bed.

That's when I saw One's body again. He was still on the bed where we left him.

I bowed my head in reverence and then ran to the lab station. As I opened the drawer containing the rest of One's memory injections, I heard a gasp.

One was breathing.

THE SCAR

Before the end of the world I often wondered how my fellow chosen survivors lived their lives.

Were they treasuring the time spent with their family? Trying to behave normally? Or like me, were they looking for ways to escape the pressure?

I imagined their varied lives, experiencing the slow destruction of the Earth from multiple different geographies, and different perspectives. I also hoped their experiences didn't match mine because, for all the good times in those final days, mine was the kind that literally scarred me for life.

A couple of months before the end I was walking home from a friend James's house. I had bailed on him after only visiting for an hour because I couldn't help looking at him and knowing that he would soon be gone. How would I have, anyway? There's no good way to tell a friend that they have weeks to live.

James was my best friend, but I never told him that I was going to be saved. I couldn't. So, a knot grew in my stomach from holding such a powerful secret. It pained me so much that I couldn't stand to be around him. And James was a great guy, so funny, such a risk taker. He pushed me to try things I was afraid to try. He was exactly the person who could have convinced me that being saved, though scary, would be an epic adventure. That just made it all more painful.

It was intolerable.

I spent the trip home convincing myself that I had done the right thing both by not telling James, but also in lying to leave early.

My head was down. I ignored the Ark floating in the sky above me, already launched under the guise of using it to stop the Destroyer. I couldn't look at it. The Ark was just another reminder of the future I was heading for, and the past I'd be losing. Then I saw it, another plumbing van parked outside our house.

I wondered if it was another messenger sent by Dr. Ghost.

Before I could react, the side door slid open, and three guys dressed in black leapt out. When one of them grabbed my arm, I cried out. If they were Ghost's men, they weren't supposed to treat me this way. I was angry.

Quickly, a second man grabbed my other arm. I yelled and kicked, but they lifted me toward the van. Then the third guy grabbed my legs. Immobilized, they fed me into the side door of the van.

I panicked. Why would Dr. Ghost's people do this? But I knew that they wouldn't do this. These weren't Dr. Ghost's people.

The new memories in my head offered me advice: "Now is not the time to fight, but the time to survive to fight another day."

I sat still from then on, not fighting back, and it did get easier.

"Hold still," one of my captors said.

Another of them strapped a device to my arm, right over where Dr. Ghost had inserted my teleportation transmitter. I couldn't figure out what the device was, but it looked almost like armour.

We drove for an hour. I had no idea where we were going. The van had no side or rear windows. Near the end of the journey we drove on what sounded like gravel for ten minutes. At some point the van screeched to a halt and from the driver's compartment I heard a woman say, "Bloody Deer."

We drove on for a bit after that. When the van stopped again, I heard the driver's door creak open. Then there were two bangs on the sliding side door, then it opened, then the men holding me captive pulled me outside.

The sky was dark, and I was standing on the well-lit grounds of a magnificent Victorian country house. It could have been a National Trust site, everything kept up beautifully, if not for the rows of dead hedges. But then, water was at a premium now.

Then men led inside the house, saying nothing to me, or to each other. In the foyer, a women dressed in expensive clothes smiled and greeted me.

"Excellent," she said. "You've arrived at last."

Her eyes fell straight to my arm, and the strap they had put on me. Her look was a hungry one.

"Sebastian," she almost sang. "The boy is here."

An overweight boy came bounding down the stairs. I hadn't seen a well-fed kid in a while, what with the rationing. The boy looked at me with the same hungry eyes, always falling to the strap on my arm.

Then he looked me up and down as if I were a contestant in a dog show, and sneered when he finally looked me in the eyes. "This is who they are sending, mummy," he said, calling back to the woman.

"I know, dear," his mother replied. "Try not to worry about that. It's your time now."

I felt like running. My heart raced.

"Just be calm," Captain Amis whispered to me.

"Julian," the woman yelled. "We have a very special guest."

Next down the stairs came a man dressed in finery with a walking cane. He carried himself as the house might've suggested, as Lord of the manor. He scrutinized me with tiny eyes. Then he turned back to the woman.

"Excellent," he said. "Let us begin immediately."

They took me to another room in the house. This room had a bed in its centre that was flanked by machines and trays of surgical implements.

"What is this?" I asked sheepishly, my heart still racing.

The adults remained silent.

But the boy couldn't contain himself.

"I'm taking your place," he said. "You're going to be the one left behind."

The boy giggled madly.

"I don't know what you're talking about," I said. "Left behind where?"

"Why are they sending this idiot, mummy?" the boy asked.

His mother just shook her head at me.

"I think he's playing dumb on purpose, son," Julian, the father, added.

The boy scowled at me. "You think you're smart, huh?"

Then he prodded me in the chest with his index finger.

"That's enough, Sebastian," Julian said. "You'll win out in the end."

"Yeah," the boy said to me, prodding again to punctuate the words. "I'll win out."

The father stepped forward and whacked me in the stomach with his cane. I folded over, gasping for breath.

"Our Sebastian should have been chosen to go on the Ark," Julian said. "Not you. You're nobody. And like any noble family has always done, we are going to stand for what is right, rectify Dr. Ghost's error."

My eyes widened, and I saw a smile grow on the man's lips.

"How did you—"

I never heard an answer. They dragged me over the bed and strapped me onto it. Then they brought out a steel table, extended my arm, and strapped it down separately.

The father tapped at my arm until he found the puncture mark where they installed the transmitter.

"Here we are," he said.

I squirmed, but I couldn't move.

"You can't," I yelled.

The father scowled at me. "Do you know who I am, boy?"

I averted my eyes and kept fighting against the straps.

Julian responded by tightening the straps.

The bands cut into my flesh, and my hand started to throb.

"Of course you don't," he continued. "That's because I live above you. My companies provided infrastructure, jobs, and shareholder returns to this country, and yet my only son would be left on the Earth to die. I will not allow that.

"You see, I have influence, but just not enough," he said. "Even bribes have lost their prestige at the high levels now. But that doesn't mean a low level lackey is above accepting a month's worth of supplies, so as to live out his last days in Babylon.

"When I discovered who Dr. Ghost had chosen, I was... deeply disappointed. Look at you, boy. You're nothing but middle class field stock," he said. "No, that won't do. The future of humanity deserves my Sebastian, and the legacy he brings."

"They'll know it's not me," I said.

"Of course they will," he said. "But by the time they do the Earth, and you will be gone. Now, doctor, if you would."

A man in a surgical gown revealed himself and strode toward me. The doctor tapped at my arm and then prepared a syringe.

"No pain medication," Julian interrupted. "This one will do fine to remember today. There's always someone better than you, boy. That's the lesson."

The doctor nodded, set down the syringe and picked up a scalpel. The blade sunk into my arm, blood oozing around it.

I wanted to scream.

Then I heard gunshots, and shattering glass.

"What's all this?" the father asked.

Another man, bloodied and coughing, entered.

"Sir, there are soldiers."

"Then get out there and kill them," the father screamed. "What do I pay you for?"

More gunshots rang out. There were men dressed in all black running past the doorway.

The father shoved the doctor aside and then undid my straps.

"Unless you want to die here, you will do as you're told," he said.

He yanked me from the bed, and then nudged me toward the door with his cane.

"Darlings, we're leaving," he said to his wife and son in the doorway

"When do I get my transmitter?" his son wailed.

The father ignored his son, leading us out to the foyer.

There were British soldiers, guns at the ready, waiting for us.

"Daddy," the son cried. "What's happening?"

The father grabbed me by the neck and pulled me back into the surgery room. His wife and son followed.

And so did a platoon of soldiers.

The father grabbed the scalpel from the surgical table and held it to my face.

"Drop the knife," one of the soldiers ordered.

"Drop your guns or this boy dies," the father spat.

The scalpel blade nicked my skin.

"He doesn't even deserve to go. My boy does," the father yelled. "Don't you understand that?"

The soldiers remained steady in their aim. Their fingers twitched on their triggers.

"Release him or we will shoot you," the soldier said.

"He's scared and unfocused," Captain Amis whispered to me. "You can get away."

Without another thought I grabbed the father's wrist. On reflex he flinched. The knife sliced across my eye socket and my forehead, just nicking my eyelids.

I threw an elbow into his stomach, and he released his grip.

Grabbing at the cut on my face, I crawled away as quickly as I could.

The soldiers saw their opening and fired their guns.

The man fell.

His wife and son screamed.

The soldiers moved into the room, half swarmed around me, the other half restrained the doctor, mother and son.

The soldiers moved me out of the house and performed first aid so quickly that I lost track of time.

They told me it was shock.

The last thing I remembered was seeing the mother and her son, Sebastian, being loaded into a military police van.

The end of the world had done horrible things to people.

29

BRAIN DEAD

I had never been so scared. I jumped when I heard One exhale.

Once I caught my own breath, I ran to his body.

I was amazed at his ability to heal. The wounds in his head and body were nearly gone. Only tiny scars remained.

"One?" I said.

He didn't reply.

I held my hand over his mouth, and felt his warm breath on my palm. He was definitely breathing. Somehow he was alive.

"One!" I yelled.

Still, he gave no reply.

"Hey," I called to the medical robot. It had already determined that no one was in bed fifteen and was moving back to the lift.

I ran in front of it and it stopped. "Medical scan, bed five," I said.

The robot accepted its new input and turned back toward One's bed. Then the medical robot scanned him, using the many tools on its arms.

It didn't take long, but it felt like a long time. I was not only worried about One, but that the colonel or the minister could storm in at any moment.

"Subject medically fit for duty," the robot said. "Scanning abnormality: subject is brain dead. No applicable treatments on record."

Content with its report, the robot returned to the lift.

I stood there dumbfounded. For a second, I hoped that One would just get up, and solve all of our problems.

Then One's last words echoed in my mind.

"My memories," he had said.

"They are *his* memories," my new memories whispered. "Aren't they?"

"Perhaps he'd like them back," Captain Amis added.

That's when I realized that I had misunderstood One's last words. I ran over the lab table and opened the drawer of nanite vials.

Each one offered a specific set of skills, except for the last bottle in the back. It was labelled: Personal. They must be One's own memories, a copy of his mind. That's what he meant. He needed this vial. I dug out another syringe and filled it with the Personal vial.

After I injected him, One stirred. I didn't know what was working, but something definitely was. I ran back to the drawer and grabbed the rest of the vials. I injected One with each, until the drawer was empty.

Then I waited for the nanites to get to work. I had no idea how long it would take, and I wondered if One would be the same person when he woke up; if he woke up.

I watched over him until my legs got tired. Then as I turned to put the syringe back on the lab table, a hand grabbed me by the collar.

With incredible strength, the hand yanked me down, my ear right next to One's mouth.

"My memories," he said. "Re-inject them."

He was finishing his last words.

"I just did," I answered.

"Yes, Callum," One said. "You did. Now, we have work to do."

30

THE PLAN

"It has been one point five hours since I was shot," One said, sitting up.

"Do you have a clock inside your head?" I asked.

"Something like that," he said. "Where are the other Arkonauts?"

"We thought you were dead, and the American soldiers took some of us hostage," I said. "They used me and Nuan to take a bomb to the Chinese... I escaped and came here to inject myself with your memories."

"Nuan is still captive?"

I shook my head and lowered my eyes. "They killed her."

One closed his eyes and sighed. His fists clenched and he shook. For a moment I thought he might go crazy and start smashing things, the way people did when they heard bad news.

He then calmed himself and breathed deeply.

"I am sorry," One said. "We will avenge her."

He stood up from the medical table and straightened his shirt.

"You came for my memories?" he asked.

"I thought you were trying to tell me to take them," I said. "So I could save the others."

"How many did you take?" One asked.

"Just one," I said. "The military training bottle."

"Though it was not my intention that was smart thinking," One said. "Your bravery is admirable."

Despite One's usual lack of emotional warmth, I swelled with pride at his compliment.

"How did you survive?" I asked.

"The nanites in my body are more advanced than those received by the Arkonauts," One said. "When I sustain physical harm, they can repair the damage, but when the damage is severe, the repairs spend their function energy, and they cannot return to my brain to resume their original programming. This is why there were replacement memories in the drawer."

"Like an extra life in a video game," I said.

"That is a reductive assessment, but it is accurate," One said. "Unfortunately, there was only one set of back up memories brought to the Ark, so I cannot be revived a second time."

I felt a rush of fear that we would lose One again, but it was overwhelmed with my joy that he was alive.

"I'm just glad that you're okay," I said.

"Thank you," One said. "Now, we must rescue the others and regain control of the Ark. What can you tell me about the intruders?"

"The Americans were last in control of the residential level. There aren't many of them, but are well-armed. The Chinese group is larger, and they were last in the engine room," I reported.

"Who leads each side?" One asked.

"An American colonel and the Chinese Minister of Defence."

"Where are the others who were with you: Gerlinde, Illarion, Koyla, and Maiara?" One asked.

"As far as I know the Americans have them."

"I have a plan," he said.

I didn't understand One's plan, but I was happy to follow his lead.

The first step was to access the computer system. We made our way to the pumping station console, and One used it to hack into the intercom and viewscreens. They would now sound and project him all over the Ark.

"Chinese and American forces, my name is One," he broadcasted. "You have illegally boarded this vessel, committed murder, and endangered the ship's crew. To protect them, I am now venting atmosphere from every compartment on the ship outside the cargo bay. In ten minutes this ship will no longer support life.

"If you wish to live, you may surrender to me in the observation room. You have my personal guarantee that you will be allowed to retreat to your ships and leave the Ark, never to return."

One tapped at the console, locking the message on a temporary loop with a passcode.

"Now, the Americans and Chinese will rush to the air pumping station, hoping to reactivate the life support manually," One explained.

"How do you know?" I asked.

"Trust me," One said. "You and I will not bother with the air, but we will use the diversion to take back the control centre."

One and I ran to the control room, but we didn't find it empty. Inside, three soldiers were talking.

"Stay here," One said. He wandered into the room.

"What is going on?" he cried. "Where is everyone?"

The soldiers aimed their guns at him, and One started to cry.

"What is going on? What is going on?" he wailed through his tears. It was a masterful performance.

"Wait didn't we shoot you?" one of the soldiers said.

I swore to myself, just our luck the troops guarding the control centre had been the ones to shoot One.

The trio of men moved in to investigate.

One struck like lightning. He grabbed two of the men's guns by the barrels, swung them around, and when the soldier's reacted and fired their shots hit each other. The two men dropped to the floor, wounded in their shoulders and bleeding.

One then flipped the weapons around and swung them at the remaining soldier, knocking him under the chin.

The third soldier collapsed to the floor.

Quickly, One knelt beside each man. He looked over their backpacks, like the one that the colonel wore, and ripped the wiring out of each of them. The straps running from the pack and down each man's limbs went slack.

"What are those packs?" I asked.

"They provide mobility assistance," One said. "Allowing soldiers who have spent long periods of time in sub-Earth gravity to maintain muscular strength."

"Or to make a weak person stronger," I said, thinking of the colonel.

"Precisely."

One went for the control centre console. He tapped into the Ark's camera system and projected what it saw in the centre of the room. First, we saw the colonel and a squad of soldiers marching through the corridors of the ship with the captured Arkonauts.

"Excellent," One said. "The colonel is in transit to the pumping station as expected. I will now set a timer to shut off the lights around them in five minutes. I will use the distraction the darkness creates to stop the soldiers. You will get the Arkonauts to safety."

"Can you take on that many soldiers?" I asked.

"I will have reinforcements," One replied.

When we neared the pumping station we heard the colonel and his soldiers speaking in raised voices.

"Sir," a soldier said. "There has been no change in the ship's life support."

"We've been tricked," the colonel growled. "Quickly, we must get to the control centre."

Then the overhead lights went out, leaving only the dim glow of the emergency corridor markers. It was like a moonlit night.

"Go to night vision," the colonel barked.

"Sir," a soldier protested. "The light level is still too high. Night vision is useless."

"Control centre," the colonel called into his radio. "What the hell are you doing with the lights?"

There was no reply but static.

"Eyes open," the colonel ordered. "Let's get to the control centre."

That's when One's reinforcements arrived. Robots started to pour out of the pumping station in droves, walking through the group of American soldiers.

"Hold your fire, men," the colonel ordered. "Not worth the ammunition."

One and I weaved among the robots, using them for cover. When we were in range, One fired the gun he had taken from the control room, hitting each target with incredible accuracy.

Several of the soldiers dropped like flies.

The captive Arkonauts screamed.

In the ensuing chaos, I slipped into the pumping station and climbed the gangways to get behind the group.

"Take cover," the colonel ordered.

I snaked around the pumping station and popped out next to my captured friends.

A single soldier was guarding them, backing them away from the fight. The guard never saw me.

I crept up and tapped Illarion in the shoulder.

He whipped around, and to his credit he stayed silent.

"The backpack," I whispered. "Pull the plug."

Illarion nodded, and stood. He ripped at the wires on the guard's pack. Sparks flew and the network of straps went slack, just like before.

Without the device's help, the guard collapsed to the floor, his legs too weak to hold him up.

Illarion punched him after that.

Koyla, Gerlinde and Maiara all popped up and looked at me. "This way," I said.

We shimmied back across the gangway to the lifts used by the robots.

"I didn't know you knew magic tricks, Callum," Koyla said. "How're you in two places at once?"

I smiled. "It's One."

"But he's dead," Gerlinde said.

"It's a long story, but you can't keep him down," I replied.

We climbed onto the lift and rode it up to the robot storage level.

"There are so many soldiers," Illarion said.

"Don't worry. One will be fine," I said. "We'll meet him back in the medical bay."

Illarion, Gerlinde, Koyla and Maiara looked at the robot storage bay in awe.

"Look at all of them," Maiara said.

"We can check this place out later," I said. "Follow me, I know a shortcut."

We went over the medical robots and took their lift down to the medical bay.

"Okay, so now we get to hide here, right?" Koyla said.

"Nope," I said. "We're going to let the American and Chinese soldiers fight each other. All we have to do is deal with anyone who gets through."

"Great. Where do we find them?" Illarion said.

"We're aren't going to them. They're going to come to us." I said.

The lift lowered us into the medical bay, and One was already there, waiting for us.

"You *are* alive," Koyla exclaimed. "Got some cat DNA in you, huh, One?"

"Thank you for your concern Koyla," One said, reloading his gun. "But I am not at all related to felines or the adage about their having multiple lives."

"How's the plan going?" I asked.

"Well," One said. "Both sides are engaging each other as we speak. I will determine their exact statuses now. Wait here."

One disappeared.

I went to the nearest computer and accessed the ship's camera system. Right outside the air pumping station there was a fire fight going on, like One said. The Chinese group had taken the bait just like the Americans, some were driving around on their electric bikes keeping up with the American forces. I checked the corridors around the medical bay. No one was coming toward us. No one was going for the control centre either.

The only person I couldn't find was the minister.

Then I checked the engine room. The minister, one soldier, and the coffin-like container were there. The minister had opened a small hatch on the large container revealing a control panel. He tapped on the panel and then what looked like a clock appeared.

It was counting down.

"I'm guessing that isn't counting down to them leaving," Koyla said.

I shook my head.

"It's a bomb," I said. "We have to tell One."

I ran out into the corridor, looking around wildly. Gunshots rang out just down the hallway. I stopped in my tracks.

"Callum, wait," Gerlinde called. "We're coming with you."

The others were right behind her.

"We can't go out into the fire fight," I said. "One's probably deep in it and we'll only distract him. We need to deal with that bomb ourselves."

The other Arkonauts nodded.

I was immediately inspired by their courage.

"Friends are a powerful force," Captain Amis whispered in my mind.

We ran for the stairs, and down to the level below. We reached the core, and snuck along the gangplanks above the engine room floor.

Below, the Minister stood at the engine controls. He tapped at the screens madly, but he didn't seem to understand how to operate the controls.

"I say we surround them," Gerlinde said. "These walkways give us the high ground, and as long as one of us makes it to the bomb we can turn it off."

"One of us makes it?" Koyla asked. "Those two have guns. I don't want to end up as Swiss cheese."

"Just a minute," I said.

I ran back toward the stairwell to where I had fought with the soldier. His firearm was still lying hanging near the end of the steps. It was empty, but it would do. Then I rejoined the others.

"We're going to have to bluff," I said. "I'll go in front and convince the minister that this thing is loaded. The rest of you, sneak in and diffuse the bomb."

The core rumbled loud enough to drown out our movements. The minister didn't look up once. He was too busy fiddling with the computer.

Finally, the minister broke into the Ark's intercom system.

"Americans, Ark crew, I have primed a nuclear device," he said. "The countdown is set to thirty minutes, and unless I am given complete control of this ship, we will all die.

"If the People's Republic cannot have this ship, no one will. I will expect your surrender in the next twenty five minutes."

Then the intercom went silent.

I inched forward, trying not to make any noise. My heart raced.

When I was right before them, I stepped out from the shadows.

"Don't move, minister," I said. "You have a gun aimed at your head."

Both the minister and his lone soldier turned to look.

"I said, 'Don't move.'"

I came up behind the soldier and pressed the barrel of the gun to the back of his head.

"Drop it."

The soldier obeyed.

"Kick it over to me."

The soldier did.

I reached down and picked up the other weapon. I aimed it at the minister.

"Good," I said. "Both of you, put your hands on our heads."

"You can't kill me," the minister laughed. "I'm the only one who knows how to disable the bomb."

I raised the gun towards his head. "Turn around," I said.

"You?" he said when he saw me.

I nodded. "I'll shoot you if you don't disarm that bomb," I said.

The minister laughed again. "Not a very good threat, boy," he said. "If you kill me you all die."

I hadn't thought of that.

"Besides, Callum, I don't think you'll fire that gun," the minister said. "I know all about you. I know why you were chosen. I know your life. You aren't ruthless enough to pull the trigger."

He was right. I didn't want to kill anyone else.

In a blink, the minister drew his own pistol and trained it on me.

"Watch out," Illarion yelled, from behind the core.

The minister and the soldier turned to see who was there.

I threw the empty gun at the minister's head. The butt of the weapon cracked him on the back of the skull, opening a gash behind his ear. Out of reflex, he fired his pistol, hitting the soldier beside him.

Illarion ran at the minister, and tackled him. I followed suit.

The minister squealed as Illarion pinned his arms down, forcing the pistol from his fingers.

Illarion grabbed the minister's arms and yanked them behind his back in a painful hold.

The minister screamed in pain.

The others came out, too, checking on the shot soldier, and then us and the bomb.

The soldier was dead.

I stood up, shaking with fear and adrenaline.

"Stand him up," I said.

Illarion hauled the minster to his feet, and the others circled him, ensuring he had nowhere to go.

"Disarm the bomb, boy," I ordered.

"You still have nothing to bargain with," he snarled. "I am happy to die for the People's Republic."

I jabbed his chest with my index finger.

"If you disarm the bomb, we will let you live," I said. "You'll be a prisoner, but at least you'll get to see the new world. The only representative of the People's Republic there."

The minster chuckled. He jerked suddenly, breaking Illarion's grip. A small knife slipped out of his sleeve into his hand. He grabbed me and set the knife against my neck.

I was his hostage.

"Now, children, back off," he said.

Koyla, Illarion, Gerlinde and Maiara stepped back, their hands raised.

"You said you read my file?" I asked.

"I did," he said, "I know everything about you."

"Did it tell you I've been in this exact situation once before? And I know how to win out in the end"

I drove my arms upwards. The minister's knife cut me across my scar as his arms flew back.

Illarion lunged, tackling the minister, with a powerful head butt to the stomach. The minister stumbled back, bumping into the railing over the lower engine core.

"I will not be beaten by children," the minister spat.

He pushed back against Illarion, sending the Russian boy to the floor.

But the momentum threw the minister into the railing, a railing added to the engine room and badly welded it seemed as it snapped and the minister tumbled over the edge.

He screamed, grasping empty air as he lost balance falling into the core. His cries for help were soon drowned out by the growl of the Ark's engines. He was nothing but fuel now.

I shot Illarion a congratulatory look and took a heavy breath.

"That was cool," Koyla said. "But, who's going to disarm the bomb?"

31

MY SALVATION

We gathered around the bomb. Only twenty minutes remained to detonation. We watched our time tick away for a moment. Each lost second was terrifying.

"One will know what to do," I said. "We have to find him."

"You think bomb disarmament is in his repertoire?" Koyla said.

"Why not?" I said. "Everything else is."

"He's probably still fighting the other soldiers out there," Gerlinde said. "We'll never survive getting to him."

"The intercom," Illarion said.

"That won't work," Gerlinde said. "If he comes here, so will they."

Illarion nodded.

"Why don't we just chuck it out the nearest airlock?" Maiara asked.

We all looked at her.

***

It took every bit of our collected strength, but we pushed the bomb to an airlock outside the engine core with just under ten minutes to spare.

"This thing is heavy," Illarion complained.

"And you're the big kid," Koyla said.

One of the Chinese ships was parked outside the airlock, complicating our plan.

"Where's the next nearest airlock?" I asked.

"We'll never make it," Gerlinde replied. "It's back by the medical bay."

I shook my head. The timer counted down. We had less than nine minutes.

"Let's just dump this thing on the ship," Maiara said. "Then we unlock the ship from the hull and it will float away."

I nodded and activated the air lock controls. The Ark's door opened, but on the other side, the Chinese shuttle's door was locked. Beside the door, a keypad with Chinese characters, beckoned us to enter a code.

"Any ideas?" I asked.

"We all speak Chinese, don't we?" Koyla said. "Get to it, Callum."

"I speak it, but I can't read it," I said.

"Seven minutes to detonation," Illarion said.

"Get help," Captain Amis whispered.

I turned away from the airlock and ran down the corridor.

"Where are you going?" Gerlinde yelled.

"To get One," I shouted back. "We need help."

I listened for gunshots, for any signal of where One could be, but the Ark was strangely silent. Sprinting, I only barely saw One, pouring over the security camera screens in the control centre.

"There is a bomb!" he said, and for the first time I heard terror and dismay in his voice.

Panting, I replied, "We're trying to get it onto one of the Chinese ships to jettison it. There isn't much time. Maybe five minutes."

"Come with me," he said.

We ran out of the control centre, away from the bomb. I didn't know where we were going, but One hadn't led us wrong yet.

We stopped at an unmarked door. One pressed his palm to it and it opened on a room about the size of my residence. In the centre of the room stood a single Cryo-Chamber.

"This is where I was kept before my activation," One said.

"I don't understand," I said.

One grabbed my arms, and the Cryo-Chamber opened.

"What are you doing?"

One didn't answer. He threw me into the chamber, and closed the door behind me.

I banged on the door. I shouted. I screamed.

One just stared at me.

"I cannot stop the bomb, Callum," he said. "I do not know how to disarm it."

"But you know how to do everything," I yelled.

"No, I do not," he replied, head bowed.

"But the Ark will be destroyed," I cried.

"Yes," he said.

"Then why am I in here?" I asked. "Let me die with the other Arkonauts."

"No," One said. "A human must survive. If one survives then we all survive. It is up to you now."

His words made no sense to me.

"Stop the bomb!" I yelled. "One!"

One shook his head.

"I have failed you, Callum," One said, "I have failed everyone."

He then stepped back. He wouldn't look me in the eyes.

I banged on the inside of the Cryo-Chamber, but it didn't matter. I watched One exit through the unmarked door. Then I was alone, inside the chamber, inside the room in an eerie silence.

Suddenly, the pod lit up. Restraints extended around my arms and legs, locking me into place. I struggled. I wasn't strong enough. The straps pinned me down.

I could only think of the others. We fought so hard. Gerlinde, Illarion, Koyla, Maiara... Nuan... Mathieu. Now it was just going to end, just like that.

We were out of time.

I finished the countdown in my head.

Four...

Three...

Two...

One...

The room shook. The Cryo-Chamber vibrated and the restraints tightened to hold me in place. I felt the shock of the explosion in my chest. The explosion would have been deafening on the outside.

The walls of the room glowed red hot but they did not fall. My Cryo-Chamber stood where it was. The bomb had gone off and I had survived. The room must be drifting among the debris of the Ark, alone and lost in open space.

Everyone else was dead, vaporised in the explosion, sucked out of hull breaches, or worse.

I cried. I screamed and I cried. No one could hear me. No one ever would hear me again. I was alone. The last human.

Why had One done this to me?

Then I heard a hiss coming from the Cryo-Chamber. The glass fogged up. It was some kind of gas. It was filling the chamber.

The gas made me sleepy. I tried to stay awake, but I couldn't. My eyes got so heavy. I felt so comfortable. My body felt weak. I tried to stay awake, but—

THE FUTURE

I dreamed.

I dreamed every dream I had ever dreamt before.

I was aware of this, conscious of this.

I could control the dreams, they entertained me, but I could not wake up.

I was here and everywhere. I wanted nothing more than to wake up and nothing more than to sleep forever.

Time no longer existed.

There was no more when.

There was only...

My eyes opened.

The Cryo-Chamber was no longer in the room where One had left me. Now, I was inside a smaller room with a large window occupying one entire wall.

I moved my arms and legs, only trying to stretch, but the restraints snapped like twigs.

That was weird.

I pushed open the door on the Cryo-Chamber. The locks resisted me only briefly, and then broke open with similar ease as the restraints.

That was definitely weird.

Was it smart to leave the chamber at all?

I didn't know where I was?

What had happened after the explosion on the Ark?

I was alone in my cell. No one stood at the window.

Across a corridor, I saw an identical room with the same dimension. It was dark, quiet, and maybe empty. Only the light from my room seeped into it, offering me no information beyond the vague impression of another humanoid drenched in shadow.

It didn't really matter. I could only think about the Ark, the Arkonauts, and all that was gone. I was the only human left. No one would help me now. There was no one.

Not my family.

Not my friends.

Not my mission.

I threw up in the corner of my cell. I coughed and spit. I had thrown up recently. Hadn't I? During the battle? When was that? Was it hours ago? Day? Years? Millennia?

Was this pile of sick the last remnant of Earth food?

I should have died with the rest of them. Wherever I was not, whatever alien world or lab or secret prison... I shouldn't have been here.

I looked around my room for anything I could use to end it. A piece of metal, rope, something... Even the restraints in the Cryo-Chamber weren't long enough. But I wanted to be with them, with Gerlinde and Maiara and One and all of them.

"You mustn't give up," all the memory implants whispered. "You're the last of your kind, a precious thing."

"Shut up," I screamed. "I'm not an artefact. I'm a fifteen year old boy!"

I closed my eyes, and the memories seemed to disappear into the shadows of my mind. And I felt stupid for feeling lonely once again.

I paced my room, trying to escape my thoughts.

Maybe I could restart the human race. Maybe I'd use advanced alien science to take my DNA and start again. I had no idea how to make it happen. Who would help me? Where would I even begin?

One should have survived. Not me. Dr. Ghost made him perfect. Who better than to carry on the human race? If One were here, he wouldn't be pacing around like a child. He would be making a plan. He would know what to do, and where he was. Maybe he would even avenge us and make things right.

I pressed my face against the window, hoping to see down either direction of the corridor. The corridor was long and dotted with more glass cells. They varied in size and shape, but seemed to go on forever.

Was this a museum, or some kind of zoo?

There wasn't a door in my room, not even seams in the wall that might permit my keepers to enter and exit.

There was only my Cryo-Chamber, and the cables running from it to the base of one wall.

Maybe I wasn't supposed to wake up. Maybe the chamber was meant to sustain me forever.

And if this were a museum or a zoo, why wasn't anyone here? I looked again out the window, and there was nothing, not even a trace of life.

I pounded on the window and yelled.

The glass vibrated at my strike.

Was I stronger, or was the glass just that thin?

I looked at my hands. They were noticeably thicker than before. My arms were more muscular too, defined and taut.

I hit the glass again and it vibrated faster.

Maybe I could break it. But where would I end up? What was outside this room, and was it any better than being stuck inside?

It was then that I saw movement in the room opposite mine.

Whatever was inside stood up.

As I squinted to see it, my eyes... changed. They started to see almost like night vision goggles, losing detail but illuminating the shape in the darkness.

What was happening to me?

Was I even me anymore?

I stepped back from the glass, blinked, and looked around my room. In full light, I saw normally. Then I looked back at the room, and the being inside, and the night vision returned.

The being was my size, with arms and legs, and a head with two eyes. But it flickered like a flame. Not a bright flame, either, but a flame made of darkness.

It moved forward, right up to the glass of its room.

My eyes adjusted themselves as light from the corridor bathed the creature.

I saw it for real now.

It was made of solid darkness, a living shadow. Its eyes were two slits and its mouth a line drawn in a smirk.

It stared at me.

It raised one arm and mimed smashing its glass window. Then it pointed at me.

It wanted me to smash the glass.

"Escape," the creature called.

Its voice was like TV static.

ANTUMBRA

"Escape," it said again, punching the glass in its room.

I felt certain that I could break the glass. I hadn't even tried before and my strange new strength moved it. The bigger questions were how I could break it safely, without cutting myself, and whether or not I could trust my alien neighbour.

The only thing I could use was the screen attached to the Cryo-Chamber. I could wrench it free and then use it to smash the window. As I studied how it connected to the chamber, I saw the last scan it took of my body.

My body had been significantly altered by nanites and surgeries performed by the chamber. My muscles were stimulated to peak growth and function. My bones had been strengthened with alloys, and my body's ability to heal itself was increased. Even my senses had been enhanced, explaining my new night vision.

Had the chamber made me like One? Was I superhuman?

I smiled at the prospect.

I scrolled through screen after screen, learning about my time in the chamber, until I reached a screen that said: No further data. In the negative space, I saw my reflection.

I had aged.

I looked like I was in my mid-twenties.

I didn't understand. A Cryo-Chamber prevented aging.

Unless this one malfunctioned?

I studied myself; the squareness of my jaw, the stubble on my face. It was definitely still me, but older.

"Escape," the alien reminded me.

I looked at it and it seemed to smile.

I grabbed the screen and ripped it from the chamber, leaving a web of broken wires and conduits.

I aimed for the centre of the window, where the impact would be most powerful, wound up, flung it at the window. The glass flexed on impact, and then cracks appeared that travelled like lightning toward the outer edges.

The glass shattered into tiny pieces and fell like a hailstorm. The screen flew on, into my alien neighbour's window, chipping a small hole in the glass.

I stepped out into the corridor, stopping to admire the damage I had done to the shadowy alien's window.

The alien smiled again, and then slid its murky fingers into the tiny hole. It filled the space almost like smoke, expanding and shaking. The glass flexed and vibrated, and soon cracks grew from the chip. And it shattered.

As shards rained down on the creature, its dark body seemed to open and dilate to avoid them, with small gaps appearing around each piece of glass, then sealing over again.

"Thank you," it said as it stepped into the corridor.

"You're welcome, I think," I said.

"I am Antumbra," it said. "You have done me a great service."

Then Antumbra looked up and down the corridor.

"Is someone coming?" I asked. "Where are we?"

"The Thieves will come for us in time," Antumbra said.

"The Thieves?" I asked.

"They are the ones who steal from all," Antumbra said. Then it walked off down the corridor.

"Hey," I called, chasing after it. "You didn't answer my question. Where are we?"

I nearly tripped over my enhanced legs when I accelerated far more quickly than I'd ever known before. I wondered if One felt this way the first time he ran. My legs didn't even feel tired by the sprint.

We passed by other cells as we moved down the corridor. Each one had different aliens inside. Some of the trapped creatures were dead, splayed out like a frog dissection in a biology class.

Whoever the Thieves were, they meant business.

"Shouldn't we save the others?" I asked.

"Later," Antumbra answered without turning.

"Where are we going?"

"To the main museum," Antumbra said. "There is something of mine there."

"Museum? I thought so," I said. "But whose museum is it?"

Antumbra stopped and peered at me.

"You can go your own way," it said. "I have things to do, and no need for a distraction."

Then Antumbra moved along at quickened pace, leaving me behind.

I followed it at a distance until we reached the end of the corridor. At the fork, Antumbra went right. I decided to go left, figuring that it wasn't going to offer me any answers, and that those were precisely what I needed, I had to find them myself.

The leftward path led to a sort of greenhouse. A large, glass, dome ceiling stretched out above, over raised beds with plants, flowers and trees. Beyond the dome I saw a city skyline.

I didn't recognise it. The architecture was not from Earth. The buildings seemed to glow along their edges, each one a tall, thin tower reaching higher than any skyscraper.

This was some kind of museum. The question was: Whose?

The plants and trees were alien too, and not knowing what was safe and what wasn't, I didn't get too close, despite the incredible colours and beauty. Then I saw something familiar, an Earth plant.

It was a rose bush.

The bush was about chest high, like the ones I had seen cultivated by neighbours back home. Ruby red blossoms of perfectly formed petals peppered the bush. I suddenly felt sad and home sick. I hadn't seen a live plant since before I teleported onto the Ark.

I reached for the flowers, gently caressing the velvety petals. It was real. I moved the bloom aside and saw the stem lined with thorns. I felt those, too, the smooth triangular design, the sharp point.

I pricked my finger and recoiled.

Where did it come from? It made no sense. The last roses died with the Earth. There were seeds on the Ark, but those could not have survived the explosion.

Was this just another dream? Was the Ark a dream?

I smelled one of the blooms one more time and then walked on toward the end of the greenhouse. There was an exit at the end of the hall.

It opened up onto another corridor, an enclosed suspended bridge lined with windows that gave a better view of the city I found myself inside. The sky bridge hung over a river that ran from the greenhouse into the rest of the city.

The dark skyline was drenched with rain. Droplets streamed down the windows around me. The occasional flash of lightning illuminated the landscape beyond the city. Far off, I saw something so large I would have thought it impossible to build. There was something familiar about the giant structure.

Something about its shape.

I stared, but the light in the corridor prevented me from seeing clearly.

I looked for a way to turn the lights off, but instead, I saw a maintenance hatch in the ceiling of the sky bridge. Rungs ran up the wall beside the hatch, so I climbed up and out.

Rain assaulted me, soaking my clothes. I shielded my eyes, with my hand.

My enhanced vision picked out the large shape of the distant structure, but still not clearly enough. I waited for another lighting strike. A bolt struck the top of one of the city spires and its flash illuminated the city and beyond.

The extra light was more than enough.

It was not a building or monument. The distant structure was a spaceship of gigantic proportions. Massive, it reached miles into the sky, like the largest mountain you could imagine.

It was the Destroyer.

ON THE RUN

What was the Destroyer doing here?

I stared at the faint outline, hoping for another flash of light to come and turn the object into anything else, as if I had imagined it. It was really there, though. It was really the Destroyer, and all I could do was wonder if I was going to watch another world die?

I wiped the rain from my face, and flicked it toward the river below. The Destroyer couldn't be attacking this world. During the last days on Earth, there was so little water left it never rained.

No. This world is something else altogether.

A crash drew my attention back toward the greenhouse. Antumbra came flying through a window, arms crossed before it, with one holding some kind of rod. It landed atop the sky bridge, tucked into a ball, and rolled to a surprisingly soft landing.

Antumbra popped up to its feet and sprinted, droplets of rain sizzling on its shadowy form.

"Out of my way!" it shouted.

I probably would have moved, but I was distracted by the long, metal tentacles snaking out from the broken window behind Antumbra.

Connected to the tentacles, a cylindrical body topped with a metal saucer exited the opening next. The saucer rotated, as if looking around, and then locked onto Antumbra. It leapt down to the sky bridge, its tentacles breaking its fall, and then quickly starting running.

"Go," Antumbra said. "Unless you want to be a prisoner again!"

What else could I do?

I sprinted along the bridge, with Antumbra close behind me, and the tentacle-robot on our tails, catching up to us.

The bridge extended another five hundred metres or so and then connected to a building in the city. We had to get there, and maybe we could lose the robot among the buildings.

I looked back, and it was even closer to us, powered by those extra legs.

"What is that thing?" I asked Antumbra.

"That is a Thief," Antumbra said.

"I don't think we can outrun it," I said. "Can we fight it?"

Antumbra scoffed.

"Not without weapons," it said.

I looked down from the sky bridge to the river below.

"You can survive this drop," Captain Amis whispered. "It might buy you time."

"How are you with water?" I asked.

Antumbra looked down.

"I can swim," it said. "But is it safe?"

A tentacle lapped at our heels, making a loud, clanging sound against the roof of the sky bridge. The beast was on top of us.

"I've heard good things," I said. "There's no choice now anyway." I leapt off the sky bridge. I saw the shadow of Antumbra dive off behind me.

The fall was exhilarating. I felt weightless for a moment.

"Feet together," Captain Amis whispered. "Body straight."

The river came at me fast. I took a deep breath and held it. My legs juddered as my feet cut the water. I was surrounded by a torrent of bubbles, each seeking the surface of the water, so I followed them.

As I gasped for air I saw a black shape slip into the water next to me. A few seconds later Antumbra broke the river's surface, with steam rising from its body.

Antumbra's quickly raised the rod it had been holding, inspecting it. Despite its lack of features, Antumbra looked confused and upset.

I looked up at the bridge above us. I couldn't see the robot, but since nothing else had fallen into the river, it seemed safe to assume it wasn't going to follow.

"Let's get to shore," I said, starting to swim toward the city's shoreline.

"No," Antumbra said. "We have to go back."

I wasn't in the mood to argue, and Antumbra's knowledge of our situation far exceeded my own. Sticking together was the smarter option.

When we climbed up on the shore, lined with smooth, rounded pebbles, I rung out my shirt and pant legs, while Antumbra sizzled with more steam.

"Why did we come back?" I asked. "You seemed in a big hurry to get away from here just a second ago."

"I need to go back inside," Antumbra said.

Then it headed for the perimeter of the building.

As I followed, I noticed that we were actually outside of a collection of three domed-roof buildings, all clustered together. The grounds around them were populated by withering trees, dead bushes and patchy grasses. Decorative fountains laced among the yellowing foliage, only some of them still working.

Two more sky bridges extended out from the other buildings in the cluster at different angles, crossing the river, and connecting to the city.

We were on an island in the middle of the river. Some kind of hub.

"Why escape if you're just going back?" I asked Antumbra.

"I thought I had everything I needed," Antumbra said. "But I was mistaken."

"You mean that rod thing?" I asked.

"It is the salvation of my race," Antumbra rebutted. "It's my mission to use it to restore my planet."

"What happened to your planet?" I asked.

"The same thing that happened to yours," it replied.

"How do you know what happened to Earth?"

"You were in the museum with me," Antumbra said. "That is where they stick the remnants of the worlds they destroy."

"A museum," I said quietly.

Antumbra ignored me, and searched for a way to get back inside.

"You did not know?" it asked.

"I was in a Cryo-Chamber," I said. "I feel like there's a lot I don't know."

"Do you remember how you got into the chamber?"

"Before the Ark blew up," I said. "I was put there so I could survive the explosion."

"What is the Ark?" Antumbra asked.

"It was a spaceship," I said. "It was supposed to save the last of my people."

"That was your plan?" it scoffed. "Escape your world in a ship?"

I frowned. "It was the best we could do."

Antumbra went quiet.

Perhaps it knew that it offended me, or maybe it was just refocusing on its mission.

"I told you about me," I said. "Now you tell me about that rod."

Antumbra ignored me again.

"I still don't know what's going on here," I said, "But if we're going back to find some missing piece for that thing, the least you can do is clue me in."

Antumbra found a suitable entrance, and kicked in a pane of glass.

I was shocked by its strength. The glass popped as if it were paper and Antumbra stepped through the opening.

I followed it inside.

"Why didn't you just kick out the glass of your cell before?" I asked.

"That glass was stronger," it said. "I needed your special strength."

"So you knew that I was stronger?" I asked. "Were you watching me?"

"I knew of your strength because the chamber displayed daily updates on your progress over the last twenty years," it said.

"Twenty years? I've been on display for twenty years?"

"The Thieves installed you in the museum that long ago."

"You keep saying 'Thieves,'" I said. "Who are they? What are they?"

"They're the ones who send the ships, the ones that suck the life from, and destroy, every world they visit."

I followed it through the museum's lower floors.

I didn't quite know why I was following it. A small part of me was drawn to the city. I don't know what answers I'd find there, but I thought that there would surely be some.

But Antumbra's mission to save its people called to me. If it was possible to save its planet, maybe it was still possible to go back and save the Earth.

Maybe I could clone new humans.

If Antumbra was one and I were just two of many beings on display, maybe the Thieves had other humans somewhere in the museum. Maybe I wasn't the last? Maybe they had some of the other Arkonauts?

With all of my enhancements, perhaps I could save them all. Was this One's plan all along? I didn't even know the complete scope of what I could do yet.

"Good luck in your search," I said to Antumbra. "I have to see if I can save my world, too."

I left Antumbra and headed back toward my Cryo-Chamber and my cell.

We didn't say goodbye. Antumbra kept walking and that was that.

Among my new abilities was a sense of direction, and I easily wove my way back to my cell and Cryo-Chamber. Along the way, I passed countless other exhibits with aliens of every shape and size, some alive and some dead. The live ones clawed or pounded at the glass, many screeching and howling to be set free.

They would have to wait, though. I had my own mission.

I reached my smashed cell, still littered with glass. If there was staff for the museum, they hadn't gotten to it yet.

I picked up the chamber's viewscreen from where it landed at Antumbra's cell. I regretted throwing it, realizing that there might be answers inside that I could use. Luckily, the screen showed only a single crack, and when I reconnected the wiring from the chamber, it lit up.

The screen displayed a list of all the upgrades the chamber had performed on my body:

Muscle growth and strengthening

Increased metabolism

Secondary heart growth

Bone density increases

Sensory enhancements

Knowledge base download

Cellular regeneration enhancement

Acidic saliva graft

Photosynthesis cell addition

I expanded information of the last two on the list, having no idea what they meant.

The acidic saliva graft was a change to the glands in my mouth allowing me to secrete and spit a slightly acidic compound that made my bite significantly more dangerous.

I had never been much of a biter, but it might come in handy if ever I was captured.

The photosynthesis cell addition was the introduction of plant like cells to my skin, which absorbed light radiation and converted it to energy for my body. This allowed me to function without food for long periods of time.

This explained why I didn't feel even slightly hungry after sprinting and swimming all over this place. Still, I felt disturbed by the changes inside me. Was I even human any longer? Had I become a superhero?

It was a strange feeling, not knowing myself. I wondered if One ever felt like this, too.

I turned my attention back to the screen, looking for any other information. In the Knowledge section I discovered that I could now speak the language of the Ark's builders. I didn't know if they were the Thieves, or someone else, but Dr. Ghost had deciphered their language at some point during the Ark Project. Additionally, I carried in me the bulk of scientific knowledge from Earth.

I had become a walking, talking, warrior encyclopaedia. And like One, I had even received memories that taught me advanced social techniques like body language reading and investigation.

I tapped through the chamber's file system, now trying to figure out why the chamber had been on the Ark in the first place. It wasn't for One, so who was it for? Was it built to save one human if the Ark failed, and if so, were that room and chamber intended to drift through space forever?

I found a listing of files on the Ark Project, and pored over them at high speed. Apparently, I also had the ability to consume information and commit it to memory quickly.

Eventually I found the file: Contingency Plan Q, Sole Survivor.

There I found a letter from Dr Ghost addressed to the occupant of the chamber.

It took me moments to read it and I was surprised by its contents, however before I could compute this information I heard someone running down the corridor.

Antumbra was once again sprinting at me at full speed. Its hands were empty. The rod was gone.

"Duck," Antumbra said, diving past me into its original cell.

Three tentacle robots, like the one that had chased us earlier, came barrelling down the corridor, and this time, their saucer-like bodies were armed with lasers.

I dove into my cell, just as a blast struck the floor in front of it.

"I need your help again," Antumbra called.

Another laser blast knocked the window frame out of my cell.

"Okay," I said. "But this time, I want something in return."

Antumbra reached its hand into its shadowy torso, the form wispily opening, and retrieved the rod.

"Convenient storage place," I said.

"I found the missing piece," Antumbra said. "Now it can be used."

"Used for what?" I asked.

"Time travel."

"Time travel?" I asked.

"Yes," Antumbra replied. "How would you like to save your planet?"

RECRUITMENT DRIVE

"You're saying that we can use that rod to travel through time?" I asked.

"It is a technological artifact of my homeworld," Antumbra said. "My species created it so that I could undo the damage done by the Thieves. We can use it to save your world as well."

I tried to read Antumbra through its body language, to discern truth and fact from its statement, but that wasn't possible given its shadowy alien form. I couldn't imagine what motive Antumbra would have to lie, and given the rapidly approaching attack robots, it seemed like a risk worth taking.

"I will help you," I replied. "And then we'll save my world."

"Good," Antumbra said. It reached into its torso again and this time retrieved a laser pistol. Antumbra tossed it to me. "Perhaps you can use this."

I looked the weapon over "I've never used one of these before."

"Just point it at the Thieves and pull the trigger," Antumbra said, then it drew a second laser gun.

"Don't worry, Callum," Captain Amis whispered. "You'll do fine."

The memory raised my confidence. I let go of trying to understand the pistol and just let my hands do what they wanted. Quickly, I pulled back a power level, and a row of lights on the barrel lit up green. Green usually a good thing, at least I hoped aliens thought so.

Antumbra leaned out into the corridor and fired off several shots.

I couldn't tell if it hit anything, but Antumbra quickly dove back into the cell as the robots returned fire.

I took advantage of their focus on Antumbra and leaned out to fire myself.

When I fired, everything slowed down, I perceived time differently as if the enemy were moving through treacle and I wasn't. I could aim and fire before they knew what was happening. I landed three shots, one on each of the robots, right in the middle saucer sections. Each tear-shaped ball of energy that left my pistol soared and burned through a robot, melting a large hole in its metal carapace and then blasting out the back.

All three robots stepped forward, still carried by inertia, before collapsing limp to the floor.

I stepped out of my cell.

Antumbra followed.

I inspected each of the fallen robots. A red puddle seeped from each of them. I knew right away that it was blood.

"I thought these things were robots," I said.

"They are part-robot and part-living creature," Antumbra replied. "It is how they have evolved to survive."

"Survive?" I said. "I thought they stole our air and water to survive."

"The machine parts extend their lives and make them more powerful," Antumbra said. "But those parts require energy. They require hydrogen as fuel, which they steal from air and water on other planets. Plus for an added bonus their thievery destroys any potential aliens that could oppose them." Antumbra said. "We must leave now. More of them will be here soon."

"Why don't we get some help?" I said. "I'm sure a lot of the other exhibits are as mad as we are."

I went down our corridor, firing my laser pistol at the glass windows containing the other captured aliens.

There were six still alive in total. One was massive, like an elephant seal crossed with a centaur and its skin rippled like waves on the sea. It had four huge legs and two thick arms. Its face was covered with a skull that it was probably wearing as a mask.

Another was cat-like, lithe and had four tails. It had claws on its hands and feet, and pointed ears. It wore a collection of straps lined with trinkets of some kind.

The third alien was similar to a giant, skeletal praying mantis. Like Antumbra, living energy played around its limbs. It stood on four legs with four arms ending in barbed energy claws and stared down at me with hollow eye sockets

The fourth creature was half my height and mostly a mouth with legs. Inside its maw were wide, gravestone-like teeth. It had no eyes that I could see.

The fifth had a snake like lower body ridged with bone. Its torso was almost human-shaped, and its face was serpentine.

The last alien was very short and made of stone. If it didn't move I would have assumed it was a pile of rocks. It walked on two lumpy legs and had two arms. It didn't appear to have a face.

Antumbra surveyed the aliens. "Why did you free them?"

"I figured they would either help us, or give the guards more targets," I said. "Besides, if we're going to save a couple of worlds, we can save a few aliens too."

"Of course, I don't want any of you to be targets for the guards. We're all going to get out of here. If you didn't have something else to do in your cells."

"I'm with you," the fat and short mouthy alien said.

The cat nodded. The giant mantis clicked its bone like mandibles. The rock creature seemed to settle in agreement.

The medusa like alien slithered away without saying anything, clearly it didn't want anything to do with us. I had no idea what it intended, presumably preferring to try its own escape plan.

"I need a safe space to set up the time travel device," Antumbra said.

"Then let's find somewhere safe," I said.

I ran down the corridor, following the mental map in my head. The city was out of the question. It was no doubt crawling with more Thieves. The whole planet was teeming with them. I realized that we'd never be safe unless we left.

If the Thieves built ships as big as the Destroyer, they must have smaller ones too.

The others were close behind me. Our jailbreak was on, but we needed one more thing first. Down the corridor I saw a door labelled "security." I broke the door open and inside we found what we needed.

The room held rack after rack of laser rifle add-ons for the Thieves. At least now we would be well armed.

"If you don't have one, grab a weapon," I said.

Only the small rock creature and giant mantis did not take a blaster.

"Don't you want a weapon?" I asked them.

The rock settled again, maybe it was shrugging. The giant mantis clamped its pincers at a rack of replacement tentacles, cutting everything cleanly in two.

"Okay," I said. "You're definitely all set."

We took up arms and headed down to the ground floor of the museum complex.

More Thieves were organising outside the museum's entrance, when we arrived, probably planning to siege the building. But lucky for us, they didn't park far from the entrance either. There were multiple small ships, each one triangular with six wings.

Rain kept falling outside, with a backdrop of flickering lightning.

"We need one of those ships," I said. "But first let's improve our odds and thin the herd a little."

As I ran attack strategies through my head, I noticed that the little rock alien was gone. Then I heard a door open and close. I watched the front doors expecting to see the Thieves storming the building, but instead it was the rock alien. It hobbled out on its short, lumpy legs to meet the thieves.

"Oh, great," I sighed.

The Thieves circled the rock alien immediately, holding it at gunpoint.

The little rock alien didn't move.

The Thieves fired at the rock. Blasts of energy struck it and pushed it backwards. A few small chips flew off the stony alien, but it didn't seem injured.

The Thieves stopped firing and let the smoke clear.

That's when the rock alien swung its body around in a violent, but smooth motion. Aspects of its granite physique flew out, making deep dents, and even outright crushing the Thieves' metal bodies.

The destroyed and crumpled cyborgs fell backwards.

The Thieves fired on the little rock alien again, and the rock alien repeated its attack, creating a tornado of swirling stone that pummelled each of the attackers.

"Nicely done, Pebbles," I said.

"We need to help him now," the fat alien said, lumbering forward like an obese centaur.

"Lay down cover fire," I said.

Antumbra and I charged behind our massive new friend, firing at the remaining Thieves.

Behind us, the giant mantis and cat-like creature took cover in the doorway. The alien with the large mouth followed me and Antumbra.

The massive alien plodded forward. Each shot from the Thieves just absorbed into its bulk. Antumbra and I fired back every chance we got.

I focused my vision, firing for the Thieves heads, and landing every shot I took.

The massive alien body slammed a Thief, crushing it nearly flat.

Our cover gone, I found myself face to face with a Thief. It pointed its gun at me, but I was too fast. I grabbed the barrel of the blaster and wrenched it sideways. Then I fired my pistol at its head.

Another Thief came at me, so I used the one I had just killed as a shield. The metal body absorbed every blast, but the force of the shots pushed me back. When the firing stopped, I shot back, taking another one down.

The large-mouthed alien lunged past me, teeth-first at another Thief. Its viselike jaws closed around the Thief's head, crushing it like a tin can. Then it appeared to eat the Thief whole.

Across the battlefield, Antumbra engaged another Thief. Its shadowy arms had turned bright white like burning magnesium, and Antumbra chopped at the Thief, severing its tentacles and then finally bisecting the evil cyborg.

I kept firing, and Pebbles, the rock alien, kept swirling stones in a brutal vortex. The massive alien flopped its girth from Thief to Thief, crushing one after another.

When I looked around, all the Thieves were defeated, the museum grounds were a warzone, littered with dead cyborgs, their tentacles twitching, or severed. I holstered my pistol and surveyed the smaller ships parked nearby.

"Our ride is here," I said to my fellow escapees. "Let's go."

"This will not be the last of them," Antumbra said. "We must hurry."

"Anyone know how to fly one of these?" I asked.

"I can," said the feline alien, now emerging from the museum. "I'm not a fighter, but I am a pilot."

"What's your name, pilot?" I asked.

"Lyger," the feline replied.

The giant mantis followed the cat-like alien. It noticed one of the Thieves still moving and deftly cut it in half with its pincers.

"Thanks for contributing," I said sarcastically.

It bowed.

"These ships won't get us off world," Antumbra said. "We'll be intercepted the moment we leave the atmosphere. We need something that can get us out of the solar system faster than light."

"Now you tell me," I replied. "Fine. Where do we get a better ship?"

Rain beat down on us. I tried to think of a plan, but even Captain Amis couldn't help me. We could fly around, evading and fighting for a few days, maybe weeks, but we wouldn't last long.

Lightning struck again, and so did an idea, a big one, parked far off behind the city across the river.

Our way off this planet was what we all hated most.

"Can you fly something bigger than these?" I asked. "Like really, really big?"

"If it has an engine and a yoke, I can fly it," Lyger replied.

I nodded. "Good."

"What are you thinking, human?" Antumbra asked.

I pointed my gun towards the horizon.

"I think we have a way off this planet," I said.

Every alien looked in the direction I was pointing.

The rain and dark skies revealed nothing. Then a lightning strike illuminated the sky and showed them the Destroyer.

"You want to leave the planet on that?" the alien with the large mouth asked.

"That's the plan," I replied.

THE DESTROYER

Lyger squirmed as she tried to get comfortable in the pilot seat of one of the Thief's small ships. The rest of us crowded behind her and looked over her shoulder.

"You can fly this thing, right?" I asked.

Lyger shushed me.

"It's just like any other ship," she said pointing at the control panel. "This is thruster control. This is a Force Dampener. And this should be the ignition."

"Great. Let's get moving. That Destroyer might be our only way off this planet," I said.

"Destroyer?" Lyger asked. "Are you sure this is a good idea?"

"Oh, that's just what my race called those giant ships," I said. "And I think this is the best idea we have."

"Alright," Lyger said. "Everybody buckle up."

Pebbles and the Mouth each managed to sit down and strap themselves in. The massive alien poured its bulk into a seat too, though it was many times too small for it, and overflowed the arm and backrest like living candle wax. The giant mantis just wrapped its legs around a chair. Antumbra and I took our own seats.

Lyger tapped away at the controls, and the ship hummed to life. Before I knew it we were lifting off the ground, with only the sounds of the engines and rain tapping at the ship's canopy in my ears.

The warzone below shrank as we climbed, flying above the roof of the museum complex.

Lyger punched our destination into the navigation computer.

"We're twenty minutes away from the ship," she said. "Any idea where we should land to get inside? It's huge."

I thought back to my time on the Ark. The control centre had not been human built. It was part of the Ark's design. Although it had been automated when it came to Earth, the Thieves were capable of piloting it if necessary.

I had been to the control centre on the Ark so many times, I knew exactly where it was located. Not in the middle of the top decks, but close to the outer hull, right next to the observation deck. All we had to do was fly by the big viewing window, and look for a crew-entrance docking bay. I closed my eyes and focused, pouring over what I remembered from the Ark's layout.

The theatre. Dr. Ghost modified the crew entrance to create the theatre. That's where we needed to go. As long as the Destroyer was just a much, much bigger Ark, that's where the bay would be.

"There's a docking bay for crew," I said. "It should be near the observation deck and a big window, but we'll have to watch for it."

"How do we get inside?" Antumbra asked.

"I don't know," I asked. "But I'm sure we'll figure something out."

"A docking bay door should be easy enough to breach," the massive alien grunted. "Maybe this ship can scan for it."

"Lyger—" I began.

"Already on it," Lyger replied.

Lyger punched at the controls and then smiled.

"Not only does the ship have records of each docking bay," she said. "The one we want is actually open right now."

"Let's go," I said.

"If it is open then there will be Thieves there," Antumbra said.

"We'll have to take that chance," I said.

Lyger engaged the ship's thrusters and we soared toward the Destroyer.

As we neared it, I realised that the sky was brightening up. A sun was rising on the horizon, illuminating the Destroyer and everything else. The massive ship was even larger than I could have imagined, a mountain of metal. It was parked in some kind of giant pit lined with machines, hoses, conduits and tubes. The Thieves must park the Destroyer here to offload the stolen resources and transport them back into the city.

Lyger brought our ship in close. We climbed from the edge of the pit, along the pyramidal surface of the Destroyer, toward the docking bay on its upper aspect.

"Human, look at this," Lyger said.

She pulled up a video screen on the console. It displayed an image of another Thief ship, like a giant floating platform, or an aircraft carrier.

"What is it?" I asked.

"I don't know," Lyger said. "But it doesn't look great."

The platform ship fired a red beam from its underside. The beam spread out like a fan, brushing along the Destroyer's hull knocking debris and ice off of its surface.

"Is it cleaning the Destroyer?" I asked.

Lyger took us higher, toward the peak of the Destroyer.

"Docking bay is just up ahead," she reported.

As we passed the flying platform, the red beam turned off and receiver dish extended, following our movement. We were being tracked.

I grabbed the yoke from Lyger and cranked them to the right.

Our ship veered, just as the red beam reactivated, firing a wide energy band at us.

An alert siren blared. On the control screen, we saw that the beam had sheered off one of our wings.

Lyger hissed and snatched the controls from my grip. She took us into a quick dive, then pulled us back up and out, manoeuvring us away from the platform.

"We're damaged, but luckily we've got five more wings," Lyger said.

"Can we still make it to the docking bay?" I asked.

"We're heading straight for it," Lyger said.

Outside the cockpit window the docking bay was open. Then red lights surrounding the bay started to flash, and the two doors snapped closed, like metal mouth.

"We're not going to make it," Lyger said, pulling back on the yoke.

Our ship careened off the hull of the Destroyer. Sparks flew all around us.

"Well, there goes that plan," the Mouth said.

"I'm detecting ships leaving from the city," Lyger said. "They're on an intercept course."

I looked out the window and my enhanced eyes zoomed in on the Thief ships. I counted five ships coming right for us,

"We need to get inside the Destroyer now," I said. "I don't think they're going to try to capture us this time."

Then I heard a weird tapping sound coming from inside our ship. I turned to see the giant mantis, clawing at the window beside it, pointing at the flying platform.

"You think we can get inside the Destroyer with that?" I asked.

The giant mantis nodded.

"The platform might dock with the Destroyer for interior maintenance," Antumbra said. "It may be able to open the docking bay."

"Sounds like the new plan," I said.

"What about those incoming ships," the Mouth protested. "We'll be outnumbered."

"Antumbra and I will find the controls to open the bay door," I said. "You, big guy, what's your name?"

"Hippopotomstroesquipedaliopherato," the massive alien answered.

"Okay, I said. "If you don't mind, I'm going to call you Hippo."

Hippo nodded.

"Pebbles," I said to the rock alien. "You, Hippo, and the Mouth find the controls for that red laser, and use it to take out those ships following us."

"Someone needs to stay with the ship, in case we need to escape," Lyger said.

I nodded. "Lyger, you stay with ship. Mantis, you come with me and Antumbra. Any questions?"

No one responded.

"Coming in for landing," Lyger said.

The ship swooped down at the top of the platform, completely avoiding the emitter on its underside. We came to a gentle stop, and then Lyger dropped the ship's ramp.

"Keep the engine running," I said. "We'll be right back."

THE PLATFORM

The air was thin outside our ship. I didn't think about how high up we were, but if the Destroyer were a mountain, we were near its peak.

The platform was completely flat, punctuated by a single tower in the centre. We ran for the tower, where the controls for the emitter, and the code to open the docking bay had to be located.

At the base of the tower was a doorway. I studied the panel next to it, but couldn't find a way to open it.

"Hippo," I said. "Would you mind?"

Hippo took a few steps back and then charged at the door like a battering ram. He hit it head first, and was deflected back, dazed. The door didn't move.

Pebbles stepped forward and flung a barrage of stones at the door, knocking it off its hinges.

Hippo staggered to his feet. "I loosened it for you," he said.

Beyond the door was a small room, and a stairwell leading up higher in the tower, and down underneath it. The platform seemed to be otherwise deserted.

Maybe we caught a break?

"The emitter is on the underside of the platform," I said. "I'm guessing the controls are down these stairs. As soon as you've taken those incoming ships out head back to ours."

Hippo, the Mouth, and Pebbles rumbled down the stairs.

Antumbra and Mantis followed me up, where I assumed the control centre would be.

Halfway up the steps, we heard slithering sounds. There was a pair of Thieves operating the control centre. This beast lacked the robotic implants we'd seen before, and were slimier, and more octopus-like. They lunged at us, their tentacles flailing.

Antumbra fired three times. The laser blasts ripped through one of the Thief's flesh.

I grabbed the second Thief by the head and kneed it in the base of the tentacles.

The creature gasped and gurgled, and then grasped for me with its tentacles. Mantis leapt in and chopped it down to size with two powerful snips of its mandibles.

The control centre was a circular room with a wide panoramic window. I sprinted to the nearest console. I struggled to read the Thieves language, but the combination of the memories and the improvements the Cryo-Chamber made to me gave me just enough information.

On the far left of the console was a communications screen, which had already linked with the Destroyer, and the other five ships closing in. Beside it was controls for the environment inside the tower, and next were flight controls. But there was nothing labelled for the docking bay access controls.

I looked to Antumbra.

"Any ideas?" I asked. "I don't see an obvious docking bay button."

"Is there a log of previous commands in the communication screen?" it asked.

I went back to the communication array, and saw that Antumbra was right. Under the list of previously executed communications, I found two entries. One was for closing the bay, and another, just a bit further down the list, was for opening it. In a few taps, I re-sent the command sequence.

The bay doors groaned as they began to separate and the Destroyer opened wide.

"Look at that," I said proudly.

"No time to celebrate. Those other ships are closing in," Antumbra said. "An open door won't do us much good if they blow us up."

I tapped at communications console and found intercom.

"Hippo, it's Callum," I said into the air. "How's it going down there?"

"We have control," Hippo replied. "But we're too low to aim at the ships."

Mantis tapped at the floor and then pointed upwards.

I nodded.

"We need to get higher so the emitter can fire down on the ships," I said.

Antumbra studied the console. "This says we're already at maximum altitude."

"So we can't get higher." I said.

"Those ships can land on the platform from above," Antumbra said. "They'll surround us."

Mantis tapped the floor again, held its fore-claws level at face height, and then cocked them at an angle.

"You want us to turn?" I asked.

Mantis stomped this time, and repeated the same motion with its claws.

"It wants us to tip the platform," Antumbra said. "That will give the emitter a clear shot."

Mantis nodded.

I hopped onto the communications console, and broadcast to our ship, as well as inside the platform.

"Lyger, I hope that ship is anchored," I said. "We're going to need to try something wild."

"It is," Lyger answered. "Should I be worried?"

"Just hold onto something," I replied. "That goes for the rest of you at emitter too."

I changed the distribution of power for the platform's thrusters, overloading one side while adding just a bit of reverse thrust to keep us from spinning in a circle.

The entire platform tipped back until we were perpendicular with the horizon.

"Hippo, do you have a clean shot now?"

"Yes," Hippo answered. "Lining up the targets now."

I heard the emitter charge. The whole platform rumbled. Then a red beam sliced through the sky, cutting two of the approaching ships in half.

The three remaining ships made evasive manoeuvres, trying to get out of the emitter's range.

"Tilt us again," Antumbra said. "We can't let them get the drop on us."

As I manipulated the controls, the three Thief ships swooped down, and headed straight for Lyger and our stolen craft.

"Lyger," I called over the com. "Get out of there. They're coming right for you."

Outside across the platform, I saw her, standing at the base of our ship's ramp.

She wasn't going to make it, and the attacking Thief ships had already begun firing their weapons.

"Shake things up," I heard Captain Amis whisper.

I jiggled the platform controls, tilting the platform sharply.

Lyger fell off balance and slid along the surface of the platform and away from the shuttle. The Thief ships continued firing, destroying our stolen shuttle.

The platform's momentum however swung up and under the Thieves and before they could realise the problem and change course, it swatted the ships out of the sky like the hand of God.

Antumbra shrieked static and pointed at Lyger, now sliding past the tower.

"I see her," I shouted, pulling the controls back to centre.

The platform moved back toward horizontal, Lyger's slide slowed, but she was still too close to the edge, desperately digging her clawed fingers into the deck.

"She will fall over the edge," Antumbra cried.

I increased the thrusters on one side of the platform, trying to level it out quicker.

I saw Lyger hissing in terror, still sliding for the edge.

"Come on," I begged the platform ship.

The platform tilt decreased to thirty degrees, then twenty, then ten.

Lyger only had a few metres of deck left.

I watched the screen and made a wish.

Five degrees.

Level.

Lyger was still sliding. She had too much momentum. Her claws dug ten long scratches in the surface of the deck. She finally screeched to a halt with her legs dangling over the side of the platform. She quickly scampered to her feet and sprinted for the tower.

"Well done," Antumbra said. "Now we have no ship."

I frowned at it.

"We've got this platform now," I replied, and then I called over the intercom. "Hippo, we need you upstairs."

Once Lyger joined us in the tower, I recalibrated the platform's thrusters to guide it into the Destroyer's open docking bay. The platform descended a gently as a hot air balloon.

Lyger burst into the control room, leapt at me with her claws out, and grabbed me by my collar.

"Never do that again," she growled. "Or you will regret it."

"You're a little more of a fighter than you let on," I said.

Lyger stepped back and collected herself. "When I'm mad."

I nodded. "Noted," I said. "We'll be inside the Destroyer in moments."

"There is not a large enough landing pad for this platform," Antumbra said, staring at the three-tiered decks inside the docking bay.

Each one was built for smaller ships, but nothing as large as the platform. Once we cleared the bay doors we would run out of room fast.

"Brace for impact," I said.

Every alien held onto a chair or console. Mouth held onto Pebbles.

The tiers inside the docking bay cut into the platform's deck, nearly splitting it into three pieces. The platform sparked, and rattled with small explosions and flying chunks of metal.

Pieces of the docking tiers broke off and fell inside the Destroyer as they absorbed our forward motion.

Eventually we came to a grinding halt.

"Everybody okay?" I asked.

My makeshift crew flashed some version of thumbs up, varying based on whether or not each alien had thumbs.

"Okay," I said. "Let's go."

I used the communication console to reclose the docking bay doors, and then we all filed out of the tower.

The platform was wedged perfectly among the tiers, giving us a makeshift ramp leading from the tower onto the Destroyer.

The docking bay doors closed behind us, biting off the back of the platform.

"Follow me," I said as the bay door finally closed. "We're almost there."

BECOMING THIEVES

The corridors inside the Destroyer were larger than those in the Ark, leading to dozens of rooms that weren't on the smaller ship. One corridor led to a balcony overlooking a cavernous well that must have normally stored stolen water.

I resisted the urge to yell "Echo!" at the ledge. The expanse was bigger than anything I'd ever seen.

We snaked around the upper section of the Destroyer, passing other storage rooms, a number of labs and mechanical closets, until we finally found the control centre.

Luckily, it was unmanned. The room was circular with a screen on the floor and a dome screen above, like the Ark. The dome displayed a three-hundred-sixty-degree view of outside the Destroyer. We saw their sun rising above a large ocean just beyond the city we had seen before. Ships poured into the sky above the city. All of them were flying our way.

"Looks like we'll have more company," Hippo said.

"They'll need good luck to catch us," I said, standing over the engine ignition controls.

Lyger helped me start everything up, blending our mutual experience and knowledge.

The last step was to warm up the engines and felt a gentle vibration through the deck plates. On the engine console, I saw six beams of light surging in the lower half of the ship.

"Engine is charging," I said. "We'll be out of here in no time."

"Where do we go after this?" the Mouth asked.

We all turned to him.

"I intend to save my people," Antumbra said. "And this human will attempt to save his planet as well. Beyond that I do not care what comes of the rest of you."

The Mouth grumbled. "That's not very resassuring"

"These Thieves killed my family, my friends, and my planet," I said. "I'm going to stop them."

I meant those words.

"How?" the other aliens seemed to ask at once.

Antumbra stepped forward and held up its artefact. It began explaining its time travel abilities.

I realized just how much I meant my last words. Perhaps this was the reason the Cryo-Chamber existed, to stop the Thieves and save all the peoples of the Universe. Was that what Dr. Ghost wanted all along?

The six beams of surging light turned bright green. The Destroyer was ready for lift-off.

"Time to go," I said.

My alien crew looked at me, and then at the fleet of approaching ships. They nodded emphatically.

I activated the engines.

The console showed the Destroyer's thrusters firing at full power.

Suddenly the whole vessel jolted.

"What's wrong?" Antumbra asked.

I checked the control panel. "There are anchors, or locks," I said. "I'll try to find a way to release them."

I scoured the console, and couldn't find anything.

"I guess we'll have to try this the hard way," I said, powering the engines to full.

It didn't work. The ship lurched and jolted.

Then Mantis rapped at the floor to get our attention. Once we were looking, it spun around in a circle like a top.

"What's it saying?" I asked.

"I think he wants us to spin the Destroyer," Lyger replied. "It could work. If the locks are meant to keep the ship from lifting off, they might be weak to torque from twisting."

Mantis clapped his claws together and pointed at Lyger.

I found the lateral thrusters on the control panel and lit them up.

The Destroyer vibrated and lurched anti-clockwise.

The metal clamps groaned.

We heard a sequence of loud pops and the Destroyer started spinning, and lifting off.

I quickly shut down the lateral thrusters, and the ship jumped into the sky. In moments, the blue sky darkened and filled with stars.

I looked out over the world below and gasped. The surface of the Thieves' home planet was peppered with other Destroyer-sized spaceships. Dozens across the entire surface, horrible metallic mountain ranges spread out across the landscape.

Stopping the Thieves would not be as easy as saving one world, or two.

I checked our route on the console. We were barrelling into deep space, and not one ship was following us. As we passed the group of moons orbiting the Thieves' I scanned one more time to be sure.

We had done it.

We had escaped.

TIME TRAVEL

With a course plotted to leave the Thieves' home solar system, Antumbra showed me the time travel rod. Our alien crewmembers stood around us in the control centre. The mood in the room was a mix of excitement and apprehension at the thought of changing the time space continuum.

"This device will allow us to send something back in time and if it is done at the right time then it will change the past to our, or in this case your, benefit," Antumbra said. "I assume we will want it to arrive on your former ship, just before it was destroyed."

I nodded, eager to see the demonstration.

Antumbra held up the rod and continued explaining.

"This will allow us to peer through time to any point we wish," it said. "We can then open a portal, and send objects, or ourselves through."

"What happens when we change the past?" I asked.

"Our scientists had two schools of thought on the issue. Some believed that by altering the past, the future timeline originally connected to it would cease to be, effectively resetting time from the point of change onward," Antumbra said. "Once the time traveller or the object reaches the date when they/it travelled back, however, the universe will either loop on itself perpetually or collapse into nothingness."

"Collapse?" I said.

"Yes," Antumbra continued. "When the new version of the old timeline reaches the point when the traveller travelled, it creates a quantum anomaly that folds the whole thing in on itself. The new timeline effectively erases the old, which is also its foundation, boom!" And its hand mimicked an explosion.

"Why would we ever try this then?" I protested.

"Oh, that theory was deemed incredibly unlikely, close to a one percent chance," Antumbra said.

"Then why lead with it—"

"Theory number two is far more likely," Antumbra continued. "It is based on the multiverse theory, wherein every decision we make creates universes based on the choice and all of its alternatives. Given that we have yet to experience a universal collapse, this seems most accurate."

"So, each timeline exists in parallel?" I asked. "We could save our planets on one timeline, but they'll still have died on another."

"Precisely," Antumbra said. "We would create a multiverse where mankind still continues as you remember it, even as our current one, where mankind ended, also continues."

"So we could use the portal to throw a bomb inside the Destroyer that landed on my planet and blew it apart," I said. "Then it blows up and never gets to my homeworld in the first place."

"That won't work," the mouth said. "You'll just create a timeline where the Thieves sent another Destroyer."

"Also let me be very clear," Antumbra said. "This rod has never been used outside of lab testing before. I don't know exactly how it will work when factoring in an entire universal timeline, or how long it will last. We must make a carefully calculated decision. This cannot be treated cavalierly."

I fell silent, trying to come up with another plan. We could open a portal on the Thieves' distant past and kill their evolutionary ancestors, but if the rod only had a few portals in it, we'd never find the beginning of their history. We didn't even know where to begin looking.

"Fine," I said. "We open a portal to the Ark, just before the explosion. We were all there, trying to get a bomb off the ship, but we didn't know the access code to the vessel we were trying to access. I didn't know the Chinese characters then. But we can see what the soldiers typed and tell them now."

"Good," Antumbra said. "A distinct point in time will be easier to find."

Antumbra held up the rod and pulled it into two pieces.

As it separated tendrils of energy danced like lightning between the two fragments. The lightning formed into a kind of control panel, with words, buttons and switches floating in mid-air.

Antumbra released the rod pieces and they floated, too.

"Now we must find the right point in time," it said.

Antumbra took two threads of lightning and swirled them until they formed into what looked like a 3D map.

"This is the universe," Antumbra said. "We just have to find your solar system, and then we can scan time until we find the moment you seek."

"Sounds too simple," I said.

"It is actually," Antumbra replied. "However, I do need you to remember some star constellations."

"Constellations? Why?"

"Because the number of places in the universe from which you can see any specific constellation is actually very small," Antumbra said. "They are like landmarks in space. Draw them here."

I walked over and raised my index finger into the space between the separated rods. I sketched the Ursa Major, Cassiopeia, Draco, Pegasus and Taurus all drawn with help from my new memories.

Antumbra nodded, and then motioned at the glowing field hovering in mid-air. "Now it will search for possible locations."

Eventually it zoomed in on three galaxies, and one stood out to me, disc-like with multiple spiral arms.

"That's it," I said, feeling a wave of nostalgia at seeing the Milky Way again, even though I had never actually seen it in person.

"We need more constellations to narrow it down," Antumbra said.

I drew again: Libra, Orion.

Antumbra set the search going again until it zoomed further in on the Milky Way, finding my own solar system.

But something about the solar system didn't look right. There were only five planets, and the sun glowed dimly, deep red. I couldn't see the Earth anywhere.

"This doesn't—" I began.

"Don't forget we haven't calibrated the time yet," Antumbra said. "We are viewing your solar system at a time after you left, but before now, remember some changes might have happened."

Antumbra swiped across the glowing map, and the solar system changed. The sun grew large, and then shrank back, turning orange and then yellow. Around it, Venus, and Mercury reappeared, and then from a ball of flame, the Earth.

"Stop there," I said.

I walked over swiped at the hovering map myself. I scrolled through time, trying to find the moment the Earth burst into a ball of fire.

"Here," I said. "This is pretty close."

Antumbra gestured again at the map, zooming in on the Earth, and then further in, to see the Destroyer, launching from the planet, a mountain with a tail of fire.

I marvelled at the display, I was seeing through time, watching my own homeworld from a perspective no human had ever had.

"How does this even work?" I asked.

"It uses quantum entanglement to extract this image, both as a way to view the universe at a past time, allowing us to accurately send a portal to the point in time we are seeing."

"Right," I said in a manner I hoped conveyed that I understood the scientific mumbo jumbo.

Antumbra gestured more, zooming in further until we all saw the Ark flying out of the solar system.

I must have been inside, just meeting the other Arkonauts.

Antumbra continued moving time forward, very slowly now. The Ark passed Mars, and the Gas Giants. Then it moved past Pluto.

I closed my eyes and for a moment, it was like I right back there.

"I can't believe we're seeing through time," I said.

"Technically we are not," Antumbra said. "You are thinking of time as a road you can travel down when in fact it is just a moment when all matter is in a previous state. The rod simply records and projects those different states in a way we can understand, which appears linear."

"Sounds like magic," I said. "Why didn't your planet just use this to stop the Destroyer when it arrived?"

"We could not stop the Destroyer once it reached us. Its power core is capable to destroying entire planets, especially in an uncontrolled explosion," Antumbra said. "By the time we realized what the Destroyer was, it was too late and unsafe for us to act on our planet, so we sent me and the rod away on a small ship that would escape the Thieves' notice. Of course, they did eventually notice and I was captured.

"They did not understand the nature of the rod and I never told them. When they stuffed me in that cell I could only wait and hope I could be free one day and reclaim the rod."

"So you knew you would be the last of your species, sent away simply to create a new timeline where you were certain your species were still alive?"

"That was our hope," Antumbra replied.

I had to marvel at its species' choice, they didn't have an Ark so they couldn't save their race like humanity had tried. What a sacrifice.

"Thank you then for this opportunity," I said. "I know what it's like to be the last of my species. Your sacrifice is not lost on me."

Antumbra bowed its head and turned back to the glowing projection.

"Here," it said. "The Ark at its moment of destruction."

"Zoom in," I said pointing. "The corridor I was in was here."

Antumbra zoomed further until I was face-to-face with a paused image of myself with the other Arkonauts carrying the minister's nuclear bomb to the docking port.

"Can you go back a bit?" I asked eagerly.

Antumbra nodded. "Just say when."

I watched the projection scroll back until we were gone, and the Chinese soldiers were disembarking their ship.

"Stop here," I said. "Now zoom in on the keypad."

The display showed a soldier tapping at the buttons.

There it was, the code to open to Chinese shuttle. I memorized the pattern.

"Now, go back to when we just saw me," I said.

Antumbra obliged.

There I was again, with my friends, holding a bomb, desperate to save the Ark.

"There," I said. "Now, how do I send the message?"

"Something physical," Antumbra replied.

I looked around for anything to write on, but the Destroyer didn't need paper. After searching for a moment, I decided to use my sleeve, which I ripped off and tore open and flat.

"Anybody have a pen?" I asked.

Antumbra shook its head. The other aliens followed suit.

I looked around again, but why would the Thieves have pens if they didn't have paper? Finally, I realized what I had to do.

"Can you prick the tip of my finger, please," I said to Antumbra.

Antumbra reached out with its shadowy hand and like a hot knife, it cut open my fingertip.

I gritted my teeth at the sharp pain and I heard the flesh sizzle. The smell was revolting.

I then painted the Chinese characters, with my own blood, on my ripped shirtsleeve. I could only hope that the Callum from the past wouldn't be freaked out by a message written in blood. I blew on the cloth to dry my ad-hoc ink.

"This should work," I said. "Send it through."

Antumbra gestured again at the glowing projection. A portal opened slowly, swirling and widening until it was about as large a porthole window.

"It is ready," Antumbra said. "Throw it now."

I balled up the sleeve and threw it. It floated in the portal for a moment, then the glowing lights flickered and flashed and it was gone.

"What happens n—?"

32

THE PORTAL

We made it to the nearest airlock with ten minutes to spare. The bomb's timer kept counting down.

"This thing is heavy," Illarion complained.

"And you're the big kid," Koyla said.

One of the Chinese ships was parked outside the airlock, complicating our plan.

"Where's the next nearest airlock?" I asked.

"We'll never make it," Gerlinde replied. "It's back by the medical bay."

I shook my head. The timer counted down. We had less than eight minutes.

"Let's just dump this thing on the ship," Maiara said. "Then we unlock the ship from the hull and it will float away."

I nodded and activated the air lock controls. The Ark's door opened, but on the other side, the Chinese shuttle's door was locked. Beside the door, a keypad with Chinese characters, beckoned us to enter a code.

"Any ideas?" I asked.

"We all speak Chinese, don't we?" Koyla said. "Get to it, Callum."

"I speak it, but I can't read it," I said.

"Seven minutes to detonation," Illarion said.

"Get help," Captain Amis whispered.

I turned away from the airlock and ran down the corridor.

But before I could go any further the air in front of us split in half, glowing gold around the edges.

I backed away at first, and then was suddenly overcome with a desire to touch it.

Before I could, a scrap of cloth fluttered through the opening and drifted to the corridor floor.

I picked it up and recognized it immediately. It looked just like the shirt I was wearing, but torn, damp and a bit more weathered. I held it up to myself and it was the same. A shudder ran down my spine.

Was it déjà vu when you thought you'd worn a shirt before?

The glowing opening in the air closed.

"What the heck was that?" Koyla said.

"I don't know," I replied.

The group gathered around me to look at the piece of cloth. I turned the cloth over and saw that on the other side was marked with a sticky red substance in the shape of Chinese writing.

"Is that blood?" Gerlinde asked.

"I think it might be," I said. "It just came through that portal thing."

"From where?" she asked.

"How would I know?"

"It's your shirt, Callum," she said.

"Yeah," I said. "That's the weird thing. I wonder if it's my blood?"

"What do the Chinese characters mean?" Koyla asked. "'Help, I need a band-aid?'"

"Chinese writing?" Illarion said. "The door. The keypad is labelled with Chinese characters."

"Maybe we should try the code," Koyla said. "The bomb is about to blow."

I took the cloth to the door and typed in the code. The shuttle's airlock opened. I pocketed the cloth and turned back to help lift the bomb.

We hauled the warhead into the Chinese shuttle, pulled the lever labelled with a picture of a clamp to unlock the ship from the Ark, and then dove back through the docking hatch.

I tapped the code in again, and then closed the Ark's port.

We all watched through a tiny window as the Chinese ship drifted away into space.

"I hope it gets far enough away," Gerlinde said.

"At least it's not on the Ark," I said. "Let's go see if One is done mopping up the soldiers. We'll tell him about the portal."

We returned to the residence level and found it to be a war zone. The walls were scarred with smoke and ash, and peppered with bullet holes. Mangled bikes were strewn about and shell cases littered the floor

There were bodies everywhere.

I nearly threw up when I saw them.

There were dead Chinese and American soldiers all over.

We stepped carefully among the bodies and discarded weapons toward the observation room and poked our heads inside.

What I saw made my stomach turn.

The American colonel had five Chinese soldiers lined up on their knees.

He stood there with two of his officers and four soldiers.

Then they executed the Chinese soldiers, firing until their guns were out of ammunition.

"The last of the vermin dealt with," the colonel snarled.

"We need to find One," I said.

"Stay right there, kids. Don't try anything stupid." An American soldier appeared from around the corner. His face dripped with blood, and his clothes were singed and tattered. He held his gun on us. "Inside," he said, gesturing to the observation room.

The colonel put on a grim smile when he saw us, "Still alive are you?" he said. "Don't worry. That won't be the case for long."

"Shouldn't you be worried about that nuclear bomb?" I asked.

"I have men looking for the minister now," the colonel replied. "He will tell us what we need to know."

"Actually, the minister is dead," I said.

The colonel frowned. "You're lying," he shot back.

"Nope," Koyla said. "Dead as a doornail. Dead as a rock. Dead as the Wicked Witch."

A vein in the colonel's neck throbbed and he clenched his teeth hard enough that I could hear them grinding.

"Luckily, I can disarm the bomb," the colonel boasted. "And your friend is going to help me."

The colonel grabbed his radio and patched it into the Ark's intercom.

"I know that you are out there," he said, his words echoing throughout the ship. "I have five of your children. Surrender to me now and I will disarm the nuclear bomb and save all of them. If you don't I will kill these hostages myself. And then the bomb will do the rest."

One responded immediately over the ship's intercom.

"Colonel," he said. "It is you who will surrender."

"Don't toy with me," the colonel said. "I will shoot every last one of these children."

"I will not bargain with you," One said. "Failure to comply will result in an extremely long and painful death for you and your men."

"Your threats are meaningless," the colonel said "I have been to hell and ba—"

"No," One interrupted. "Your threats are meaningless. You were once a member of a great army, destined to protect the innocent, and yet you now take the coward's route, threatening children in your disgusting selfishness. You're no leader. You're no patriot. You are a coward. And I am everything that you have to fear."

One then shut off the intercom.

The colonel and his soldiers froze. I could tell that the soldiers were considering One's words. They each broke eye contact with their leader, instead looking down at the floor. The soldier aiming his gun at us lowered it.

The vein in the colonel's neck surged and his jaw clicked.

Footsteps running hard down the corridor, broke the moment. It was One, speeding to our rescue.

"Defend this room," the colonel shouted.

His soldiers didn't take the order at first. They kept looking at the floor, and then to each other, as if unsure what to do anymore. Maybe it was too many years of military training, but they fell in line the moment One burst into the room, aiming and firing at him. But One was a blur.

He charged in, holding one of the metal doors to the Ark's original alien rooms. He used it as a shield, darting among the soldiers, absorbing their bullets, and then smashing them in the face with its broad surface.

Quickly, three soldiers were down, knocked out or dead.

The remaining two, flanking the colonel, aimed, but One was still too fast. He dropped his shield, and retrieved a piece of metal from the pocket of his shirt. He leapt across them, and in two fast swipes, slit both of their throats. They fell to the ground, hands still on their guns, faces frozen in a state of confusion.

The colonel couldn't react quickly enough, and One swung around behind him, driving the blade through the older man's hand, forcing the colonel to drop his pistol. The gun bounced and came to rest in a damp puddle of red.

One stared the colonel dead in the face. The old man backed away clasping his ruined hand.

"You will return to your ship and leave this vessel," One said. "This is my final offer of mercy."

"I must protect the interests of the United States of America!" the colonel screeched.

"That place is no more, sir," One said. "All of the old places, and their ideas are gone now. These children are the new future. Do not be so foolish as to stand in their way."

The colonel seethed.

"You think you're smart don't you?" the colonel said. "These packs aren't just for zero gravity."

He touched a button on his pack and the straps to his limbs tightened.

It was the colonel against One.

If One lost we were dead.

The colonel was fast, but One was faster.

The man threw a quick punch aimed at One's head. One dodged at the last moment, slipped under the colonel's swinging torso and threw an uppercut and flung the colonel back.

The colonel lunged forward, throwing a punch that sailed over One's head. However a kick from the colonel connected with One's leg which buckled, but only barely.

One grabbed onto the straps connecting to the colonel's arm and ripped them free.

The colonel's arm went limp, but he charged at One again, performing a powerful kick and caught One in the stomach.

One doubled over, but grabbed the colonel's ankle as he did, again tearing the straps from the limb.

The colonel stumbled back, wincing when he tried to put weight on the leg.

One stood tall and wound up for another attack, but the colonel had already turned away and was running out of the control centre on one still-powered leg.

One made to go after him however his left leg was weak, one of the colonel's strikes had injured him. I assumed he would heal quickly.

One sat down and sighed, despite his superhuman body he was tired, not surprising after a long and brutal gun fight.

"We have to catch him," I said.

"He will return to his ship to regroup," One said. "Then I will sort him out. I just need a quick break."

We gathered around One and looked down at him waiting for him to ask the obvious question.

"What?" he asked.

"Aren't you going to ask us about the bomb?" Maiara said.

"I saw what you did with it on the cameras," he said. "Thank goodness you did, I did not know how to disable it."

One looked off into space, I think he was contemplating the ramifications of the bomb going off in the Ark.

"We snuck it onto a Chinese shuttle and released its anchors," Maiara said. "It's floating out in space right now."

One seemed to have an idea. He grabbed the colonel's radio, dropped on the floor during the fight, and turned it on.

"Colonel, do not leave the Ark," he said. "You are safer here."

"What are you doing, One?" I asked.

"The colonel will die if his ship passes through the explosion," One said. "It would be wrong of me to let him die that way. If I did I would be no better than him."

The colonel never replied.

"I think you were too late," Koyla said, pointing at a streak of light outside the ship. "Nemo's about to watch him get blown up."

Despite the fracas, our fish swam contentedly in his tank on the control centre windowsill. I felt a sense of relief in seeing him again, but I didn't know why.

Outside, the colonel's ship flew far away from the Ark and then circled back towards us. His shuttle positioned itself right outside the observation window.

The radio crackled to life.

"Crew of the Ark," he growled. "I have a powerful missile aimed at your one and only window. I will fire and expose your ship to the cold vacuum of space. Place your protector in chains, and bring the bomb to the airlock, or I will destroy you a—"

That's when the Chinese shuttle, with a nuclear bomb inside, exploded.

A wave of energy rippled from the ship, catching the colonel's ship and tossing it like a rowboat during a hurricane. The waves of force shook its hull until it broke at the seams, finally shattering into more pieces than we could count.

"He didn't survive. Can we?" Koyla asked.

"The colonel is dead," One replied. "But the Ark's hull is strong enough to withstand a blast from the outside."

The shockwaves from the explosion then struck the Ark.

Vibrations rumbled all around us, I was worried the rivets in the hull might shake loose.

The shaking stopped and the light of the explosion faded.

"So it's over?" I asked. "We did it?"

"Not yet," One said watching us drift toward Pluto.

33

GOODBYE WORLD

"The blast has knocked us off course," One said, running back to the control centre.

"How can we help?" I asked.

"We have to prepare the ship to land," he said.

"Land?" I said. "We can't live on Pluto."

"We have no choice, we're caught in the gravity of the planet or asteroid or whatever this rock is called now."

"Let's fire the engine," I said.

"Yeah get us back on course," Maiara said.

"It is a significant power drain," One cautioned.

"Better that than landing on an inhospitable world," Illarion replied.

One seemed convinced.

"We need to prime the core," he said.

"I can do that," Gerlinde replied.

"You have four minutes," One said.

"There's no way to get to the engine room in time," Koyla said.

Koyla was right, but I had an idea.

I ran out into the corridor and found a working bike. I got it back on its wheels, revved the motor and drove back into the control centre.

"Get on, Gerlinde," I said.

She got on the back and she wrapped her arms around my stomach.

"You're crazy," Koyla said.

I smiled and did a donut before I drove out of there and down the corridors.

"Hold on tight," I said as we zipped down the stairs. Gerlinde screamed as each step caused the wheels to shudder uncomfortably.

We arrived in the engine room. We had to disembark from the bike and run along the gangplanks to the controls.

"One minute to terminal trajectory," One said over the intercom.

The Ark started to shake. We were starting to go through Pluto's thin atmosphere.

"You know the engine will probably destroy Pluto, it's not as big as the planet Earth," Gerlinde said solemnly as she activated the engine.

"It hasn't been a planet for a while anyway," I said.

Gerlinde logged into the computer and primed the engine.

"Use that other console to open all the exhaust ports," she ordered.

I went to the panel and followed her command.

The engine rumbled as the exhaust started pouring from the core.

"Engine is primed," Gerlinde said. "There's no shielding on the engine. We have to get out of here before the core pulses, or we'll be vaporized."

"Fun," I said.

We ran back to the bike and drove away, getting as far away as possible. I couldn't get the bike to go up the stairs, its battery too drained, so we had to run.

The Ark shook as the engine pulsed. A hot and blinding light poured from the room behind us as we darted up the long stairwell. Then the ship jolted, the engine suddenly boosting its velocity, and we were thrown against the steps.

"I think we made it," Gerlinde said, groaning as she picked herself up.

When we got back to the control centre, One looked at us and smirked.

"We are back on course," One reported.

I sat down on the floor.

"Now it's over," I said.

34

BACK TO NORMAL

Nuan's body lay reverently on the table in the observation room.

We had gathered in the same way we had for Mathieu.

One invited us to say a few words.

We all bowed our heads and stood silently for a few moments. Then I took my place back in the crowd.

Sanna led us in a prayer again, and we tried to repeat after her flowing Arabic.

Maiara spoke of Nuan's bravery too, and shared a conversation they had had on the first night aboard the Ark.

Others came forward, too, all speaking love for Nuan, and for what her sacrifice, and Mathieu's meant for us.

We owed them a better world, one built in their memory.

As the last to speak to Nuan before she died I knew I had to say something.

"Nuan did not betray us or leave us. She never felt like she had to serve two masters. She was loyal to us. Her last words were 'I was proud to be an Arkonaut,'"

People sighed in joy at hearing that.

"She was one of the bravest people I knew and she faced her death without fear. I hope I can live up to what she did."

One spoke the lasts words.

"These words are from a great Chinese epic," he began. "'Look at that wonderful moonlight. It makes me long for the time when I can return home.'"

He lowered his head.

"Nuan is now at home and at peace, standing with her ancestors."

We all bowed our heads, too.

I prayed for her again, and I prayed for us, One, and the Ark.

One carried Nuan's body out of the room for storage in the cargo bay alongside Mathieu.

Now there were two nations whose legacies lacked a bearer: China and Canada. I hoped that this was the last loss we'd take.

As the crowd broke up and we scattered about the room, I allowed myself to smile. We would carry their legacies. All of us. And Mathieu and Nuan would live forever in our memories.

One sidled up beside me without making a sound.

"May I see the cloth?" One asked. "Gerlinde said it appeared as if from thin air."

I took it out of my pocket and handed it over. Past One I could see that all the other Arkonauts were staring at us.

One had already shared the footage of the portal with the entire crew, but he hadn't asked me about the note yet.

One held the piece of fabric up to my shirt and studied both.

"They are exactly the same," One said. "And this is human blood, enhanced by nanites."

One touched the blood with his finger. "It is yours, Callum."

I didn't know what to say.

The other Arkonauts gathered around and One held up the torn piece of shirt.

"I do not understand how, but this has been sent to us by Callum from another time," One said.

"Someone is watching over us," Sanna said.

"Man, why couldn't it be Batman or someone cool?" Koyla joked.

They all laughed. Even I laughed.

"I will perform more tests and notify you all of my findings," One said, taking the cloth and leaving the room.

Gerlinde, Illarion, Koyla and Maiara all joined me at the window. We stood there in silence for a moment. We looked out the window at the last glimmers of the Sun's light, a small dot in the distance. Even Saturn looked small now. The Ark was leaving our home solar system.

"This is it, isn't it?" Koyla said.

"What?" Gerlinde asked.

"We're never going back," Koyla said. "Ever."

We all sighed.

This was it, wasn't it? We were leaving it all behind. Everything we knew, of home, and even of space.

I put my arm over Koyla's shoulder. The others followed, until we were all linked, arms to shoulders in a long hug.

We were our own family now. We were our own solar system. This crew was all we'd ever need again.

"We'll be alright," I said. "We're Arkonauts."

SYSTEM ONLINE

COURSE STEADY

ARK WILL REACH WORMHOLE IN 10 MONTHS 14 DAYS.

CANADIAN REPRESENTATIVE DECEASED: AUG 29

CHINESE REPRESENTATIVE DECEASED: SEPT 30

CONTINUE ON PROJECTED PATH...

ENACT PHASE 6

ACTIVATE: TWO

THE NEW FUTURE

"—ow?" I said.

Antumbra shut off the rod and then looked around at us.

"The destruction of this timeline should have been instantaneous if the first possibility was correct," it said. "So I think we can conclude that we were successful in creating an alternative timeline in another part of the multiverse."

"Let's see it," I declared.

"I'm afraid we cannot," Antumbra said. "It is one thing to view the past of our universe but the rod cannot locate another universe entirely."

"So what do we do now?" I asked.

"We have saved your people," Antumbra said. "When the rod has recharged itself we will save mine. In the meantime I would like to take action against the Thieves, purely for revenge, if that is agreeable to you?"

"I don't see why not," I said.

Suddenly, something shoved me aside. I stumbled to my left. It felt like a giant hand had just slapped me across my whole body.

"What was that?" I asked.

My voice was different, a mix of my own and a girl's voice, both speaking the same words with the same inflection.

There was a human girl standing next to me. She wasn't there before.

We both turned to Antumbra.

"What's going on here?" the girl and I asked in unison.

Antumbra peered at us.

"Our scientists did not predict this."

Acknowledgements

A big thank you to Ralph and Hazel Walker for their advice, support and encouragement.

My thanks to Nate for all his work during the editing process.

About the Author

M. Drewery has been writing for 20 years and is a life long Sci-Fi fan. He lives in a little village in Surrey, England. The only people who know it exists are the people who live there. One day he'll write a book where it becomes the nexus for multiple realities from which burst out monsters and heroes, just to put it on the map. You can find him at http://www.thebinarylibrary.com/

About the Publishing Team

Nate Ragolia was labeled as "weird" early in elementary school, and it stuck. He's a lifelong lover of science fiction, and a nerd/geek. In 2015 his first book, *There You Feel Free,* was published by 1888's Black Hill Press. He's also the author of *The Retroactivist*, published by Spaceboy Books. He founded and edits BONED, an online literary magazine, has created webcomics, and writes whenever he's not playing video games or petting dogs.

TJ Stambaugh received several commendations for his bravery as a battalion commander in the Meme Wars. TJ retired to Catonsville, MD, where he paints and enjoys movies you have to read. He's the founder and El Presidente of MoleHole Radio.